# EMPIRE OF LIGHT

# EMPIRE OF LIGHT

## 1

## THE SPIRIT OF INNOVATION

A NOVEL BY

# CARCER KANE

ISBN: 979-8-9915025-1-1

Publisher's Cataloging-in-Publication Data
provided by Five Rainbows Cataloging Services

Names: Kane, Carcer, author.
Title: Empire of light 1 : the spirit of innovation / Carcer Kane.
Description: Detroit : Mind Factory Press, 2024. | Series: Empire of light, bk. 1.
Identifiers: LCCN 2024920843 (print) | ISBN 979-8-9915025-2-8 (hardcover) | ISBN 979-8-9915025-1-1
    (paperback) | ISBN 979-8-9915025-0-4 (ebook)
Subjects: LCSH: Fantasy fiction. | Steampunk fiction. | Adventure stories. | Romance fiction. | BISAC: FICTION
    / Fantasy / Gaslamp. | FICTION / Science Fiction / Steampunk. | FICTION / Fantasy / Action & Adventure. |
    FICTION / Romance / Fantasy. | GSAFD: Fantasy fiction. | Adventure fiction. | Romance fiction.
Classification: LCC PS3611.K36 E47 2024 (print) | LCC PS3611.K36 (ebook) | DDC 813/.6--dc23.

Library of Congress Control Number: 2024920843

Academy of Worldly Science
Grand Library Control Number: KC-01111867HC001

Work of fiction. Any similarity to persons living or dead is purely coincidental.
The Bureau of Records wouldn't allow such a blatant transgression of law.
No wood nymphs were harmed in the making of this book.

100% written by a human!

Cover design by DR@Gon

Printed and bound in the United States of America
First printing November 2024

Paperback 1st edition

published by
**Mind Factory Press**
Detroit, Michigan USA

www.carcerkane.com
www.mindfactorypress.com

 *For Wendy, who loves to read* 

# EMPIRE OF LIGHT

The 19th century was an age of wonder. Following the victories of the Purge, mankind looked to the future with a renewed sense of hope. Unshackled from that dark age of terrible beasts, everything seemed possible. Inventions and innovations exploded with pent-up fury. Culture and industry flourished. Men became as gods. And of course, whenever such prideful vanity reigns supreme, a fall of great consequence is inevitable.

Mason Moore—*A History of the Empire*, 1921

# Chronology of Occurrences

# CHAPTER ONE
## *Solitude*

The trout had just taken the bait when Elphias heard the child screaming. He tugged the fish from the rolling water, sunlight gleaming off its speckled scales, and tossed it into a pail on the embankment without bothering to remove the line and hook. Scrambling up the slope he could see a woman running in his direction while pushing a wheelbarrow down the road. The child was in the bucket, gripping the sides and wailing with pain. Elphias rubbed his hands across his charcoal grey vest and started toward his vardo, sheltered beneath the dappling shade of an ancient oak tree. He mounted the stairs into the living wagon to retrieve his doctor's bag, then bounded back down to meet the approaching woman, careful not to lose his top hat in the process.

"Hoy," she called as they drew closer. The wheelbarrow bumped over a rut and the child, a young boy Elphias could see now, screamed in pain. "Hush, Jonathan," the woman said, setting the wheelbarrow down and huffing with exhaustion. She was middle-aged, face tanned from the sun, with her sandy brown hair drawn up in a messy bun. Damp spots of sweat showed on her blouse and road dust clung to the bottom of her prairie skirt. "The doctor will help you," she said to the boy, then looked at Elphias. "You are a doctor of medicine, I hope?"

Elphias tipped his hat. "I am indeed. How can I be of service?"

"The lad, he—"

"I cut my foot," the boy interrupted, staring at Elphias with wonder. He rubbed tears from his eyes then thrust his left leg out, dirty bare foot wrapped tight with a strip of cloth. Blood was seeping through the layers.

Elphias squatted and placed his bag on the ground. "I'll need to take a closer examination," he said and began to unwrap the bandage. Jonathan huffed with pain. Elphias glanced at him and smiled. "Why don't you tell me what happened?"

"I stepped on a rock," the boy said. Then his eyes widened. "Harpies was chasin' me."

The woman groaned. "Jonathan…"

Elphias glanced up and discovered it to be a very flattering angle to her features. He quickly turned back to the boy, hoping it didn't look as awkward as it felt.

The bandage fell away, revealing a gash in the sole of Jonathan's foot.

"Well, you certainly did step on a rock. You'll need stitches to close this up."

Tears welled in the boy's eyes. "You gonna sew me?"

Elphias nodded and smiled. "Yes, but I'll take the pain away first. You won't feel a thing after." He reached into his kit bag and retrieved a bottle of anesthetic and clean cloth. He uncapped the bottle and soaked a spot on the cloth, then began blotting the wound.

Jonathan winced. "Ow! You said it wouldn't hurt!"

"I said I'd take the pain away. That takes both time and this numbing agent, which also cleans your wound too. We don't want it to become infected."

Jonathan whined as the cloth pressed gently against his skin. Elphias knew he'd need to distract the boy while preparing the needle and suture thread. He set the anesthetic aside and considered his options.

"Harpies, eh?" *That should do the trick.*

Jonathan nodded, lower lip trembling. "They was at the Carson barn. They saw me and started to chase me."

Elphias glanced up at the woman. "Chickens," she said and gave him a tired smile.

Jonathan glared at her. "They was harpies!"

Elphias grinned and began to stitch the wound closed. "I don't know, Jonathan. There've not been harpies in these parts since long before you were born."

Jonathan looked at him suspiciously. "How would you know?"

Elphias' smile faded. "They all died in the Purge." *And if they had been harpies, your flesh would be feeding their chicks, your hair would be lining their nest, and your mother would be wondering where you'd went,* he amended silently. Some truths need not be shared.

"Purge? What's that?"

Elphias chuckled. The woman laughed too, face flushing. "I've not read him much history."

"Well, no matter. You'll learn all about it when you go off to boarding school, you must almost be of age?"

The boy nodded, eyes suddenly downcast. "Yes. I'll be six in two months." His lower lip began to tremble again.

"Everyone's afraid of going off to school," Elphias said quietly. Jonathan looked up to meet his gaze.

"They are?" The boy glanced up at his mother, who nodded.

Elphias nodded too. "Sure. You're leaving home to go live somewhere else for several years, someplace strange and unknown. But that's also the most wonderful thing too."

"It is?"

"Yes. It's an adventure, really. You'll learn many wonderful things, see sights you can't begin to imagine, and make friends. It's an adventure to find out who you are, and who you'll become." Elphias pulled the last stitch into place.

Jonathan smiled. "It would be nice to meet other kids."

Elphias knotted the thread. "There you are, young master. You have been properly 'sewn'."

Jonathan's brow knit. "You did? I didn't feel you doin' nothin'!" He turned his leg to examine the bottom of his foot.

"I still need to dress the area," Elphias said, then stood to face the woman. "He'll need to stay off the foot for a day or two. Not easy at his age, I'm sure."

The woman laughed. "Thank you, Doctor." She gave him a curtsy. "Nell Emery."

"Elphias Root." He smiled and tipped his top hat. "Now if you'd like to accompany me to my wagon we can settle the fee of services."

"Yes, as you wish."

They set off toward his vardo. His horse grazed beyond, tethered next to the river bank. A crow cawed from its perch somewhere above as a gentle breeze stirred the trees. Clouds dotted the deep blue sky.

Nell studied the sign painted on the side of his living wagon.

The Spirit of Innovation
### DR. ELPHIAS ROOT
### PHYSICIAN & CHEMIST
#### Healer of Maladies
#### Concoctions and Curatives for all conditions!
#### Elixers, Tinctures, Liniments, Ointments, and Tonics

"You are a traveling man, I see," Nell said. "Have you traveled far?"

Elphias nodded. "Far and long. I've been from Ostravia to Torbuld and back again so many times that I sometimes forget where I am." He looked at her. "I am in Torbuld now, right?"

Nell laughed. "Aye. And I should know, it's all I've ever been."

"There's nothing wrong with making a home somewhere. Here for instance." He swept his arm around at the surrounding landscape. The river cut around a field of wild grass and meandered through a scattered gathering of trees. Across the river a gentle slope ran up into a forest. "There's a tranquility to this place."

They reached the vardo and Elphias bounded up the steps and inside, leaving the door open as he rummaged through his cabinet. Nell peeked in from outside. "How is it? Living in a little house on wheels?"

Elphias laughed. "Comfortable, actually. Would you like the grand tour?"

Nell nodded and he motioned for her to climb the steps. She hiked her skirt safely above her boots and climbed up to stand on the footboard, peering into the vardo with curiosity.

Elphias patted the cabinet to the right of the entry. "I keep my medical supplies in here, and across from it as you can clearly tell, is the stove for cooking and heat." He stepped further in and gestured to a well-worn wooden bench near the stove. "This is where I eat most of my meals. The standing desk opposite and next to the medical cabinet is where I concoct curatives. This solid lower panel on the front of it swings up to become a table when I eat at the bench. To the rear you'll see my bed is elevated above a chest of drawers. Normally there'd be another bed in the lower space, but I had the dresser placed there to make room for my chemistry station."

"It's very efficient," Nell admitted, taking it all in.

"I've found that to be true."

They stepped down from the footboard and stood in the peaceful shade together. Elphias passed a small ampule of red liquid to Nell.

4

"For his pain, if it becomes acute."

"Is this one of your concoctions?" she asked.

"No. Certain chemicals are restricted, even from me. That's manufactured by Parkwell Pharmaceutical Potions. You'll find Red Rose is an effective opioid analgesic. Best perhaps before bedtime."

"Thank you, Doctor Root. How much do I owe you?"

"A five note will suffice," Elphias answered, and began to wash dried blood from his hands in a basin of water. Afterwards he slipped on his grey frock coat, comforted by the slim shape tucked within an inside pocket. *If only it felt heavier*, he lamented. Such discomforts needed addressing.

"Can you tell me where the nearest town is, Miss Emery?"

Nell counted out five single notes. "The nearest town? That would be Lancaster." She pointed up the road, the opposite direction from which she'd come. "A day's ride to the east." She looked him up and down. "I suppose you need supplies every now and again. Don't you worry about running out while you travel?"

Elphias smiled. "Again, the better points of making a home somewhere."

She nodded and handed over the money. "Thank you again for tending to Jonathan. He's my twain. Once he's gone to school there'll be no more children for me." Their eyes met. "I wonder what I will do then."

Elphias' mouth became dry. "Yes, well I should bandage his foot."

He slipped away, feeling foolish. Here he was, forty years old and still deeply vexed by his last relationship. His long dark hair and neatly trimmed beard were showing streaks of grey, there were wrinkles at the corners of his eyes and mouth, but inside he was still the same as ever. He absentmindedly patted his inner breast pocket and the slim metal case within.

Elphias sat on a fallen tree next to his campfire, cooking the trout over some hot coals and staring into the flames. Perhaps it was time to settle down. He certainly had saved enough money to buy land and build a home, and as a veteran of the Purge he had the right to do so. He could build a small office to practice his medicine while continuing to reside in the vardo. After living in it for a decade it had become an extension of him, a tangible thing that would be there when needed. A thing that could never die.

He realized that the trout was starting to blacken and cursed himself for becoming distracted. He removed the fish from the heat and waited for it to cool. Maybe he would build a proper kitchen too. Eating from campfires and the vardo's furnace stovetop had lost its rustic charms. An oven roasted chicken every once in a while would be a welcome change of pace.

Footsteps sounded behind him, coming from the road. He turned his head to witness Nell approaching with a wrapped plate in her hands.

"Hoy, Doctor," she said. "I hope you don't mind me paying a quick visit."

"Is all well with Jonathan?"

"Oh yes, he's right as rain." She approached and held out the plate. "I wanted to bring you this as thanks."

He took it from her. The towel was warm in his hands and the wonderful smell of baked apples filled his nose.

"I just made it," Nell said, cheeks flushed pink. "I thought maybe you'd like a taste of home, since you travel so much."

Elphias peeled the towel back. The smell of pie wafted up and his stomach rumbled with anticipation. The crust was a perfect golden brown.

"It looks amazing, Miss Emery. Almost too good to eat."

"Oh, I hope you do though."

Elphias nodded his head. "I said almost."

The apple pie was as delicious as it looked. Elphias ate his fill, forgoing his scorched trout. Nell watched him eat, hands folded in her lap as they made polite small talk. She owned an orchard and made her living selling produce to the marketplace. "I have no time to sell apples in a farmers market, I earn more by shipping them in bulk. I never see the folk I sell to." She shook her head at the absurdity of it all. "It must be nice, doing what you do. Seeing the folk you're helping, seeing what the skills of your hands can accomplish."

Night was beginning to fall, stars poking through the blue twilight.

"I should be taking my leave," Nell said.

"That pie was the best I've ever eaten, Miss Emery. If you sold those in bulk you'd be wealthy in no time."

Nell shook her head. "I'm glad you enjoyed it." She started off toward her home, then turned to look over her shoulder.

"I'm glad you've made camp here, Doctor. The folk around these parts will be too. I hope you truly consider making it a home."

She flushed, then turned and set off at a brisk pace.

Elphias watched her go, then sighed. *You've got to stop running someday,*

*Elphias,* he chided himself. *It needn't be today, though.* Elphias stood, then went to fetch water so he could douse the flames.

Twenty minutes after the fire was fully extinguished Elphias had the horse hitched to the vardo and ready to go. He unhooked the steps and secured them in their traveling position on the bottom of the back-carriage. Taking the reins, he climbed onto the footboard and sat with feet propped on the struts. Elphias took one last melancholy look at the serene campsite then snapped his horse into motion. They set off, headed east toward Lancaster.


An hour later they reached a stretch of land where the road led into a dense forest. The horse stopped short of the dark woods, snorting nervously and shifting its hooves in the dirt. Elphias debated. Wide open fields rolled away to each side of the road, he could just make camp here until daybreak. But he wasn't far enough away, he needed to press on. It was a good thing he'd filled the pail with water before leaving the stream.

A series of compartments were mounted to the back of the vardo, containing mostly tack and other items for the horse. Elphias pulled a large bottle labeled Courage from one of the compartments and inspected the contents. Half-empty. Elphias uncovered the water pail and emptied the calming agent into it. He let the horse drink the pail dry before getting back inside the wagon.

He removed the slender metal case from his inner pocket and opened it. Ampules of different colored liquid occupied only four of the twenty slots available, which was his main reason for heading to Lancaster. It wasn't all about avoiding the apple woman. Elphias selected an ampule of dark green potion then put the case away. He snapped the top off the glass capsule and downed the Green Glory. Its familiar sour taste enveloped his tongue and he relished the flavor. Not that it was always that way. He used to suck on a Kavan sugar cube after administration. Things change, however, and he'd grown accustomed to the Glory's vinegary tart flavor over the years. *Why can't other parts of me change as well?* he wondered.

As he waited for the sedative to take effect he studied the forest. He hadn't lied to the boy. There were no more harpies as far as he knew. But there were other things. The Purge, effective as it was, had only done so much.

Elphias' pulse rate slowed. His pupils constricted as a warmth snaked up the back of his neck and filled his mind with a calming venom. The horse also stood still, ears flicking. It was time. He remained inside and shut the lower half of the double-hinged door, keeping reins in hand. *No sense taking any chances*, he thought. Elphias spurred the horse to motion and they drove forward, slipping into the dark forest without hesitation.

The woods were pitch black and eerily silent. Elphias turned a hand crank mounted next to the door, creating an electrical current to ignite the carriage lamp. A lux stone within the housing began to glow, casting a beam of light through the lamp's thick protective glass lens. It didn't do much to illuminate the road but did permit a pale glow to the tree trunks rolling past, enough light for the horse to clop its way along. Small insects began to flit around the lens, drawn by its glow. Elphias had heard conflicting stories from soldiers during the Purge—monsters were either drawn to light or repelled by it. He had no idea which was which, but hoped it was the latter. He did know one thing for certain. They all seemed to be drawn by the scent of blood.

A loud crack sounded from his left, like a large limb snapping free of a tree. The fact that something of considerable weight would be the cause didn't escape Elphias' attention. He'd had an additional top forged for the vardo's double-hinged doors, a set of iron bars mounted opposite of the standard wood half. He swung the bars closed, fed the reins through a slot at the bottom, and then bolted the caged section shut.

The horse was on its own. He'd never bothered to name it. Names caused attachments, and attachments only led to pain when death took its due. He'd learned that long ago. Elphias had cried himself dry then and had no desire to refill the reservoir. He resisted the urge to reach into the cupboard and take out the daguerreotype portrait. It was too dark to see her face anyway.

Elphias needed to distract himself. Green Glory only stilled physical reactions to emotional stimulus, only subdued the instinctual fight or flight response. It didn't prevent mental anguish. There were other drugs in his case for that, but he couldn't be guiding a horse or much else for that matter. He needed to make camp first.

Twenty minutes later they broke free of the forest. The woods to his left still ran the length of the road, but to his right were broad rolling fields of long grass. A cluster of old tombstones thrust up from atop a hill and Elphias urged the horse in that direction. It had been nearly a hundred years since people had buried their dead, so there was little chance of anyone visiting it come the morning. Superstitions would keep night wanderers and thieves away. All in all a good place to blot out his memories.

He made camp as quickly as possible, tying the horse to a bent and rusted iron fence partially surrounding the graves. The twin moons cast a soft glow to the landscape, rendering the world in black and bluish grey hues. The wind stirred up, rustling the forest across the road. Elphias could hear an eerie whistling, odd piping musical tones barely audible through the trees. The sound was unmistakable. Wood nymphs playing wind instruments carved from the bones of men. The strange melodies had an ill effect on humans, lulling them to follow the sound and seek out its source. All they would find is their own deaths. And after their bones had been picked clean they'd likely become instruments of their own. If Elphias were a normal man he might already be plunging into the dense forest, stumbling wide-eyed to a wicked end. His third year of medical school had ensured that would never happen.

He'd been a student during the thick of the Purge, when all manner of rash measures had taken place. The conflict had been raging for four years at that point, and men were suffering great losses. Elphias' immunity to charms came from enduring treatments of listening to the call of captive sirens. One week of being strapped in a bed for three hours and then allowed a recovery of six hours before beginning the process again.

Elphias couldn't remember the first few treatments, only coming to awareness in the recovery room, flesh bruised where he'd strained himself against the restraints. Gradually, as if awakening from a dream, memories of what happened during treatment began to return and eventually he was aware of the entire three hours. He'd strain against the restraints, an erection raging, needing to get to the siren, needing desperately to throw himself at it. It was the most beautiful creature he'd ever seen. Until the spell finally broke, and he'd seen a siren properly for the bloated, mottled green skinned monstrosity that it was. Slit shaped orifices on the sides of its thick neck produced the lulling song, leaving the wide fanged mouth available to eat as it called even more prey to the harvest. It was a creature of ravenous instinct, its large black eyes devoid of compassion. A siren was utterly terrifying. He shrieked in terror, alerting the facilitators he'd become immune to its malign influences, just like every other student that broke the hypnotizing spell had done. Those that were fortunate. Most were driven mad by the experience, others convulsed to death. At the start of their third year there were one-hundred and eight students in Elphias' class. After the siren treatment there were forty. Rash measures indeed.

Then began the venom immunities.

More bad memories to alleviate, and he had the means to do so.

Elphias entered the vardo and secured the doors, making use of the top bars to freshen the air overnight. He removed the case from his frock coat and opened it before turning the hand crank a cycle to bring the lux stone to light. Vitally important to identify the different colors from one another, especially the inky black one he always kept in the upper right corner. Elphias removed a blue ampule and tucked the case away. He moved with familiarity through the dim interior, lit only by scant moonslight filtering through the mollicroft roof windows. Elphias exchanged his clothing for a nightshirt from the dresser, then climbed up onto the mattress with ampule still clutched tight. He snapped the Blue Oasis open and drank its bitter contents, then lay back and made himself comfortable. He slid aside curtains to the rearward facing window and opened the pane to discard the empty capsule and let some air in. A gentle cross breeze stirred towards the door, freshening the stale smell of the room and diminishing the chemical odors of his trade. He could still hear the wood nymph's music, but the memories it brought were falling into the background of his mind, engulfed by a deep unconscious void. Elphias let them go without resistance, secure he could drift free without interruption. The void expanded like a black wave, sweeping over his thoughts and washing them asunder.

# CHAPTER TWO
*Preparations*

A harsh rapping awoke him.

"Hoy," called a hoarse voice, "are you alive?"

Elphias squinted toward the door, wishing he'd shut the solid top half. An elderly man with an unkempt white beard stood outside, squinting back at him through the bars. The senior wore a boilerman's cap thrust down on his head with a vengeance, strands of long grey hair trailing across the collar of his brown duster. The man also held a walking cane which he rapped against the lower door of the vardo once more.

"Hoy, I say."

"Hoy, dash you!" Elphias sat up and held his forehead in his hands.

"There's no need for profanity," the old timer snapped. "I'll wait out here while you dress your manners." He turned and wobbled down the steps.

Elphias swung his legs out of bed and took a deep breath. He was still feeling residual effects of the Blue Oasis, a dullness in his thoughts and a low headache above his eyes.

He dressed slowly, taking deep breaths in and out to clear his mind. Finally he slipped into his frock coat and donned his top hat. He took another cleansing breath, then stepped out of the vardo to see what the elder wanted.

The aged man was sitting on a nearby tombstone, gauntlet covered hands resting on his walking stick. A thin, saddled horse grazed nearby, untethered and content. Elphias took note of a collection of animal hides secured behind the saddle. *A huntsman?*

The man squinted at Elphias as he approached. "I need a doctor, a real doctor, not the spineless bone bags that are all the rage these days."

# The Spirit of Innovation

"Well, perhaps I can be of assistance. What ails you?"

The old man shot him a sharp glance. His face was deeply carved by wrinkles but the eyes were a bright shiny blue. "With me? Naught! Naught besides age." He emphasized the last word bitterly. "What I want is a doctor who served in the Purge, one who understands what must be done if things go badly."

Elphias studied the skin on the man's face. There was a subtle hang to it, as if carved in slightly melted wax. There was only one thing that would cause that effect.

"I both received my training and served." He gave the stranger a salute, right hand flat against his shoulder, arm bent across his chest. "Doctor Elphias Root."

The old man nodded and returned the salute from his sitting position. "Cobb," he said with a small grin. "I was just a grunt, and still am I suppose." He squinted up at Elphias with a neutral look. "How did you know I served?" Then, before Elphias could answer, he reached up a gauntleted hand to touch his face. "Aye, you've a good eye, Doctor. Most think I'm too old to have fought. I think you're just the man I'm looking for."

Elphias sat on a tombstone opposite Cobb.

"What can I do for you?"

Cobb reached into his duster pocket and pulled out a folded piece of paper. He thrust it out to Elphias, hand wavering.

Elphias took the sheet, folded into quarters, and opened it up.

DANGER TO THE UNION!

MONSTERS ARE RETURNING!

MASTER HUNTSMAN NOW MUSTERING A MILITIA

TO SAVE OUR GREAT NATION.

MEET IN THE VILLAGE

OF LANCASTER ON PATERO 22ND.

SOME EXPENSES PAID.

B. COBB, MASTER HUNTSMAN

Elphias studied the flyer. "That's today, isn't it?"

"Aye, Doctor, tis. Hunt will be on the morrow or such."

Elphias nodded. "About this 'some' expenses paid."

Cobb coughed a small laugh. "Aye, cutter, you'll be paid for your services. A man living on the road is always in need of coin." He cast a glance at Elphias' vardo. "I should'a done that. See'd the land while I had a chance."

"You still could."

"Bah, where would I go? These days I mostly just travel from my hut to the town and back. That's how I found you. I see'd this wagon house on the hill and thought who'd be ignorant enough to camp there?"

Elphias smiled and tipped his top hat. "At your service."

Cobb flashed a grin, revealing a missing molar. "Nay, Doctor, nay. Once I see'd your doctor sign I knew you were no fool."

"I'm still trying to decide that one for myself," Elphias said with a smirk.

Cobb shook his head and smiled. "To keep such sense of humor, you've either never see'd tragedy or see'd too much of it."

"I wish it were the former."

"Don't we all, Doctor Root," Cobb said and looked off to the distant woods. "Don't we all."

Elphias nodded in agreement. "Yes, I suppose you're right, Master Cobb." He rubbed his hands across his thighs. "I'll need to procure some supplies before your hunt. Does Lancaster have an apothecary?"

Cobb touched a hand to his chin. "Mmm, I'm not sure of that. Mayhap they do, I would guess. Lancaster turns a fair trade in provisions and equipment. Tis where I'm headed to get my needs."

"Would you care to ride together? The footboard of my wagon makes for a poor seat, but we could tether your horse to the back-carriage. Or you could ride alongside if you'd prefer."

 Cobb's brows went up. "Aye, tis a great kindness, Doctor. I'll ride with you, if we get on to Lancaster as short as possible. I'd like to take stock of them that come to hunt."

Elphias planted his hands on his knees and stood. "Let me harness the horse and we'll take our leave."

Cobb stood with a wince of pain. "I'll help if you don't mind. I'm not much the slouch." Wind stirred the long grass, caressing the tombstones in hushed tones.

Elphias gave a nod. "No, I don't suppose you are. Come then, let's be off."

They rode in silence for the first hour, rocking with the sway of the vardo.

"What do you expect to be hunting, Master Cobb?"

Cobb waved a hand at him. "Bah, just Cobb will suffice, Doctor. I never went beyond the boarding school."

Elphias nodded. "All right, Cobb it shall be."

"Thankee, Doctor Root. As to the hunt, I expect to find anything."

"I heard wood nymphs lasternight," Elphias said. "In the wood across from the graves."

Cobb's head whipped to face him with a speed that was almost comical. "Wood wenches? This close to the road?" He hunched forward, fists clenched. "Oh, tis worse than I'd imagined, Doctor. Fools!" He slapped his thigh. "Fools!"

"Who's that now?"

"I've warned them. Warned them over and again." Cobb was worked up. Spittle flew from his cracked lips. "Tis the folly of ignoring the beasts. Pretend they don't exist til you find one on your stoop! And then tis too late, ain't it?"

It sounded like Cobb was well-versed in this argument, and given his condition Elphias couldn't blame him for such passions. But he himself wasn't ready to be so disparaging.

"I suppose that's true," Elphias said, "but following the Purge everyone wanted to move forward and build a better future. You can't blame them for not wanting to look backwards."

Cobb shook his head. "Nay, tis foolish to walk ever forward and never look every now and again over your shoulder." He scowled off into the deep forest along the road. "That's how you end up prey. Be it from beast of the wood or a cutpurse of the city. That's how they feed on you."

Elphias drove on. He could think of nothing else to say.


They reached Lancaster an hour later, rolling from dusty road to clatter across a cobblestone thoroughfare running through the center of the town. Brick buildings of two stories lined the street, displaying signs for material goods and services of all types. Elphias didn't see the familiar structure of an apothecary but that meant nothing. Closed to the general public, they weren't a main street operation.

Cobb asked to get off the wagon in front of a rustic wooden building bearing the name Edna Hudson Provisioneers.

"I'll meet you at the Bernd Tavern," Cobb said, climbing down from the vardo with difficulty.

"A burned tavern?" Elphias asked.

Cobb untethered his horse from the back-carriage and grinned. "Only a surname, Doctor Root. Tis that way a spell." He pointed further up the thoroughfare, then tipped his hat and led his horse toward the storefront.

Elphias parked his vardo in an open lot and unhitched the horse. He tethered it near a water trough then set out to seek an apothecary. He'd barely begun his journey when Cobb hobbled into his path, face set into a scowl.

"Won't sell to me! Been ordered, they say! Whole blasted town has!"

Elphias rubbed his jaw. "Under whose orders?"

Cobb shook his head with exasperation. "An inquisitor they say! I'm to meet him at a hotel up the street." He removed his boilerman hat and rubbed a shaky hand through his stringy grey hair. "What query could an inquisitor have of me?"

Elphias shrugged. "There's only one way to find out. May I join you?"

Cobb nodded, brow knit by worry. "Aye, Doctor. T'would be a comfort. You can tend me when my heart gives out."

They walked up the street to an ornately gabled four story surrounded by stylish traveling carriages. An elegant sign on the front ran from roof to entry awning and proclaimed itself the Ellison Hotel.

Elphias opened the front door for Cobb and they entered the lobby. A scattering of high backed chairs flanked a woven carpet leading to the front desk. Females wearing uniforms of the Imperial Guard occupied most of the seats, smoking cigarettes and playing cards. They cast casual glances at Elphias and barely acknowledged Cobb at all.

"So far so good, Cobb," Elphias whispered. "They've not shot us yet."

"That sense of humor ain't always welcome," Cobb groused.

A silver haired woman greeted them at the front desk. "Welcome to the Ellison, the finest hotel from here to Beltram," she stated with head tilted back to show how highly she thought of the place. Elphias had seen better, but some truths need not be shared.

"An inquisitor wanted to see me," Cobb said.

The woman's eyebrows shot up as a hint of a smile touched her mouth. "Oh! That would be Inquisitor Oulcott, a most charming gentleman. You must be the master huntsman. He told me to expect you." She bustled from behind the front desk and beckoned for them to follow. "This way, if you please. He's in the dining room at the moment and wanted to see you immediately, no matter the hour."

The dining room of the Ellison was open and spacious, comfortably fitting ten large round tables within its confines. Inquisitor Oulcott presided over a center table, reading a sheet of paper and holding a cup of coffee in his left hand. He set them both down as the silver haired woman escorted Cobb and Elphias in his direction.

"Ah, Miss Templeton," he smiled. "What may I do for you?"

Elphias figured the inquisitor to be about his own age. The man had a kind, bearded face and grayish green eyes that peered over a pair of spectacles. He wore vest and cravat, and had his sleeves pulled up by a garter on his biceps.

Miss Templeton smiled at the inquisitor and flashed a well manicured hand in Cobb's direction. "This is the gentleman you were waiting for, Inquisitor Oulcott."

"Ah, yes. The master huntsman. Very good, very good. Thank you." He indicated the vacant chairs around his table. "Please gentlemen, be seated. Would you care for some food or drink? My treat of course."

Miss Templeton hovered, waiting to take their order.

"A cup of coffee would be wonderful," Elphias said as he pulled out a chair. "It's a rare occasion I'm allowed the pleasure."

Cobb settled into a seat. "Tea for me. And toast if you have it."

"I'll return with your orders shortly," Miss Templeton said and scurried off toward the kitchen.

"Zediah Oulcott," the inquisitor identified himself.

Cobb fidgeted in his chair. "Brogan Cobb," he said cautiously. "And this be my hireling, Doctor Root."

"Ah," Zediah smiled, "a fellow man of science. A pleasure."

Miss Templeton bustled up to the table and set their drinks in front of them. "But a moment for your toast, good sir," she told Cobb and then set off to get it.

"I should sit with inquisitors more often," Elphias said with good humor. "The service is impeccable."

Inquisitor Oulcott laughed. "Ah, yes. I've become so accustomed to the dramatics I hardly notice it anymore." He sat back in his chair and took a sip of his coffee, then looked at it with distaste. "Cold. I've let myself become distracted again."

"What do you want of me?" Cobb asked firmly. "None will sell to me on your demand."

Zediah set his cup down and reached for a sheaf of papers. He shuffled through them, pulled one free, and then held it so they could read the print. Cobb's flyer.

"This is your billboard, is it not?"

Cobb gave a quick, firm nod. "Tis."

Zediah nodded and set the paper down. "This is why I wished to speak with you upon arrival."

"I'm within the law to gather a hunting party," Cobb said and gripped the tabletop, bunching the white cloth beneath his gauntleted hands.

"Oh, I've no issue with that. I'm not here to stop your hunt. In fact, just the opposite. I have a proposition." The inquisitor sat forward, an excited gleam in his eyes. "I'll fund your expedition under two conditions. One, that my party and I accompany you in an observational capacity. Two, that I may acquire any specimens should your hunt prove successful."

Cobb eyed him with suspicion. "Why do you want the dead things?"

Zediah sat back and shrugged. "For research, what else? There are still gaps in the Academy's knowledge about the monstrous species. The Bureau of Esoteric Inquiries is seeking any of such creatures, providing they weren't hunted to extinction during the Purge."

"Oh they exist," Cobb said. "They exist indeed, don't they Doctor Root?"

Elphias nodded and took a sip of coffee. "I can confirm the existence of wood nymphs several hours west of here."

"Really?" The inquisitor sat forward and picked up a nearby fountain pen. "What exactly did you witness?"

"To be quite honest, I only heard their charm music coming from the forest. I'd know the melodies anywhere, there's nothing quite like it."

"Ah, I see," Zediah said, laying down the pen and sitting back. Then he gave Elphias a curious, thoughtful look. "Their bio-hypnosis had no effect on you, then? Yes, of course. You're a medical doctor, and appear of proper age. Tell me, were you among those who received the immunity conditionings?"

"I was," Elphias admitted and sipped his coffee. Seems he would not escape those memories as easily as he'd wished.

Zediah rubbed his chin, deep in thought. "Fascinating. Hmm." He looked up as Miss Templeton approached and placed Cobb's toast on the table. "Have you additional rooms available for my guests?"

Elphias held up a hand. "There's no need on my part, I've brought my accommodations with me. I'm very accustomed to my mattress."

Cobb nodded. "Nay for me as well. I've lodging secured down the street where the hunting party will be gathering."

"Fine, gentlemen," Zediah said, "that be all Miss Templeton."

"As you please, Inquisitor," she said with a small curtsy, then walked away.

Zediah watched her go, then returned his attention to the table. "So Master Cobb, do we have an arrangement?"

Cobb scratched his bearded chin and took a nibble of toast. They waited as he chewed. "You'll pay for all provisions?"

"You have an open credit, but please confine purchases to the hunt or the Central Treasury will have me tossed into the pits."

Cobb motioned at Elphias. "I've agreed to provide for the doctor's services as well. Should things go badly, his supplies will need to be compensated for."

"Very well," Zediah said, "I'll have an additional contract drawn up for you, Doctor Root." He pulled a set of papers from his pile and handed them across the table to Cobb. "In the meantime here is our contract, Master Cobb. You will see it is plainly written. The Academy of Worldly Science will fund your hunt in exchange for acquiring anything you've captured or slain. At my discretion, of course."

Cobb studied the papers for a few moments. "Aye, tis as you say." Zediah handed him the fountain pen and Cobb shakily scrawled his name in the proper places.

Elphias drained the last of his cup and set it down. He gazed around the dining room, noting that a few other people had drifted in at some point. A woman sat near the window, facing away from Elphias. A long plait of auburn hair trailed midway down the back of her green jacket. She turned her head to look out the window and Elphias' heart nearly stopped.

Lydia. It wasn't actually, nor could it be. But the resemblance of this woman's profile to Lydia was strikingly similar. The same firm set to the chin, the same gentle slope of her nose. Elphias' mouth ran dry and he patted the case within his frock coat without noticing he had done so. Cobb's sharp elbow to his arm snapped his attention back to the table.

Zediah eyed him curiously and flashed a smile. "I asked if you were feeling all right?"

"Yes, forgive me. I—yes, I'm fine." Elphias adjusted his puff tie. "Would you happen to know if there's an apothecary here?"

Zediah shuffled through his papers and removed a hand drawn map. He examined it for a moment. "Ah, yes. Here we are." He handed the map over to Elphias and tapped a rectangle representing a building. Elphias studied the location, trying to imagine the route from the Ellison.

"Take the map," Zediah said. "Return it to me tomorrow and we can finalize your contract as well."

Elphias stood and gave a polite nod to Zediah. "Thank you, Inquisitor. I shall see you then. And you as well, Cobb."

"You know where to find me," Cobb said without looking up from his tea and toast.

Elphias exited the dining room, casting a furtive glance back at the seated woman. She was still looking out the window, firm chin resting on her palm.

*I wonder what she's waiting for?* Elphias wondered, then thought, *What am I waiting for, for that matter?*

He exited through the lobby, oblivious to the glances of the guardswomen.

The outside smelled of smoke and horse droppings, adjusting Elphias' perspective immediately. He surveyed the map, turned it to match the direction he faced, then set off up the street.


The apothecary was located down a back alley, tucked behind a carriage maker's factory. Elphias could hear hammering from the factory and the air smelled of sawdust. He was disappointed by the state of the building, a dilapidated narrow structure with only a black door and no windows on the first floor to identify it as an apothecary. Even the skull above the door was a painted representation, not an actual artifact. Regardless, he hoped they would have what he required. He approached the black door and tilted his head towards a speaking tube running into the building.

"Ahoy," Elphias said. Long silent moments passed, with occasional interruptions by the carriage maker's muffled hammering. He prepared to speak again when a man's hollow voice echoed from the speaking tube.

"Who stands at Death's door?"

"Root, Elphias. Three-seven-four-six-two." He waited as the speaker verified his information in the Physician's Annual.

A bolt was drawn back from the door with a rusty grind. "You may cross the threshold."

# The Spirit of Innovation

The inside was worse than he'd feared. There wasn't even an inner chamber to pass, the valet merely motioned for him to follow. The man appeared older than Cobb, but naturally aged with wisps of hair covering his liver spotted head. They passed across a threadbare carpet to a wooden counter. The valet crossed behind it and faced Elphias. Of course he'd be the pharmacist as well.

"What d'ye need, brother?"

Elphias handed him a list. The man scanned it and nodded.

"Good that," he said. "Save for the ampules."

Elphias' spirits sank. "You've none at all?"

"I've Black Poppy, but naught else from the Parkwell."

"That seems highly irregular."

The valet shrugged with indifference. "No Black Poppy, for ye then?"

Elphias sighed. "Just provide what you can."

He walked to a nearby chair and flopped down onto its tattered cushion, waiting while the ancient pharmacist filled his order.

That night Elphias dreamed a familiar dream where he stands bare chested before a mirror, illuminated by the flicker of leviathan oil lamps. A tray of surgical instruments lays to his side, and Elphias selects a gleaming scalpel. It slices easily through his flesh, traversing from sternum to mid abdomen. He uses his reflection as a guide while he cuts, noticing the mirror image is weeping silently. Setting down the scalpel, Elphias reaches into the chest cavity and extracts his beating heart. He drops it without hesitation, then begins to suture his chest closed. Afterwards he studies himself in the mirror. The incision is closed in the Y stitch of an autopsy, and his reflection is no longer crying. It has been cured.

Elphias awoke sweaty and tangled in his blanket. Harsh morning sunlight glared in through the rear window and he fumbled the curtains closed. He shut his eyes and tried to drift back to sleep. After twenty minutes he knew it was useless and flung back the covers with exasperation. He dressed himself, then took Zediah's map and set off toward the Ellison Hotel.

Cobb was outside the Bernd Tavern, facing a line of nine rough looking men. Cobb paced back and forth in front of them, like an officer examining his troops.

"Hoy, Doctor," Cobb called. He turned to the hunting party and pointed at Elphias. "This here's the man that will mend your wounds should you run afoul of misfortune. Pay him the respect he deserves."

The men regarded Elphias with dark eyes. They mumbled greetings as he tipped his top hat to them.

"Hopefully you won't need my services," he said.

"Aye," Cobb agreed. "Will you be ready to leave in two hours, Doctor?"

Elphias nodded. "I'm headed now to meet with the inquisitor. Other than that I need only ready my horse, the vardo is already stocked with medical supplies."

Cobb nodded with approval. "Then I won't delay you. I need to run these lads through some drills. Benson!"

One of the older men jerked at the name. "Yes?"

Elphias started off toward the Ellison, listening as he walked away.

"You ever used a fire sprayer?"

"Nay, Master Cobb."

"Then it's time you learned. You'll be the fireman."

Elphias had known a few firemen during the Purge. Wearing a tank with a hose that could spray burning leviathan oil, their job was to stand outside of wooded areas and burn any creatures driven out. As this was also where most field hospitals were staged, Elphias had been able to speak with many of them in the boring lull between engagements. He could still picture their sooty faces, but their names were long gone. He'd begun the curious habit of forgetting people's names after parting their company. He couldn't really recall when it had begun. Or at least he chose not to remember.

The dining room was full. Elphias noticed that the guardswomen were seated together at a rear table along with a female officer. The officer stared at Elphias as if memorizing his face, then turned back to her table mates.

Zediah was sitting at the same table from the day before, but this time he was not alone. The young woman, the one who reminded Elphias of Lydia, was sitting with him. She looked up as Elphias approached, fresh faced and hazel eyed, and his guts did a flip. Her eyebrows were arched differently, the cheekbones more pronounced, and her jaw more rounded, but the resemblance was even stronger than he could have imagined. Her auburn hair was pulled forward over her shoulder, spilling down across her white blouse. Elphias maligned himself for staring at her and shifted his focus to Zediah instead.

"Good morning, Doctor Root. Please join us."

Elphias fumbled for a chair, hands shaking slightly. He thought of his ampules and fought the urge to take the case out then and there.

"This is my secretary, Miss Crevan," Zediah said. "This of course is Doctor Root."

"Please call me Bella," she said. Her voice was different too, lower and with a precise pronunciation. Elphias suspected she'd overcome a regional dialect to sound more cosmopolitan.

Elphias removed his top hat. *Say something you fool!*

"Elphias. A pleasure to make your acquaintance, Miss…Bella."

She laughed, her cheeks full and flushed with color. A pool of blood flashed in Elphias' mind. He fought the memories with everything he had.

Elphias sat quickly, feeling foolish. If it showed, Zediah and Bella gave no indication. "Thank you for use of the map," he said and returned it to Zediah.

"I hope it was of use. Were you able to procure everything you required?"

"Fair enough." He resisted the urge to stare at Bella. She wasn't Lydia. Lydia was lost in his past.

A platter of scrambled eggs and bacon sat in the center of the table, next to a pot of coffee.

"Help yourself, please," Zediah said.

Elphias took the plate in front of him and scooped some eggs on, then added two strips of bacon. He set down the plate and then stared at the food. He'd been starving on the way here. Now he felt nauseous. *I should have stayed by that river*, he thought with regret.

Zediah handed some papers across the table. "Here is your contract, Doctor Root. You will find it similar to Master Cobb's."

Elphias took the contract and pretended to study it. His mind was too unfocused to make proper sense of the words, the sentences fragmented into incoherence as he tried to read them. *This is madness. Come to your senses, she's half your age! And she isn't Lydia!*

He took Zediah's fountain pen and signed the contract. The signature looked strange to him, as if it belonged to someone else. He held out the contract and pen.

Bella leaned forward and took them from him. Her fingers were slender, the nails neatly manicured and trimmed short. "Did you travel far to come here, Doctor Root?" she asked.

Elphias laughed. "More than you could imagine. I travel from place to place, rendering assistance where I can." He stared down at his hands. "I've been moving about the Empire now for more years than I care to remember."

He forked some eggs into his mouth and chewed them. His hunger returned suddenly and he nibbled on some bacon.

"That must be terribly exciting," Bella said in her earnest tone, hazel eyes sparkling with imagination.

Elphias swallowed and took a sip of coffee. "You must see some excitement, traveling with Inquisitor Oulcott?"

Bella grinned. "This is only my second field work with the inquisitor, and my excitement is mostly confined to transcribing his adventures and queries." She cast a sidelong glance at Zediah. "A shapeshifting wolf man last time, wasn't it?"

Zediah laughed and looked at Elphias. "Some rumors are bull wash," he admitted. "But don't let her modesty fool you, she's a skilled observer. She drew that map you used by memory. She'd make an excellent inquisitor of her own."

Bella shook her head and grinned. "There's a special inquisitor and a grand inquisitor, but I've never heard of a secretary inquisitor."

"There's a time for everything," Zediah said. "Times are changing. That's the nature of progress, and the progress of nature: always moving forward, transmuting to something new."

"There are female inquisitors, are there not?" Elphias asked.

Zediah nodded. "Yes, though not as many as should be." He smirked at some private thought and Elphias suddenly wondered if inquisitors ever faced questioning, and if so, by whom? Zediah looked at Bella and continued. "They represent half our population, but less than a quarter of the inquisition staff. It is a mystery that still eludes me."

"Must be our mysterious natures," Bella said jokingly.

The guardswomen stood as one and filed past their table. The officer stopped and faced Zediah.

"We are ready to depart upon command, Inquisitor."

"Excellent, Commander. Prepare our charge for travel."

"At once." She gave Zediah a curt nod, then strode from the room with head held high.

Bella began to gather Zediah's papers. "And I will perform my duty of transcription." A smile played at her lips.

Elphias watched her movements, trying to resist bewitchment. *I'm supposed to be immune to charms*, he thought with irritation.

"You're not joining us?" he asked. Bella shook her head and he felt a contrasting tug of disappointment and relief.

"No, I will be guarding this hotel with my teletype and keen observation."

Zediah laughed. "You see, I told you. She's more than just a secretary."

"Don't I wish," Bella said.


"Nay! Tis forbidden!" Cobb's face was red, his eyes narrowed and glinting with rage. He stood in front of Zediah, his arm thrust in accusation at the female guards. "Women are prohibited from the hunt! You should know this! Have you no respect for tradition?"

Zediah held his hands up in a show of surrender. "They are in my accompany, and in an observational capacity only. They will act in a defensive manner if my party is at risk, but will otherwise remain apart from your activities."

Cobb screwed up his face. "But tis dangerous! They could be killed!"

"It is a chance they have committed themselves to, Master Cobb. They've taken vows of procreative abstinence and have pledged their lives in service to the Empire. There will be no violations of law." He stared at Cobb. "Besides, we have a contract as you recall."

"And does it include whomever you've got in there?" Cobb pointed off to a witness box flanked by two guardswomen. It was a wheeled cart with a wood structure fixed to the bed. The enclosure was seven feet tall and thinly designed, forcing its occupant to stand until released. Only a narrow slot set high in the bolted door provided light to the unfortunate soul within. It was never a good sign to see a witness box.

Zediah nodded. "It does."

Cobb darkened further. Elphias was afraid he'd have an apoplectic fit but he turned and stalked off instead.

"Tis unnatural," Cobb muttered as he moved away. "Naught good will come of this."

Elphias looked at Zediah. "May I ask who's inside the witness box?"

"You may," Zediah said with a smile, then turned and walked away.

Elphias watched him go, wishing he'd read his own contract when he'd had the opportunity. Now it was far too late.

# Carcer Kane

Teletype Transmission [Decoded]:

ADMINISTRATIVE EYES ONLY
Re: SUBJECT background check
23 Patero, 1867
Auris,
I made acquaintance with SUBJECT to-day when he signed an Academy contract of Temporary Hire (included in official transmission). He confessed to be a traveler, which may explain the lack of residency records. I detected no ill-will towards the Inquisitor, though SUBJECT gets a furrow between his eyebrows when looking at me. I detect no menace. Perhaps he is uncomfortable around women.
The Inquisitor is currently on hunt with SUBJECT and others. I will give additional update should the need arise. Until then I await further order.
Dutifully,
Oculus

Bella sat back from the teletype and rolled her neck and shoulders. So much paperwork to transmit to the Academy, even before the addition of the doctor to the party. She pushed the padded chair away from the desk, grateful that the Ellison provided such amenity. On her last assignment with the inquisitor they'd been forced to take meager accommodations, so she'd balanced the teletype on a rickety side table that swayed with every key press.

She stood and crossed the thick floral carpeting to the room's tall window, opened to allow fresh air, sunlight, and the ambient sounds of Lancaster in. Her room overlooked a bountiful garden at the back of the hotel, and one of the kitchen staff was down there picking tomatoes. The woman's dark skin contrasted starkly with the bleached white uniform to beautiful effect. The surrounding sea of vegetable plants looked robust and vibrant with a colorful bounty of fresh peppers, beans, and squashes. No wonder the food had tasted so wonderful.

Beyond the magnificent garden an open field sloped down to a winding creek shepherded by occasional trees. Bella could see a few women washing clothes down at the water, while a group of small children chased each other around the field shrieking with delight. She smiled, her eyes betraying the opposite emotion.

*I hope you have normal lives,* she wished for the kids. The boys would be fine—unless a war broke out—as would most of the girls. But perhaps one or two of those young ladies would be taken along a different path. One of secrecy and necessary lies, like Bella had. A path where people think you're just an ordinary secretary.

The teletype clattered behind her as an incoming message began to print. Bella took a steadying breath and straightened her skirt, then returned to the device to receive her orders. An illustrated mouth was printed at the top of the page, a clear sign it was not from official Academy channels. She's thankful it's a beautiful day. She can set the trashcan by the window to burn the transmission after reading it, as she did with every message from the Body. All spies were required to do so.

# CHAPTER THREE
*The Hunt*

Elphias drove alone to the hunting ground, following the procession of wagons as they wound their way back to the cemetery. Lydia haunted his mind, personified through Bella. Sometimes it was Bella with Lydia's voice, other times the reverse. He tried to recall all the diseases he knew of in a futile attempt at distraction but Lydia plagued the back of his thoughts anyway. Memories arose unbidden, like the first time he'd set eyes on her. She'd been walking through Memorial Park with some friends, an amber sunlight lining their profiles. Lydia's companions had been striking and glamorous, but it was her wholesome features and vibrant personality that captured Elphias' attention immediately. He approached and introduced himself, unable to let her pass without making an attempt of conversation. To his delight, Lydia was drawn to him as well. Her friends had tittered and left them to talk, and they'd spent the afternoon wandering the city and enjoying each other's company.

*Was I really that young and bold once?* With a bit of shock he realized it had been ten years ago, in 1857, the year after he'd opened his practice in Arkoff. It had occupied the lower floor of a brick two story, and featured an office, washroom, examination room, and waiting area. After the horrors of the Purge it had been a welcome change of pace, free of painful shrieks, gouts of blood, and ragged strips of flesh. Elphias had a steady stream of patients, middle class merchants and tradespeople for the most part. Decent people with average injuries and illnesses. None had ever come to him afflicted with basilisk venom, or hexed by a red witch.

## The Spirit of Innovation

On their second date Elphias had given Lydia an after hours tour of the practice, relating what duties he performed. They finished back in the waiting area, and that was where they first kissed. They'd been standing next to each other, Elphias had said some silly thing and Lydia had laughed. They looked at each other and their eyes locked. He could still remember the moment, the silent vacuum of awareness between the both of them, as if some switch had been flipped. And then they were tilting their faces to each other, mouths opening and lips brushing together, the heat of their breath upon their tongues. Her body pressed against him, his right hand grasped her lower back and drew her closer. Feeling the stiff fabric of her jacket beneath his fingers and the press of her breasts against his chest. His previous infatuation with her transformed in a single beat of his heart. It exploded, boiling with alchemical fury, forging passion, white hot and scorching. It was all they could do not to violate the law. They were breathless, as bonded as the Dualvinity. They filed an application for a Permit of Procreation the next day. There would be more kissing as they awaited approval. And they were.

The vardo bounced over a rut in the road, snapping Elphias back to his surroundings. He rubbed at his face and wasn't surprised to find his cheeks wet. His familiar home creaked around him, swaying with the pace of the horse. He'd owned it since 1858, bought it with the money he'd gained by selling his practice. That was the year of the tragedy, the year he'd rolled out of Arkoff and began his wandering. He'd never been back. He doubted he ever would. That old life was dead to him.

They reached the cemetery as the sun began to dip from its zenith. One of the men was a packmaster and had loaded his hunting dogs on Cobb's newly purchased wagon. Their alert yellow stares made Elphias' horse nervous, so he eased his vardo away from the hunters and parked it near the ancient cemetery. He stepped down off the vardo and blocked the wheels, tied the reins to the cemetery fence, then set off to join the others. He left the horse hitched so he could immediately depart after the hunt, find the nearest fully stocked apothecary, and deliver himself from pain and unwanted memories.

Cobb was shouting orders at the hunters, who reluctantly complied with his terse instructions on unloading their weapons and supplies. Elphias approached as the hunter Benson was struggling a metal tank outfitted with shoulder straps and a spray hose from the wagon.

"Watch it," Cobb snapped with irritation. "That's fifteen gallons of leviathan oil. Spark that tank and you'll burn all night."

"I'd rather not have the honor," Benson whispered, eyes wide and never leaving the tank as he gingerly set it on the ground.

Cobb turned to the others and pointed to the packmaster and a pale-faced man.

"Fang and Whitey will take the dogs in the woods to drive out the quarry. The rest of us will form our firing line along this way, and the fireman will take care of any that pass us. All understood?"

The surly and brooding men nodded and gave their assent.

Cobb turned to Elphias. "Doctor Root, are you prepared?"

"Yes. I'll stage the field hospital there."

"Next to the graves." Cobb grinned slyly. "You doctors are a funny lot." He adjusted his boilerman's hat and then went to the wagon to retrieve his gun.

They'd armed themselves with bolt action carbines, loaded with jacketed dragon powder ammunition and fixed with bayonets. Purge tech, Elphias mused. Jacketed ammunition had been invented late in the Purge, the result of desperation and desire for victory. The Purge had begun in 1844, when men were armed with muzzle loaded rifles, notoriously slow to reload when facing a charging beast. Jacketed ammunition and bolt action rifles had debuted in 1854. Two years later the Purge ended. And once the threat of the beasts was removed, progress exploded with a rapidity that few could have ever imagined. Elphias had toured enough of the Empire over the years to have witnessed the beginnings of forged iron frames for buildings. Height was no longer a concern for brick structures, the rigid steel would support the weight. Steam powered sky trains navigated cities, underslung from elevated tracks to pass safely above pedestrians and carriage traffic below. The track itself, the inner structure of the brick towers that supported it, all from the power of steel. It was truly a wondrous time to be alive.

The inquisition party had made camp a short distance from Elphias' vardo. Zediah was overseeing two guardswomen carrying a trunk from their provision wagon. He was dressed in an Inverness jacket and wore a slouch hat to shade himself from the blazing sun. The women set the trunk down, then joined their fellow guard standing around the witness box. As Elphias approached he was shocked to see the guards armed with sleek new rifles. A lever curled around the trigger, forming a trigger guard and Elphias noticed one of them cock the lever, loading a round into the chamber. Others were loading ammunition into a small slot set below an ejection port. Elphias had never seen a rifle that held additional rounds within itself. Dragon powder was a rare commodity, the dried shite of an extinct beast. Ammunition was almost as expensive as the weapons that fired them. Technology was advancing more rapidly than he'd realized. It was being developed for threats yet unimagined.

"Hoy, Doctor," Zediah called as Elphias approached.

"Hoy, Inquisitor." Elphias looked down at the chest. The official seal of the Academy of Worldly Science was emblazoned upon the lid, as was an icon of an open eye, the seal of the Inquisition. "I must admit, I'm curious what's inside."

Zediah smiled. "No reason to deny you, your taxes helped pay for the contents." He bent to the chest and fiddled with a combination lock holding it closed. The lock snapped open and he slipped it free and tucked it in the pocket of his jacket. Zediah opened the lid. The lower part of the crate was compartmentalized, small drawers and nooks for various vials and bottles. Elphias' eyes were drawn to two items mounted to the underside of the lid, held in place by pegs and straps.

"I recognize the televox," Elphias said, looking at the smaller device. It was a handset, inset with a harmonium fragment attuned to the harmonium fragment of another device. Speaking into one televox caused the harmonium to vibrate within both devices, transmitting a raspy replica of the speaker's conversation on the other unit. Although it could only be paired to one televox, the distance between them was limitless. "Is that attuned to the Academy?"

"Ah, yes, normally it would be. Currently it's affixed to my return transport, an airship." Zediah removed the televox and displayed it to Elphias. "It's the latest model, you see this screw here? If you remove it you can open the handset and swap out the harmonium chip." He lowered the televox and slipped it into his jacket pocket. "I hear they're working on a model that will hold multiple chips. Rotate a switch and it will connect you to a different televox. Imagine the possibilities."

Zediah unstrapped the other item from the lid. "I'll bet you've never seen the like of this," he said proudly. It looked like a long barreled pistol, with a rubberized grip and a pair of metal prongs at the end instead of a muzzle. A small hand crank was set to the side of the device.

"Truly put," Elphias admitted.

Zediah gripped the gun with his hand and rotated the hand crank several times. Then he pointed it away from them. "I present the shock gun," he said and pulled the trigger. A spark of electricity shot out of the end about the distance of a foot and danced like lightning. He released the trigger and the skittering discharge vanished.

"The number of rotations determines if it incapacitates or kills," Zediah said. "I wished they'd given it a better name, but I think you'll agree it's an impressive weapon." He leaned down and placed the prongs to the ground, then discharged the gun. "Safety first," he grinned, then pulled back his jacket to hitch the weapon to a loop on his belt. He glanced off towards the woods. "Ah, the hunt begins."

Elphias turned. The dogs were loping into the forest, ears and tails low, noses bobbing to scents only they could detect. Fang and Whitey followed, armed with short barreled shotguns. It had been a long time since Elphias had seen this many weapons in one place. The dogs and men vanished into the undergrowth and Cobb strung his men out in a line distanced several yards from the trees.

He looked over to his vardo, and the lonely graves beyond. "I should prepare my station."

Zediah nodded. "Let's hope there won't be the need."

"I couldn't agree more," Elphias said, and then set off through the high grass to ready himself for bloodshed.

The sun dipped lower as Elphias waited. He'd already prepped syringes and bandages, filled the basin with jugged water he'd acquired in Lancaster, and readied tourniquet strips and his bone saw. He also had a bottle of ether and cloth, just in case he needed to use the saw. In the fury of the Purge, Elphias had been forced to sometimes rely on his amputation patient biting down on a stick for anesthetic. He'd not do that to anyone ever again if it could be avoided. For his final preparation, Elphias had taken an ampule of Green Glory from his case and slipped it into the watch pocket of his vest.

Clouds scudded in, pushed by a lazy current. The guardswomen stood their positions, shifting their weight from foot to foot as they waited. Elphias rearranged his surgical tools and tried not to think about the empty slots in his ampule case, especially the Blue Oasis. *Should I backtrack to Binderpeak?* he wondered. *The apothecary was fully stocked. I could—*

# The Spirit of Innovation

The baying of dogs echoed suddenly from the woods, startling Elphias to awareness and chilling his blood. Their barks increased in tempo, descending into deep pitched growls. Shrieks followed, high and piping. They'd found the wood nymphs.

Cobb was shouting at the firing line but Elphias couldn't hear him over the chaos from the forest. The guardswomen were standing at the ready, rifles unslung and pointed toward the ground. Zediah stood by them, staring at the dark woods with arms folded over his chest.

The din grew closer. Elphias' heart pounded. He pulled the Green Glory from his watch pocket and snapped the top off. Then he swallowed the liquid in one quick gulp and tossed away the empty ampule as if it were something unclean. The shrieks grew louder, the dog's barking more frenzied. Elphias could hear a great crashing of underbrush now, drawing ever closer. The firing line was reforming, compensating for the frenzied movement coming from the wood. Benson stood behind them, flame flickering at the end of the spray head. He was quivering with fear.

*I should have given him the Green,* Elphias thought. He stared into the woods and could see the underbrush swaying, leaves jerky and whipping beneath a mad dash of fearful creatures. The shrieking was almost deafening, multiple voices chorused in instinctual terror. It sounded like there were a lot of them. *There's too many,* Elphias realized suddenly as he caught sight of the thin brown shapes crashing through the foliage. *Cobb, you fool! What where you thinking?*

And then the nymphs began to burst forth from the forest. They were tall and slender, and feral faced with fanged teeth, emerald green eyes, and skin the color of bark. Their long, slender fingers tapered down to thin, sharp points. Deceptively fragile looking, those claws were anything but. Elphias had seen what they could do. It's what they used to drill out the bones to make their instruments.

Sensing the men the wood nymphs shrieks of terror turned to rage and they charged the firing line. The men fired, smoke filling the air from the muzzle blasts. Wood nymphs staggered and fell, but more were still pouring out of the forest. The huntsmen were quickly working the bolt action of their rifles and filling the empty breech with fresh ammo. Those few nymphs of the first wave, three that survived the hail of bullets, dashed forward in the lull, finding an opening in the firing line and taking advantage of it. One of them flicked out a long arm as it passed a hunter. He screamed and fell, weapon tumbling from his hands and a gout of blood spraying from his open guts.

The three wood nymphs raced for freedom. Benson turned his nozzle towards them and squeezed the trigger. Flaming leviathan oil sprayed in an arc, igniting the creatures immediately. They shrieked louder, tumbling and clawing in agony, flame and black smoke roiling from their thin bodies.

The firing line exploded with another barrage, downing another tangle of wood nymphs exiting the forest. A few of them still stood, but by then the dogs had reached them and hauled them down, savaging the screaming creatures with their sharp teeth. The huntsmen surged forward, bayonets readied, and began to stab at the writhing bodies.

The disemboweled man moaned and twisted with agony. Elphias grabbed his doctor's bag and ran to the patient's side. It was a lost cause. The man's abdominal wall had been cleanly slit open as had his viscera. Elphias could see ragged sections of his small intestine and ascending colon where the claws had rendered them open, spilling their toxins into the body cavity. There was nothing he could do but end the man's suffering. Elphias reached for his ampule case and extracted the Black Poppy. The man was watching him, eyes glazed with pain and blood slicked teeth bared in a grimace.

Elphias snapped the top off the Black Poppy. "This will end your suffering," he said. The man nodded and opened his mouth, gore speckled lips quivering with the effort. Elphias emptied the ampule and the man choked it down. He lay his head back and closed his eyes, face contorted with pain. Eventually the facial muscles began to relax and his breathing grew shallower and shallower, until at last his chest stopped rising and falling.

*Another death,* Elphias thought darkly. *How many more will I witness before my own draws me into the black?*

Approaching footsteps shuffled through the field grass. Elphias looked up. "Cobb."

Cobb stared at the eviscerated corpse and shook his head with pity. "Gut cut. Blasted way to die, that."

Elphias rubbed his chin. "There's a good way?"

Cobb nodded, mouth thin. "Better ways, at least." He looked off toward the inquisition party and frowned. "Oh, now what's this?"

Two guardswomen were facing the witness box, flanking their commander and Zediah, as another unbolted the door and swung it open. The commander stared into the box. "Come out," she said, her voice firm and loud from thirty yards away. A young woman shuffled out of the witness box, dressed only in a dark chemise. She raised her thin arms, bony hands shielding her eyes from the glare of sunlight. Blinded from its intensity, she missed her footing on the steps and tumbled to the ground with a cry of surprise. The guardswoman closest to her leapt back with a startled shout. The two next to the commander raised their rifles and stood firm, as did she. "Get up," she ordered the prone woman.

The woman tried to rise, thin arms quaking and head hanging slack. Zediah shook his head and strode forward over the protest of the commander. "Oh, for the love of the Divine!" he shouted with disgust. "Can't you see how weak she is?" He squatted next to the woman and spoke softly to her.

Elphias started in their direction. "Maybe I can be of assistance."

Cobb snorted with anger. "Tis naught to do with me," he snapped and hobbled off toward the remaining huntsmen.

Zediah helped the frail woman up, taking her by the forearm and giving her support. "This way," he told her, "it's not far." The guardswomen trailed behind, following Zediah and the woman. The commander walked behind them all, scowling with disapproval.

Elphias met them part way. "Is she all right?"

Zediah met his eye and gave a nod. "Yes, thank you, Doctor Root." He glanced at the woman. "It's distasteful how she is treated, but that is the law." His expression firmed and his brow wrinkled. "And I must obey."

Elphias suddenly understood. "She's a witch."

Zediah gave a curt nod. He led her towards a scattering of dead wood nymphs, laying sprawled where they had died. Zediah stopped before the nearest one and pointed to it, addressing the witch. "I want you to preserve the bodies, preserve them for transport. Do you understand?"

The witch stared down at the corpse and said nothing. Her mouth hung open and Elphias began to wonder if they'd sedated her when she nodded, ever so slight.

Zediah gave her arm a squeeze. "Good. Good." He released her and stepped closer to Elphias. "Have you ever witnessed a witch at work?"

"No," Elphias said, then glanced to his left where Cobb was overseeing the hunters. "I've seen their results though."

"Ah, yes. I suppose you would have during the Purge. Red witches are a nasty lot. Celindra is a green, if you're aware of the differences."

Celindra kneeled in the grass next to the nymph corpse and began to gently rub her palms on its forearm. Her lips moved in a whisper of syllables but neither Elphias nor Zediah could make them out.

Elphias rubbed his brow. "It's their virtue, I've heard. The green witch is a virgin, the red not. And there's the old saying 'A green will take your ills away, the red will curse you to the grave."

"Yes, you're correct. But the differences go even deeper than that."

The dogs began barking somewhere in the forest, followed by a woman's terrified scream. Elphias hadn't noticed that they'd gone back in. If not for the sedative he'd have jumped with fright. Everyone else did, however. All but the green witch, Elphias noted.

Cobb wheeled about, eyes wide. "Ready yourselves! Weapons up! Make sure you've reloaded!" The huntsmen scrabbled with their rifles, ejecting the spent shells from their last salvo. From the wood the dogs continued to bark, drawing closer. A woman's voice was pleading something incoherently, overridden by Fang's voice.

"Shut yer yaps, mutts! Leave her be!"

The dogs fell silent, save for a few residual yips. Now the woman could clearly be heard, pleading through hysterical tears. "They had me captured, didn't they, the willow folk. I was up a tree to hide of the dogs. They scare me terrible."

Cobb shook his head. "Ease off. Lower the guns, lads."

Dogs began to bound out of the underbrush, stopping to look back with tails wagging. A dirty faced woman dressed in ragged clothing stepped out next, followed by Fang. The woman took a look at everyone staring at her with weapons in hand and shrieked with fright. She dropped to her knees and covered her head, weeping in terror. "Oh, please don't a kill me, like them willow folk."

Zediah strode forward and stopped before her. "Good woman," he said amicably, "please stand up. No one means you harm."

Her weeping subsided. She unclasped her hands and tilted her head to face Zediah. Her eyes were red from crying, the tears having washed trails of grime from her filthy cheeks. A twig stuck out of her wild black hair. Zediah motioned for her to rise and she warily got to her feet. And there she stood, hands clasped together and eyes looking to the ground.

"What's your name?" Zediah asked.

"Ena," she said softly.

"What were you doing in the forest?" Zediah's voice remained smooth and calming. Elphias wondered how many people he'd questioned over his career.

Ena flicked a sly glance off to her right and Elphias turned his head to see what she'd been looking at. His vardo?

"I was captured by the willow folk. Then I was up a tree of the dogs."

"Ah, I see. But what were you doing in the woods before the willow folk captured you?"

Again the furtive glances towards his vardo. Elphias frowned. Had this woman been following him?

Ena glanced up into Zediah's eyes and then her expression broke. Tears began leaking down her face, cleansing more skin. "Oh, I cain't help it," she said in a shrill tone, "I think on it all the time."

Zediah's smile froze. "Think on what?"

Ena looked about, cast another glance at Elphias' vardo, then thrust an accusing finger in his direction. "He knows. He's of the same."

Elphias blinked with surprise, feeling exposed as everyone turned to look in his direction. All but Celindra, he noted. She was watching Ena. "Me? What do I have to do with any of this?"

Ena looked at him with wild eyes. "The feelings, right? The thinking about them?" Zediah looked back and forth between Elphias and Ena, cautiously amused.

"What are you talking about?" Elphias shouted. "Thinking of who?"

Ena thrust her hand towards his vardo. "The dead!" she screamed, then looked in that direction and fell into a reverent and hushed whisper. "The dead."

Elphias felt like a fool. She'd been looking at the cemetery, not his vardo! Because he'd parked there she'd assumed he carried a similar fascination with the buried dead. He was about to explain this to Zediah when he noticed the inquisitor sharing a look with Celindra. The green witch nodded her head solemnly. "She's a one," she said.

Zediah suddenly stepped backwards, drawing his shock gun and winding the hand crank. "Red witch!"

Cobb's voice came piercingly high. "Weapons up! Weapons up!" Everyone that bore a weapon had it pointed at the red witch. She turned back to the forest but Fang and his dogs blocked her way.

"I surrender, I surrender!"

Zediah kept his shock gun pointed at Ena. "You will come peacefully."

"Yes! Yes!" She looked towards the cemetery and sobbed. "Can I see them a last time afore we go?"

Zediah cast Elphias a glance. "Doctor Root, do you have any sedatives or sleep aids in your wagon?"

"I do."

Zediah smiled. "Wonderful. Then yes, you may visit the cemetery again. But under guard. And you will do as you're told."

She nodded. "Yes, Master, yes! Thankee."


They walked toward the cemetery, the red witch at the fore and the guardswomen behind. The fireman walked to Ena's flank, cutting her off from dashing back toward the forest. Zediah paced next to Elphias as they followed the pack.

"As I began to explain previously, Doctor Root, on the differences between the red and green witches."

"Oh, yes. You were saying?"

"A side effect of red magic is a strain upon the mental wellness of the witch. Overwhelmingly they suffer from simultaneous maladies; an obsession with one thing and an abject terror of another, a phobia as the alienists call it. What these things are, the things that warp their personality, is unique to each individual."

"So based on her obsession with graves you deduced she was a red witch?"

"I certainly had my suspicions at that point. Celindra's confirmation finalized it."

Elphias considered this for a moment. "What do you suppose her fear is?"

Zediah cast a glance up to the sky and adjusted his glasses then looked downward for several paces. "I'm sure they will discover that at the Academy," he said solemnly.

A horse clopped past on the road, pulling the empty witness box. Celindra had been left behind with two guardswomen. The driver brought the witness box to a halt near the cemetery then walked to the back and opened the door.

Ena stopped moving. "What's that?" She shook her head wildly back and forth. "No, no, no, no! I cain't! I cain't go in there!" She whirled suddenly, head bobbing as she tried to look past the guardswomen, desperately trying to meet

Zediah's eyes. "Kind Master, please! I cain't go in there! Tie me to a horse, drag me if you must, but…"

Benson the fireman rolled his eyes. "Shut your mouth and move witch!" He stepped forward to menace her to movement. And she moved. Screaming with terror and rage she lunged at him. "Oi!" Benson shouted but she dodged around his fire nozzle, babbling something that made their ears sour. Then she slapped him across the face and was off toward the woods.

Benson screamed and staggered forward, free hand clutching his face where the witch had touched him. Deep wrinkles were already spreading out from the spot, rapidly aging the flesh as it moved, causing decades of damage in seconds. He screamed again and Elphias moved to help. There was nothing he could do to stop the aging, but he could ether the fireman until the pain had stopped. Or he died of some age related dysfunction.

The guardswomen raised their strange rifles and were tracking the witch as she ran. The commander drew in a breath. "Aim, and…"

"Alive, if possible," Zediah said.

"…Fire!"

The rifles popped and the witch screamed with pain. Ena tumbled into the long grasses, wailing with agony. Her screams mingled with Benson's. His voice was aged and hoarse, the wrinkles had already claimed his head and neck and were racing down his arms and through his body. He suddenly grunted and stiffened with pain, clutching his chest with a free hand. His eyes rolled up and his finger contracted upon the trigger of the fire sprayer.

A gout of flame shot forth, the heat baking Elphias' face. He staggered backwards and fell, bumping his head on the ground. Eyes to the sky he never saw Benson drop to his knees, the gout of flame spraying through the open door of the vardo. But when he sat up, when he gained his perspective of what he was seeing, his world shattered. A vortex of fire blazed out of the door, blasting glass from the windows. The horse rose up in terror, engulfed in flame, and rocked the vardo violently back and forth before springing it free from the blocks. The dying animal surged forward in a futile gallop, smashing the front wheel into the cemetery fence. The wagon bounced onto two wheels and, already top heavy by design, crashed on its side with violent impact. The sound of shattering glass came from within as beakers and vials of pharmaceutical liquids fell from cupboards. The horse collapsed. Green flames flared from within the vardo, fed by the chemicals and wooden interior.

Elphias was running towards the inferno, yelling at the top of his voice. He didn't remember getting up and didn't remember starting to run. A sudden and strong impact to his side knocked him to the ground in the tackling embrace of a guardswoman. She held him down, telling him something over and over but he couldn't understand what she was saying. He didn't care. All he was seeing was Lydia; Lydia burning. His only picture of her was in there, burning up with everything he owned. Everything. The one thing in his life that couldn't die was doing just that in front of his eyes.

Elphias snaked a hand into his coat, reaching for the slim case, then remembered he'd given the Black Poppy to the huntsman. He turned his head to the side, unable to watch the fire any longer. Off in the distance he saw Cobb, red faced and thrusting his bayonet over and over again at something on the ground. Cobb was screaming in rage. Elphias closed his eyes and turned his face to the ground, pressing his forehead against it.

And then he screamed too.

# CHAPTER FOUR
### *No Choice*

Elphias sifted through the ashes, unsure of what else to do. There was nothing to be saved really, besides melted bits of metal and a few small bottles, their glass scorched black. Even the stove was a loss, warped from the heat of the blazing inferno and buckled from when the burning vardo finally collapsed in upon itself in a dying plume of spark and flame. After the fire had died down enough to get close, Elphias used a long branch from the woods to drag his cashbox from the embers. The metal was as blackened and buckled as his lost stove and he waited anxiously for it to cool enough to touch. One of the guardswomen, perhaps the one that had saved him from dashing into the fire, gave him a jug of water which he used to pour over the box. Once the sizzling, steamy protest had stopped he set down the jug and opened the damaged container.

Ashes. A few singed corners of the bank notes that once filled the container remained, but that was all. His deposit records, identification papers, and field surgeon license had also been consumed by the flames. He squatted before it, hollowed out. *I have nothing*, he thought miserably. Even his ampule case was empty.

"Have you no coin?" Zediah's voice was soft and low. They were alone at that point, everyone else busied by some task. The guardswomen were crating bodies of the preserved dead for transport to the Academy, while Cobb and the huntsmen were off in the brush, seeking where the wood nymphs had been dwelling.

Elphias shook his head. "Only what's in my purse, and that was mostly emptied at the apothecary." He placed his head in his hands.

"Your bank will have deposit records," Zediah suggested. "If you present your identification papers, they—"

Elphias laughed, though it was bitter and hopeless. "They were destroyed as well. And I don't have *a* bank, I have several." He looked up at Zediah and shrugged. "I've been traveling for nearly ten years now and made deposits whenever and wherever I could." He looked back down into the ash filled cashbox. "I can remember some of them, but…I mean, just the logistics of it… Besides, how could I?" He gestured to the pile of ashes and burned horse skeleton.

"Ah, yes. I see your predicament. Hmm." Zediah scratched at his chin thoughtfully. "In that case, I have a proposition for you. One I've been considering since lasterday."

Elphias gave him a wary look.

"There's still the matter of settling our contract. I will pay you now, but it won't be nearly enough to compensate your loss. The Treasury will only approve the materials used to perform your duties, not the losses from the fire."

Elphias stood and stretched his shoulders. "I didn't imagine that they would."

Zediah nodded. "I may have a solution, however. I must return to the Academy now, but in three days time I'll be embarking on a journey to Verdun. I could use someone with your unique skill set after I arrive there. You have done autopsies before, have you not?"

"I have. What is the—"

Zediah held up a hand. "I cannot say. Nor will I. It's extremely confidential, only a select few individuals know about it, and I shouldn't even have told you that much. For all intents and purposes, I'm traveling to attend the Empire's science exposition. As will you, should you agree. I can tell you this, however. If you accompany me, I will compensate you greatly once our mission is completed. You'll certainly be able to afford comfortable transport to recoup your lost deposits with."

Elphias stared beyond the cemetery, where the road rolled back into the woods. *I could start walking right now,* he thought. *Walk through the night and I'd be back at that bend in the river. Then I could find that woman and eat apple pie every day.* He turned to Zediah and nodded. "Sure. What choice do I have?"

"Wonderful," Zediah said and smiled broadly. He reached within his Inverness jacket and pulled out a small coin purse, then handed it to Elphias. "Here's your payment, plus a small advance to facilitate a means of travel to Beltram."

"Beltram? You're starting out from the opposite coast?"

Zediah nodded. "Yes, and we'll arrive in Verdun three days later."

"Three days? That's impossible. Unless...they've finished the transcontinental sky rail?"

"Indeed they have, Doctor. We'll be traveling aboard the *Spirit of Innovation* on its maiden run, a special express from coast to coast with only a stopover in Lacroix."

Elphias shook his head. "Three days. Remarkable times we live in."

The commander of the guard raised her arm and signaled to Zediah. "Ah, we're ready to depart. May I offer you a ride back to Lancaster? We'll be passing through on our return to my airship."

The huntsmen had returned from the forest and began to load their weapons onto the wagon. "I'll get a ride from Cobb," Elphias said, "don't let me detain you any further, Inquisitor Oulcott."

Zediah gave a swift nod. "Very well, then I shall hope to see you at the Beltram Station on Patero 26th. The *Innovation* departs at 1 in the afternoon, so let's meet on the platform around 11. I'll be waiting for you beneath the large clock. You can't miss it." Then he turned and strode off towards the inquisition wagons.

Elphias watched him go, then went to dig through the ashes once more.


Elphias rode in silence on the back of Cobb's wagon all the way to Lancaster, waving off the hunting dogs that would occasionally come to inspect him. There would be a snort of air, then a touch of a wet nose, or a lick to the side of his face. The huntsmen were silent as well, an acknowledgement of their two fallen comrades wrapped in cloth and laying on the bed. Elphias was grateful for the solitude, he didn't feel like talking to anyone. He didn't want to return to Lancaster, and he certainly didn't want to travel beyond to Beltram. He'd have been perfectly content never seeing Zediah again, but such choices were no longer available. It was then that he wondered if Bella would be accompanying them on the journey. A nervous twinge gripped his stomach and he was torn by a duality of feelings again, one part hoping she wouldn't be there and the other wishing she would. Dualvinity save him. Three days together. *I'll likely go mad*, he thought.

They reached Lancaster well after dark. Elphias debated going to the apothecary for shelter. Besides a dispensary, they commonly housed short-term sleeping accommodations for physicians as well as a reading room with the latest medical journals available for perusal. Based upon his observations from the day before, Elphias had little hope the accommodations would be better than the rest of the place. And so with a feeling of subtle despair he took a room at the Bernd Tavern, where Cobb was staying. There were a smattering of rooms on the second floor, and Elphias was thankful to get one to himself.

The mattress was too lumpy, the pillow too thin, and the room too large compared to the comforting density of his vardo. He lamented being out of the proper ampules to escape his sorrow, and in the darkness of the room wept once more, for losses deeper than perhaps even he understood. When sleep did finally come it was fitful, dreamless, and unrestful.

Sunlight and external sounds awoke him hours later, and he felt somehow more exhausted. He dressed slowly and then shuffled from the room to get something to drink. Preferably with alcohol.

"Hoy, Doctor. Sit with me, will you?" Cobb occupied a table by the window, drinking a cup of coffee.

Elphias slid out a chair and lowered into it. "Cobb. How of you this day?"

Cobb shrugged, then looked out the window. A steady flow of morning traffic was passing by; carriages, horses, and pedestrians. "There's an ache in my bones. Tis going to rain, I think."

"Would you like something for the pain? I have…I could get something from the apothecary."

Cobb shook his head. "Nay, tis kind of you to offer though." He studied Elphias for a moment, his eyes sharp. "What will you do now?"

"I…" Elphias shook his head slowly, thinking how absurd it all seemed. "I am going to accompany the inquisitor to Verdun, where I am to be paid for some secretive service."

A harried looking woman wandered over to the table and cast her eyes on Elphias. "Get you something, lovely?"

Elphias considered for a moment. "Kingsbury Dark Ale if you have it."

The woman grinned, displaying crooked teeth. "We do, and from the look of you, you need it." Cobb waited for her to pace back to the bar before giving Elphias a smirk.

"Dark ale for dark times if you're traveling with that man. Still, he seems fair enough as inquisitors go." Cobb patted the outside of his jacket and smiled at the sound of coins clinking in a coin purse. "I got a better horse and a wagon out of the deal too." Cobb's smile suddenly vanished. "Sorry, Doctor, twas rude of me to say, given the circumstance."

The woman brought Elphias' ale back and took a copper in return.

"Is he to pick you up here then, in his great airship?" Cobb laughed. "What a grand adventure you'll have, like in them sky pirate books." Cobb held out his coffee mug for a toast and Elphias obliged him. The ale was warm and bitter. Elphias was pleased.

"Actually I'm to find my way to Beltram. Then we'll travel by—" He stopped as Cobb's face went still. The huntsman set his mug down hard enough to rap the table and slosh coffee out.

"The *Spirit of Innovation*?" Cobb said it reverently, aged face nearly as innocent as the boy Elphias had stitched up just days ago.

Elphias laughed. "Yes, I see you're familiar with it."

Cobb nodded enthusiastically. "Aye, tis true! I been a fan of the sky trains since I first rode one. After the Purge they shipped us to Austra in a brand new 2-4-4 to muster us out. Them tracks are loud above you, like a giant rattling a cage. But below? Below tis like you're flying." His eyes took on a far-off look and Elphias couldn't help but smile.

Elphias took a long drink. "You should be going in my place."

"Wish that I could, Doctor, wish that I could." Cobb looked out the window again. "But there's not much use for me. Bah, listen to me cry, forgive me Doctor. So, how are you to get to Beltram then, the coach?"

Elphias hadn't really given much thought to how he'd get to his destination. The thought of being crammed into a stagecoach, mashed with a stranger on each side and three facing, knees knocking together for two days was almost ridiculous. "I have no idea," he said and downed some ale. The sooner this feeling of being untethered ended the better. He felt like an airship torn free of its mooring and drifting aimlessly. Cobb's hand slapping down on the table snapped him back to reality.

"I'll take you."

"Oh, Cobb. That's not necessary, you—"

"Have naught else to do but wait for the long sleep. I'd like to see the *Spirit of Innovation* afore that happens. Besides, I was grousing about not traveling anywhere the other day, remember?"

Elphias gave him a lopsided grin. "I'm afraid I'll be a horrible traveling companion. I'm still feeling very sorry for myself."

Cobb winked and tapped his skull. "I ride with the same every day, so tis no trouble at all. And won't we make a fine pair. Doctor Sorry For Himself and his driver, Old Man Miserable."

"We'll be famous, Cobb. I can already see the stage play."

Despite their individual woes they laughed and toasted each other once more.


"The first number is the number of guide wheels, the second them that drive the motion. The last number is the wheels supporting the engine. The entire wheel bogey setup is atop the train, configured to grip the overhead rail."

"Fascinating," Elphias said and resisted the urge to leap down from Cobb's wagon and run screaming into the field stretching off from the road. Today he had learned everything he had ever wanted to know about steam engine trains and that hadn't been much to begin with. Cobb, it turned out, was more than just a sky train enthusiast, he was a fanatic. Over the first several hours of their journey he had waxed enthusiastically about the development of the sky train, the challenges of such a track design, and the inevitable disasters that such new technologies failed to foresee.

"But that's the greatness of the Union, ain't it? That we rise back up and figure out a way of making it work. The might and willpower of Toravia!"

Cobb then proceeded to get into the minutia of steam engine mechanics and how the *Spirit of Innovation* had been built to take advantage of steam with little loss at all.

"It can travel at fifty miles an hour, imagine that! That old 2-4-4 I rode on only did thirty at full chisel. They say if you travel faster than that your brains will come out of your ears."

"That's ridiculous. It would do no such thing."

"And you would know this because…"

Elphias looked at him sharply. "Because I'm a doctor of medicine."

Cobb laughed, short and raspy. "I know that, I'm just having my fun. No offense meant, I can see you've not an interest in the trains as I do."

"Forgive me, Cobb. I told you I'd be a horrible traveling companion. You've been kind enough to drive me to Beltram just to see the *Spirit of Innovation*, the least I can do is share your interest. What more should I know?"

"Bah, I'm tired of talking about trains," Cobb said and spat off the side of the wagon.

They ate lunch under the shade of a willow, eating bread and dried jerky they'd purchased before leaving Lancaster. They were surrounded by fields of wheat, save for the worn dirt strip of the road. Occasional traffic passed by, riders on horses and some workers in a wagon. They exchanged greetings and tipped their hats at each other. At one point a stagecoach roared by, the red-nosed driver ignoring them completely. Elphias caught a quick glimpse of miserable faces looking at him with envy as they flashed by. He suddenly felt better, things could be worse after all. The day was pleasant, a light breeze stirring the sun hazed wheat. Elphias looked back the way they'd come and saw that the sky was the color of slate. It flickered as thunder rolled ominously across the sky.

"There's that rain," Cobb said and rubbed his knees.

They drove through the downpour, accompanied by the occasional blast of thunder. The rain was cold and stinging. At Cobb's urging, Elphias had purchased a duster before leaving Lancaster and now he was glad he did. He had flipped the collar up to try and keep the rain from his ears but it only did so much. He understood now why Zediah wore a slouch hat for travel. At least his top hat was beaver pelt so the rain wouldn't damage it. His clothes were the only things he had left, he didn't want to lose them too.

"Why didn't it rain like this lasterday?" Elphias muttered. "Maybe I'd still have my home."

Cobb gave a short laugh, a spray of water flying off his lips. "Aye, seems the Wet come early, but not early enough." He fell silent for a few moments and then gave a huff of disgust. "Foul witch. I should'a killed her when the truth came out."

They sloshed through a muddy puddle. Elphias tucked his hands into the pockets of his duster. "When did it happen? For you, I mean."

Cobb stared at the road, water dripping from his face as the rain continued to fall. Elphias began to think he should apologize for asking when Cobb's cracked lips parted.

"Twas in '46. Sixteen. I was sixteen years old. Oh, Dualvinity how I could run then. Like a deer." They slogged into another series of puddles, the road squelching beneath the wagon wheels. "I joined the year afore, ran away from school and lied about my age. I was the youngest one, imagine that. Ain't that a treat?" He rubbed at his eyes. "They called me Pup, like a little dog cause I was following the older fellas around, trying to learn from them. All the other kids was finishing boarding school and moving on to academies, but not me, I just wanted to get out and serve. I was the only one."

Elphias hunched forward, trying to protect the back of his neck from rain. "The youngest I worked on was eighteen, but the rest were graduates. Farmers and laborers to be sure, but they'd finished their educations."

"I envy them," Cobb said. "I never stayed to find my calling, I left afore the placement tests. I wonder what I would have become?" He shook his head. "Tis useless to think on. The thick of the matter is I got touched by a red witch, she put the touch on me afore my bayonet pierced her evil heart. In two steps I went from sixteen to sixty-six, from being the youngest soldier in the battalion to the eldest." Thunder rumbled and echoed off through the fields. "They still called me Pup, though. A new recruit thought to call me Pops, but they turned him right around, the fellas did. They beat the manners into him. I never had trouble of him again."

"I'm curious about your speech patterns too, you speak like you're the age you appear. Certainly you didn't speak that way when you were sixteen?"

Cobb shook his head. "Nay, tis true, that. You're an observant sort. You'd have made a good inquisitor, Doctor Root."

"I'm not sure about that," Elphias chuckled, trying to imagine such a thing.

"The truth is, after I mustered out I began to seek the elderly and copied their words so I wouldn't stand out as strange. After all these lasteryears, tis just the way I talk."

Elphias turned to study Cobb. "You said you were mustered out at the end. You served ten years after the curse?"

"Aye, that I did. For all I lost? Aye, I had more than enough rage to push me the whole blasted time."

Elphias did the math. "So, your true age is what? Thirty-six, thirty-seven?"

"Aye. Thirty-seven."

"You're three years younger than me." Elphias shook his head.

"And look old enough to be your father." Cobb wiped the rain from his face. "Tis a funny, funny world, this."

An hour later the wagon became mired in mud. The storm had passed them by and the rain had slackened to a light mist, but they were still wet and uncomfortable. Cobb tugged the horse by its reins from the front while Elphias pushed at the wagon from the rear. He'd neglected to buy boots, so he had stripped off his shoes and socks and rolled up his pant legs. The mud squelched beneath his feet as he leaned into the wagon, pushing for what he was worth. It begrudgingly moved, mud-caked wheels rotating to only advance an inch or two. Cobb eventually worked the horse over to the side of the road, where the long weeds gave them more purchase than the mud. Once the horse was on firm ground the wagon soon followed. After it was free Elphias pulled himself onto the rear and flopped down on the plank bed, staring up to the grey clouded sky as he tried to catch his breath. His feet were cold and there wasn't a single part of him that was dry. *I'd give anything for a Blue Oasis ampule,* he thought dully, *anything at all to close my eyes and wake up in Beltram.* He closed his eyes anyway, shutting out the dismal sky above.

The wagon rocked as Cobb climbed up and settled onto the spring seat. Elphias kept his eyes closed. He wiped water from his face. "Cobb, are there any larger towns between here and Beltram?"

"Like Lancaster you mean?"

"Near enough. One with an apothecary, to be more precise."

Cobb gave a cluck to the horse and Elphias heard him snap the reins. The wagon gave a lurch and began to roll forward.

"Well, as I recall there's Clarksburg to the south, but tis out of our way a good thirty miles or so. Tis naught but villages from here on out, if you'd even call them that."

Elphias opened his eyes and sat up, swaying with the rock of the wagon. They were traversing the roadside, avoiding the mud while they had space to do so. Elphias stood and carefully made his way to sit next to Cobb. Reaching under the spring seat, he took his socks out of his shoes and wrung them dry. Then he cleaned as much mud from his feet as he could before slipping them on. His damp shoes were next, but at least his feet were a bit warmer.

"I have to say, I'm looking forward to the inn tonight. It will be decent to be dry for a change."

Cobb gave him a pitiful look. Elphias' spirits sank lower. "Don't tell me we have to sleep outside."

"As you please," Cobb said and faced forward once more.

Elphias didn't find his literalism comforting.

The clouds moved out by evening and when they finally made camp the night was full of stars. It was too wet for a fire so they ate a quick meal of bread and dried bacon and prepared for bed. Fortunately for Elphias, Cobb had purchased extra bed rolls for the huntsmen and was able to provide him one. The bedrolls were damp too, but at least Cobb had rubber sheets to place on the ground that kept them from getting worse. Elphias had folded up his duster to use as a pillow and lay in his bedroll staring up at the sky. Cobb snored lightly a short distance away, having dropped off to sleep almost immediately. Elphias had no such luck, he'd rarely been able to slip into slumber so easily, not without extreme exhaustion or the comforting aid of narcotics. Night was when the phantoms rose up in his mind, reminding him of past mistakes, regrets, and things left undone. Night was the curse of an active mind when all one wanted to do was sleep.

Despite the delay, they were still making good time. If they pressed on tomorrow they could make Beltram by the following morning. Elphias would have plenty of time to visit the grand old apothecary there and fill his case. It was a comforting thought, unlike his usual run of worries lately. *One more night at the most,* Elphias thought gladly.

A shooting star flared across the sky over him before vanishing. Though not superstitious, Elphias decided to take it for a good sign. After the past two days, things couldn't get much worse.

# CHAPTER FIVE
## *Dark Water*

"The bridge is out."

That much was very clear. Elphias could see just the tips of what had once been posts of a side railing poking up out of the mud brown river. He looked at the person who had delivered the bad news, a stout woman with a dirty face and a shock of curly hair atop her head.

"This is from the rain?"

The woman shook her head and smiled, revealing an uneven row of tobacco stained teeth. "Nah, nah. The Wet come early to the north, so the river was already cresting. Lasterday's deluge made it worse. Now it's too swift, even for me."

The woman had set up a ferry, a large raft constructed of lashed together logs that she could push across the wide river. The raft was tied to a tree now, secured with heavy rope to keep it from floating away in the current. Water pushed against it, washing partially over the logs where they offered the most resistance. A short distance away a slouched man sat on a stump, head in his hands. The ferry operator caught Elphias looking that direction.

"There's a sorry piece of work, there," she said. "He was driving a stagecoach through here lasterday. Gave me a good choice of words when I told him the bridge weren't safe. Course the water weren't as high as it is now, but it was still flowing over the bridge something fierce."

Elphias took another look at the stagecoach driver and thought it was the same one who'd passed them by the day before.

"So off he went, driving all them folk across the bridge. About halfway across the water took a toll and started to float the carriage. The stagecoach flipped over, tumbling off the bridge with horses and all. I could hear the folk screaming as it went over, but not for long." The ferrywoman shook her head sadly then gave the coach driver a hard stare. "He swum to shore thereafter. Of course he would, after was his foolishness that killed them all. But what did they expect, putting a man at the reins. Er, no disrespect, gentlemen. I helped fish him out though, I'm not a brick-heart. I helped fish him out of the river, and that's where he's sat since. I reckon he's trying to decide whether to walk back from where he come, or just throw his self in the river and be done with it. I opine it should be the latter, but that's cause I can still hear them folk's last screams. It was worse when they cut off though." She scratched her head and walked over toward the river, staring off into the rolling waters.

"Well, there's a fine tale," Cobb said lowly, "just as I was starting to feel good again."

Elphias watched the river snaking swiftly by, trying not to imagine what it would have been like inside the stagecoach.

"If not for you, I may well have been one of those poor souls, Cobb."

"I'm glad you weren't, Doctor. That ain't a good way to die." Cobb sighed. "I hope mine is a good one. Going in my sleep would be fine by me." He sat forward and put his chin in his palm. "But we've more immediate problems, don't we?"

Elphias had the same worry. Unless there was another way around, they'd have to wait for the river to lower before they could cross. It could take days. If he missed the train he could also forget the money Zediah promised. He'd nearly spent everything he had in his coin purse, and once he visited the apothecary in Beltram he'd have nothing left but a copper or two. Then it would be time to begin backtracking his life, working backwards to visit each bank and pull what scant deposits he'd filed there. In the meantime he'd risk arrest for vagrancy and being labeled a deadweight, one unable to contribute to the Empire. Elphias had heard horror stories of their fates, hard labor in the pits or toiling on constructions funded by the duumvirate. Those too weak to work served other purposes. Test subjects were always in demand at the Academy. Either route led to only one outcome: you went in a deader and came out as a dead body. No one escaped the sentence, they could never earn enough to pay for their freedom and there was no job waiting for them if they did.

"Do you know of another road we could take? Something with a higher bridge perhaps?"

Cobb shook his head. "Nay, Doctor Root. I already run it through my mind. There's naught to the north and the south will be worse."

Elphias took off his top hat and set it next to him, then leaned forward to run a hand through his hair. He was not a religious man, but he began to wonder if he'd done something to be cursed by the Dualvinity. He didn't really believe in the Father Sun and Mother Betha, not literally anyway. There appeared to be a hidden order beneath the chaos of the world, so he believed something was at hand. But the sun was just that, a sun and nothing more. And Betha was just the planet they lived on, stirred by the same hidden order as everything else. Beyond the raging seas, beyond the great leviathans that prevented exploration, there could well be other countries and other people. Would they worship the same gods or would they believe in something wholly different? It was a foolish thought for another time. Elphias needed to think about the present. He hopped down off of the wagon and approached the ferrywoman.

"How much lower until you can cross?"

The ferrywoman rubbed her nose. "If it were only the height we could cross now. The problem is the current. It's too strong for the pole."

"Could it be pulled across?" The voice was scratchy and unfamiliar. Elphias and the ferrywoman both startled at the sound of it and turned to see the stagecoach driver behind them.

"Mothers love, you gave me a scare," the ferrywoman said unkindly.

The stagecoach driver stared at her, his face haggard and eyes bloodshot. There was a set, angry look to his features. "Could it be pulled across?" He pointed at the tree that the raft was tied to. Elphias noticed that a great length of rope was coiled on the ground, the ferrywoman had only given the raft so much.

The ferrywoman shrugged. "I guess. Except there ain't nobody over there to toss a line to, now is there?"

"I'll swim it across."

The ferrywoman gave a bitter laugh. "Why don't you just make a noose and hang yourself, if you only want to die."

"I want to help." The stagecoach driver turned his flat stare to Elphias. "I need to help. I need to do something."

The ferrywoman rubbed a palm across her forehead, then shrugged with resignation. "Okay. I can see that you're set to do it."

Ten minutes later they had the rope tied around the stagecoach driver's waist. He decided he'd cross at the bridge, to try and walk across by floating and pushing his feet against the side rail. The other end of the rope was still wrapped around the tree and tethered to the raft.

"You'll need to lift the line over them posts as you go," the ferrywoman told him. "Otherwise you'll tangle it."

The man nodded. "The name's Jessop."

"And I'm Milby, what's your point?" the ferrywoman replied.

"If I die…" Jessop shrugged and then turned and started into the river.

Elphias climbed back up onto the wagon where Cobb still waited. "We may be getting across today."

Cobb shrugged. "Or watching a man drown."

Jessop shuffled forward onto the bridge where the current was least and then settled into the water, leaving only his head and shoulders visible. He leveraged his feet against the rail and started moving sideways. The current grew stronger, flowing up behind him and splitting to both sides of his shoulders. He approached the first post and flicked the rope over it. The slack flowed down river, dropping out of sight beneath the dirty water.

"That's one," Elphias said.

"Aye, but he's still far to go. That rope could get tangled on something under the water."

"You're full of optimism."

Cobb scratched his chin. "I've see'd too many a man suffer from optimism to put much in it myself. But one of us will be right, that's for sure. And tis better to be proven wrong as a pessimist than an optimist anyway, don't you agree?"

Elphias gave a lopsided grin. "That makes a disturbing amount of sense, actually."

Jessop had made further progress, passing two more posts and with only three more to go. The current was even greater out in the center of the river, the water sluiced at the back of Jessop's neck, fanning out to both sides like wings. He struggled against the flow, teeth gritted with the effort.

"He needs to move faster," Elphias said with concern. "The cold and exertion will fatigue him before he's across."

"He's halfway, he'll make it."

Elphias shot Cobb a look. "Don't be switching sides on me now, Cobb."

"You started it," Cobb replied smartly.

Elphias laughed. "Yes, I suppose I did. In that case—"

There was a shout from the river and a dampened cracking sound. "It's breaking!" Jessop yelled and then surged forward as the rail snapped free of the bridge.

"Dash it!" Cobb swore, clenching his fists.

Elphias stood and watched helplessly as Jessop washed past them.

Milby cupped her hands to her mouth. "Swim! Swim for the shore!"

Jessop began swimming for the far side, water splashing as he struggled to cut against the surging river. He was rapidly drifting away, head bobbing up and down with the current as he floundered to stay afloat. He kicked and paddled, spray flying.

"Go," Elphias muttered under his breath. "You can make it."

Jessop disappeared beneath the surface. Long seconds passed.

"No." Elphias sat down on the spring seat. Another death. How many more? Cobb tapped Elphias' arm and pointed.

"Oi, look there. I was wrong after all."

On the far side of the river Jessop was emerging from a shallow, frame bent with exhaustion. He staggered out of the water before collapsing to the ground. They could see his labored breathing, torso rising and falling.

"Oi!" Milby shouted. "Are you all right?"

Jessop continued to lay in a panting heap but one pale arm lifted and gave a listless wave before falling once more.

Elphias let out a nervous laugh. "He must have swum underwater. Thank the Dualvinity he made it. I thought for sure..."

"We all did, Doctor," Cobb said seriously. "For one and true, didn't we all."


It was nearly night before they were ready to cross. While they had waited for Jessop to recover his strength, the ferrywoman had been busy modifying her raft. She'd chopped down some thin trees and fashioned them into an A frame at each end of the raft, making sure the rope was inside of them.

"We'll use the current to help us cross," Milby said. "I'll have him secure it down river of us and then use the pole to keep us angled the right direction. The current will push us to the other side."

Cobb and Elphias had said nothing. After the past few days, they weren't prepared to accept anything going according to plan. Elphias was already discouraged at having made so little progress. They'd need to make camp soon after reaching the other side, provided they even survived the crossing. He could almost see it, the raft flipping and sending them all into the river. And with the trend of his luck lately, he'd likely get snagged on the submerged stagecoach and drown anyway.

They loaded the wagon onto the raft and unhitched the horse to stand along side it. Elphias and Cobb got on and Milby untethered the mooring. She pushed them away from the shore and out into the muddy brown water. The damp smell of it filled Elphias' nose and he held tight to the side of the wagon for support. He did not want to test his luck against its treacherous current.

Cobb also gripped the wagon, his aged face pale. He looked away from the water and met Elphias' eyes. "I never learned to swim," he said and shook his head. "Figured what were the point, I ain't a fish. How of you? Do you know how to swim?"

Elphias nodded and thought back to the last time he'd been swimming. It had been with Lydia, they'd gone to the beach together that day. She had something important to tell him. Elphias shut the line of thought down quickly. "It's been a long time. I'm not sure I'd even remember how."

"Oh, you'd remember," Cobb nodded. "You may think you forgot, but it'd come back to you. It always comes back to you. You never forget the things that matter."

Elphias stared down at the river and wished that he could forget. He'd certainly been trying long enough.

They made camp on the other side, building a small fire and brewing a pot of coffee to share with Jessop and Milby. A few other travelers had shown up on horseback, so after the coffee the two ferry operators took their leave and began orchestrating a return trip across the river.

Elphias settled into his bedroll as the fire was dwindling to hot coals. He stared into the glowing red embers, comforted by the heat and trying not to think of his vardo burning. He felt unnatural, as if constructed of opposing halves. Everything in the Empire was clad in the fabric of duality. The merging of Ostravia and Torbuld into the nation of Toravia, jointly ruled by the duumvirate, while the faithful praised the two gods of the Dualvinity. Woman was the sacred alchemist and man the catalyst that produced further life. From the symmetry of living things to the twin moons in the night sky, it was all a symbiosis of two, the sacredness of conjoining and compatibility. Elphias closed his eyes, feeling the heat from the coals on his face and wondering if he'd ever be whole again.

They encountered the bandit early the next morning, having departed their camp before dawn stained the sky with its violet hues. They'd just entered a dense pine forest when Cobb pulled his wagon to a stop and shook his head with disgust.

A soiled man wearing the dirty, tattered uniform of the Royal Guard stood in the middle of the road, a mischievous look in his pale eyes.

"Hoy now, lads," he called loudly. "You need a travel permit for this area. Rest aside so I may spot yours."

"Clear the road!" Cobb shouted. "I'm in no mood for nonsense, especially from a bark bottom."

"Nay, elder father? How of you, Top Hat? Will you deny my request to spot your permit or shall I call the guard?"

"The same guard that ensures bandits receive the treatment?" Elphias asked with irritation. "Please, by all means call them forth." When would these troubling delays cease?

The soiled man squinted at them and shook his head. "Have as you will," he said with a sneer and then gave a shrill whistle. His accomplices began to emerge from behind trees on both sides of the road, equally as filthy and foul-faced as the next. The squalid seven stopped once in view, brandishing wooden weapons with their grubby hands.

The soiled man grinned. "What say you now?"

"I thought wood nymphs were the ugliest things in the sticks. Tis clear now I was mistaken," Cobb said and snapped the reins hard against the horse's hindquarters. It sprang forward, jolting the wagon into motion and nearly upending Cobb and Elphias off the spring seat.

The bandit's accomplices began shouting curses as they dashed to catch them. The closest one leapt up on Cobb's side, trying to grab the reins. Cobb snatched up his walking cane and swung it backhand with all his might. It struck the bandit in the face, shattering teeth and snapping the walking in cane in half. The filthy man grunted with pain and tumbled from the wagon.

"I thought you liked eating sticks!" Cobb shouted.

The soiled guardsman still stood in the road, waving his arms in an attempt to stop Cobb's horse. Cobb snapped the reins again and they plowed into the bandit, the horse knocking him supine and trampling an arm on its way past. The man screamed with pain and Elphias had a brief look down at his contorted expression before it vanished beneath the buckboard. The rear wheel bounced over something and the man screamed again.

A wood club clattered into the back of the wagon, a last ditch throw by one of the others as they quickly fell behind.

"You all right, Doctor?"

Elphias cast a glance back over his shoulder. The standing bandits had given up the chase and were turning back to the two laying sprawled in the dirt. "Yes. Better than those lot."

Cobb scowled. "Twas a good walking cane, that. Shame to wreck it on a bone bag."

They rode in silence for a few moments.

"Do you think the leader was truly a former guardsman?" Elphias asked.

Cobb scratched his chin. "Mayhap. I did know a few that gone rogue after the Purge, mostly them that was destined to be deaders after mustering out. Could still be happening with the Royal these days, though I hope not. Don't seem quite right. Them that serve shouldn't have to face the pits. Not for poverty."

"Truly put," Elphias said. "I've provided aid to deadweight veterans during my journeys, men trying to avoiding such conscription by keeping low and trying to earn their keep with chores and such. I never charged them. What would be the point?"

"You're a good man, Doctor Root. But I know'd that the moment I saw you. Even with your 'hoy, blast you' business."

Elphias laughed. "I never did apologize for that, did I?"

Cobb grinned and patted him on the shoulder. "No need, Doctor. If it weren't for you, I wouldn't be off to see the *Innovation* with my own eyes."

"I'm glad it's a passion of yours," Elphias said, and meant it. Everyone deserved the panacea of passion. *Almost everyone,* he amended. When would he finally prescribe it for himself?

# CHAPTER SIX
## *New Horizons*

The Academy of Worldly Science was a sprawling monstrosity of conjoined buildings and cavernous halls, claiming nearly a square mile of space in the city center of Austra. The entirety of the Empire's knowledge was held and conducted beneath the Academy's high vaulted roofs and domed ceilings. It was said by some that if a bit of knowledge wasn't to be found in the Bureau of Records or the Grand Library, then it was being discovered in one of the Academy's labs. Bella thought that to be a bit grandiose, as it took more than lab work to facilitate the Academy's ravenous hunger for information.

There were the inquisitors, for one. Their sole purpose was to go out into the world and seek answers and new discoveries. Inquisitors acted with full authority of the Academy, it was why they'd been granted such broad powers. They could question and detain anyone, commandeer transportation, or press citizens into service to get the answers they sought. They could also pick whomever they chose from the Academy staff to accompany them on their inquiries.

*Like me for instance,* she thought, looking at the Department of Inquisition summons in her hand.

It had come via the vacuum tube at her desk, scrolled within a mail container. Hers was but one of the 225 desks in the secretarial pool, distributed over three stories at the end of a vast atrium. Bella was on the second floor, close to one of the spiral staircases that wound above and below. She descended it to the ground floor and looked across the atrium, where the facade of the Grand Library rose up through the distant curved glass ceiling and beyond. The number of books within boggled her mind, it was said to contain everything ever published and with space reserved for those yet unwritten. *One day I shall write a book,* she thought, *called How to Live an Unsatisfied Life.*

She walked to a set of double doors to the side of the atrium and pulled them open. A long hallway with tall windows to her right stretched off a vast distance before her. Lux lanterns were interspersed the entire length of the hall, hanging on long cables from the ceiling high above. The effect, Bella surmised, had been to make people of high ego feel small. And there were certainly an overabundance of egos within the Department of Administration, if not the Academy as a whole.

The Department of Inquisition was near the far end of the hall, so Bella set a rapid pace, the heels of her boots clacking against the marble tiled floor. The first door to her left was the Bureau of Cartography and she couldn't resist taking a peek through the office windows at the large map painted on one wall. It represented the continent of Valgrad, an enormous display composed of Ostravia to the west, Torbuld to the east, and the wedge-shaped Freehold of Agaria nestled down south between the both of them where the Dragon River sluiced out of the Cragback Mountains. The massive mountain range had been embossed with plaster by the designers, and rightly dominated the center of the map. It was aptly named the Great Divide, and split the Empire in two.

A crescent shaped illustration to the southeast of Valgrad represented the island nation of Kava, which was only accessible by airship and maintained a steady trade relationship with the Empire. Toravians certainly appreciated Kavan sugar as a sweetener to their baked goods and bitter drinks and tonics.

Bella moved on down the hall, thinking of the map and what it truly represented: the limits of their knowledge about the world around them. Besides Kava, approximately a nautical mile of sea was as far as any had traveled and returned to tell the tale. For out beyond the protective reefs that allowed sea travel at all, were where the mature leviathans roamed, massive sea serpents that made short work of the pitiful ships of mankind. For all their advancements in metal hulls and armaments, even hunting the juvenile leviathans that breeched the reef seasonally was a challenge. For every three leviathans hunted one ship was lost with nearly thirty hands aboard. Such was the profit of leviathan oil that the industrialists continued to send men out to sea. And that the men continued to go.

As for airships, any that attempted to explore anywhere beyond the favorable trade winds between the Empire and Kava were never seen or heard from again.

Many years ago, before she took a dead girl's name, Bella used to dream about what lay beyond the horizon of those unexplored seas. She'd imagined piloting an airship of her friends to mysterious lands for exploration and adventure. She was commander, naturally, and Kasey was first officer, Trina the navigator, and Bella, dear sweet Bella, was officer of the watch. She closed her eyes, hearing the clack of her heels against the tiles.

*You're Bella, silly, have been for years.* She opened her eyes just in time to see the man before they collided into each other. He grabbed her upper arms with his hands, softening the impact but still mashed her breasts up against his body. The smell of him overwhelmed her, a mix of body odor and musty clothing. She shuddered with sudden revulsion, knowing his identity before he even spoke.

"Now Miss Crevan, if you want to get closer to me you need only ask."

She pulled back from him, forcing a smile. "Forgive me, Inquisitor Martel, I wasn't watching where I was going," she said and thought, *but you were, weren't you, you old lecher. You put yourself in front of me, that's why you reacted so fast.*

Inquisitor Magnus Martel was one of the eldest inquisitors, a venerable part of the Department of History where he spent most of his time instead of the inquisition offices. His notoriety as a perverted womanizer was common knowledge amongst the females within the Academy. His eyes were pale, his face bloated, and if he'd ever been handsome his features had long since surrendered to the vices of his soul. He licked his lips, hands still grasping her.

"I'll watch out for you, if you'd like." His eyes drifted to her torso bits. "I really wouldn't mind at all."

Bella nearly gagged, his breath was as foul as the rest of him. She forced another smile, though it felt tight on her lips. "I'm fine, thank you," she said and shook free of his grip.

He leered at her, taking enjoyment in her discomfort. "Oh yes, that's right, you're Oulcott's, aren't you? Yes, he's got his fingers all over you. Mmm, can't say as I blame him."

Color rose to Bella's cheeks. "Inquisitor Oulcott is a decent man, unlike some."

Martel rolled his eyes. "Yes, the great Oulcott. His love is his work. He doesn't take time for the benefits of his position." He swept his sticky gaze over her body once more. "I can certainly come up with a position for you. Many, in fact."

An image came quickly to mind, of smashing his head in with a rock. She even knew the sound it would make. *That wasn't you, silly. Ambrosia did that.*

"You're being foul, sir. Please behave more appropriately."

Martel sneered. "Come now, we're both adults. You must be in your mid twenties at least. Have you been bred yet?"

She saw and heard the slap before realizing it was her hand that did it. Her anger suddenly subsided as she realized what she'd done.

"Inquisitor Martel, forgive me. I…"

A bright red handprint began to glow on Martel's cheek. He flicked out his arm and snatched hold of her wrist. "That's a capital offense," he said, digging his fingers painfully against her bones. "You'll be in my chambers tonight, you little bitch, or I'll send you to the pits mysel—"

"Release her at once, Magnus!"

Martel looked over his shoulder, then laughed and released Bella's wrist. "Saved by your true love," he said and turned to face Zediah.

"You're a disgrace," Zediah said flatly. "Why don't you crawl back to History and slither amongst the fossils where you belong."

Bella rubbed her tender wrist and glared at the back of Martel's head. *One strike, that's all it would take,* she thought darkly.

"No need to be hostile, Oulcott, I was merely looking at her best interests."

Zediah stepped forward and looked Martel in the eyes. "Then for your best interest, I suggest you look elsewhere."

Martel took a step back. "My goodness me, Oulcott, I think I was wrong about you." He turned and gave Bella a wink. "He may be interested in the benefits of his position after all."

Martel shuffled away with an arthritic gait, eyeing the swaying bottom of a woman walking before him.

"Has he been giving you much trouble?"

Bella shook her head. "No, but he's growing more bold." She looked at Zediah. "I slapped him. He—"

"Deserved it," Zediah finished and glared at Martel's retreating form. "It's a…technique of his. Goad a woman to strike him, then threaten punishment if she doesn't accommodate his perversions."

"Thank you for interceding, Inquisitor. Truly."

Zediah shrugged. "Any gentleman would." He stared at her a moment. "If you need some time to gather yourself before we meet, it's no discomfort on me."

Bella shook her head. "No, now is fine. I'd rather put all of this out of my mind by getting back to my day. What did you wish to see me about?"

Zediah stared at her again and Bella had an uncomfortable feeling. "It's about your file." He looked around the hall to see if anyone was in listening range. "We should go to my office. This isn't the place."

"Lead on," Bella said with forced indifference, though her pounding heart suggested otherwise. *What does it say about me?* she wondered. *How much does he know?*

Zediah's office was a small wood paneled room with an arched window overlooking a courtyard. His bookshelves were crammed with educational tomes on a wide assortment of topics, not unusual for someone within the Bureau of Esoteric Inquiries, Bella imagined, and a troll skull was prominently displayed within a glass case near the window. Rumor within the younger Academy staff was that he'd personally slain the beast on some adventure during his early days in the inquisition. Having traveled twice now with Zediah, and seeing only his kind and gentle nature, Bella couldn't imagine him killing anything. *Does he feel the same of you?* she wondered, and certainly hoped so.

Zediah's face betrayed no emotion of any kind at the moment. Sitting at his desk with his back to the large window, he adjusted his spectacles and stared down at Bella's open file. She sat opposite, looking out at the thin scrap of sky visible above the Academy buildings clustered beyond.

"You attended Rosewater School for Girls from 1848 to 1858, is that correct?"

"Yes, Inquisitor." Her heart pounded. Why was he asking about Rosewater?

"That's a very prestigious boarding school, from what I understand."

"It has that reputation, yes."

"There's an ornate clock tower there, isn't that right?"

Bella shook her head. "Not when I was attending."

"Ah," Zediah said. "I must be thinking of someplace else."

*Or trying to poke holes in my cover story and see if I really attended there,* Bella thought. Such queries had been accounted for, since her records were constructs. She'd never even visited Rosewater, but had instead attended a nameless school in the village of Hempwick, near the Agarian border. By a fluke of careless boundaries established in their peace treaty, a small area of land had escaped inclusion in either the Empire or Freehold and was for all intents a sovereign domain. As far as the Academy was concerned, Hempwick did not even exist since it was absent from any maps, even those maintained in the Bureau of Cartography. This befitted shadowy organizations loyal to the duumvirate that needed to break the Empire's laws to protect its interests. This and other secrecies were maintained by the Body of the Empire, the powerful organization to which Bella belonged, and hidden within the innocuous Office of Female Affairs. As such, part of their individual assignments had been to learn as much about the school they'd allegedly attended so that even an alumni would believe it.

"After which you entered Enton Trade School to learn the secretarial arts, graduating in 1860. Why?"

She blinked at him with surprise. Some inquisitors were known for tricky questions, letting you talk yourself into trouble. What did he suspect?

"Why did I graduate?"

"No. Why did you decide to become a secretary? Your aptitude and placement test results suggested a career of higher station."

"And here I am," she said and smiled.

Zediah stared at her. "That's evasive."

Bella swallowed. "Am I in some sort of trouble, Inquisitor?"

Zediah looked down at her file again and drummed his fingers. "Upon graduation you began working for a newspaper, the Toravia Herald."

"Now who's being evasive?"

Zediah ignored her and flipped to another page. "Employment records show you did a commendable job, so much so that they made you a reporter in 1863."

Bella nodded, mouth dry. *What is he after?* She tried to smile. "The Bureau of Records is thorough, aren't they? Do they have my articles in there too?"

"No, but there's a letter from your editor."

Bella sat up a bit. "There is? What did she say?"

Zediah closed the file and sat back in his desk chair. He stared over the rim of his spectacles and studied her for a moment. "She was very upset and wanted to know why you left. Specifically, why the Academy recruited you to be a secretary."

Bella shrugged. "They liked what I wrote apparently."

"A month later there you are, assigned to the inquisition pool. Most girls work years to get there."

Bella licked her lips and felt distant, like she was looking at herself. "I'm just lucky, I suppose."

Zediah pushed back his chair and stood, then walked to the window and turned his back on her. He looked out the window, head tilted skyward.

"There is a rumor within the Department of Inquisition, mostly unspoken but there all the same. It alleges there is a hidden organization within the Academy."

Bella's stomach dropped.

Zediah turned away from the window and faced her. "An organization whose one purpose is to observe the inquisitors and report our true nature outside the Academy grounds." He paced forward and sat on the edge of his desk, looking down at her.

"Have you ever been part of such an organization?"

"No," Bella said. It was a crime to lie to an inquisitor, though spies had an exception. And it wasn't exactly a lie. The Body was based outside the Academy and did far more than just observe inquisitor behaviors. That still didn't make her feel good for being evasive though.

To her relief, Zediah smiled.

"Ah, yes. I suspect that if such an organization did exist, those under its employment wouldn't be allowed to confirm this fact. Would you agree?"

Bella studied him. His eyes twinkled with a sense of merriment. She sensed he already suspected the truth. "That would be a very reasonable assumption. If such an organization existed, Inquisitor."

He smiled again and stood. "Please, call me Zediah." He walked around his desk and sat in the chair once more. He leaned forward and steepled his hands. "I'm assembling a team of people for something important. People I can trust. Beyond what is required of your duties, no one else must know. Can I trust your confidence, Bella?"

She looked him in the eye, feeling a sense of relief. He wasn't trying to expose her secrets at all, just taking a measure of her character.

"Yes, Zediah. Truly and freely given. Yes."

Zediah grinned. "Wonderful! Pack your bags for travel." He clapped his hands together and rubbed them with excitement. "How do you feel about sky trains?"

# CHAPTER SEVEN
## *The Spirit of Innovation*

The road into Beltram was clogged with traffic and the going was slow. Elphias and Cobb had only moved about a mile in the last hour and they were still on the outskirts of the city.

"Seems everyone's to see the *Innovation* depart," Cobb observed.

"Hopefully I'll be aboard before it does."

"Aye." Cobb pointed to the massive arched towers that supported the sky rail, thrusting up through the coal smog of Beltram's vast industries. "Elsewise you'll have to grab ahold as she rolls on past."

Elphias smiled. "I'll take my chances on the usual method of boarding."

"Had enough of adventure, then?"

Elphias nodded. "Yes. Though I don't think I'm free of it yet. The inquisitor has something planned in Verdun, so until then my adventure continues." He fished his pocket watch out of his vest and consulted the time. It was nearly 10, he was supposed to meet Zediah in an hour. The train was to leave at 1. It would all be very close. Elphias had hoped for a chance to reach the apothecary but there seemed little chance of that now.

They rounded a bend in the road and discovered the source of the backup. A wagon had lost a wheel and overturned across the road. A few men were trying to clear it from the street while people pushed past on both sides. Huddled together in a crush of bodies, they were making the situation worse.

Off to the side of the road a group of school boys in uniform clustered around a dead dog laying in the dirt. They were poking it with a stick and making disgusted laughing sounds.

"Have any spawn of your own?" Cobb asked.

Elphias' heart clenched. "No," he said. Some truths need not be shared, and it was close enough to the truth anyway. No need for Cobb to know all the sorry details. A puddle of blood still flashed through Elphias' mind anyway. Her hand had been so little, the fingers impossibly tiny. Elphias pushed the memory away.

"Tis a surprise, I must admit. I assume the women find you pleasant to look at, and you're a doctor to boot. I'd think your seed would have plenty of willing fields for planting."

Elphias shrugged. "Must be my sparkling personality." *Running from every woman you see helps too,* he thought and decided it was also additional knowledge Cobb needn't know. "How of you, Cobb? Have any?"

Cobb shook his head. "Nay. Tis forbidden, didn't you know?"

"No. Why would you be forbidden to sire your allotment?"

"The curse," Cobb said and gestured at his face. "The Bureau of Genetics was afraid I could pass something on from the hex. I'm not allowed to procreate."

"They've told you this?"

Cobb nodded. "Aye. As soon as my injury made record at the Academy, one of them come out to the front as quick as you please to tell me the truth of it."

"I'm sorry to hear so, Cobb. It doesn't seem a fair deal."

Cobb shrugged. "The Empire were straight enough to tell me at least. Saved everyone the troubles of denying me a Permit of Procreation. Bah, who'd want to mate with a wrinkled old coot like me anyway?"

They had made it to the overturned wagon finally, and were starting to edge around it. The traffic beyond was breaking up and dispersing itself to the various roads, alleys, and walkways of Beltram.

"Looks like we may get there yet, Doctor Root."

"I have faith in you, Cobb."

Cobb smiled. "Tis nice that someone does."

The transcontinental station was surrounded by bustling crowds of curious onlookers. Pennants waved in the wind, strung from the towering terminal to the ground below. A raised stage was set before the wide staircases leading up to the platform, and a brass band was performing as Cobb and Elphias approached on foot. The band played a merry tune, entertaining the public as they waited to watch the *Spirit of Innovation* begin its journey.

Traversing the city had taken longer than Elphias had anticipated. There had been more delays as they'd tried to find a livery stable vacancy for Cobb's horse. It seemed everyone had come to see the *Innovation* depart and brought their mounts with them. Elphias glanced at his pocket watch and noted it was nearly 12:30. He pushed and weaved his way through the crowd, headed for the stairs. Cobb was at his heels, huffing with exertion, as eager to get to the train as Elphias was.

The band ended their song with a grand flourish and basked in the applause of the assembled. Officials were gathered upon the stage, talking amongst themselves as the conductor raised his baton and set the band to music once more. The familiar strains of the national anthem began to play and men began to remove their hats. Elphias took off his top hat but kept in motion, growing ever closer to the stairs. He finally reached the first step as the band finished the anthem. The crowd erupted into wild applause. Elphias glanced back to see Cobb wipe tears from the sides of his eyes.

"Beautiful music, that," Cobb said. "Makes you proud to be a Toravian."

An elderly woman loitering near the steps clapped Cobb on the back. "Long live the Union!" she cried.

"May the Empire remain strong," Cobb answered.

Elphias began pushing up the steps. He hoped Zediah was still waiting, though he doubted it would be the case. The inquisitor was likely aboard by now, Elphias couldn't imagine he'd wait there this long. He wove his way upward, annoyed by the number of people just standing at the side of the stairs to gawk at the crowds.

Speakers hanging on the station exterior and surrounding buildings crackled to life. "-esting, testing. Oh, it's on now." The audience laughed and the man down on the stage blushed red. He handed the harmonium linked microphone to a heavyset man in top hat and tails. The man held the microphone to his mouth. "Thank you, Lord Roberts."

Elphias reached the top of the steps as the heavy man introduced himself as the Baron of Beltram and began to rhapsodize poetic about the glory of the Empire and its marvelous technology.

"When you look at the success of our nation," the Baron said, "does anyone doubt the Divine smiles upon us all?"

Elphias did. He doubted it very much.

Up ahead he saw a large clock at the center of the passenger platform. There were too many people milling about for him to see if Zediah was at its base or not. He heard Cobb give a sudden gasp from behind.

"Tis more magnificent than I'd pictured."

Elphias had been so focused on the clock he hadn't even noticed the sky train to his right.

The *Spirit of Innovation* hung down from the sturdy sky track, sporting a sleek, streamlined, black iron exterior. Exhaust pipes flared out of the smokebox at the front of the engine and curved back, reminding Elphias of animal horns. Thanks to Cobb's descriptive education on steam engines, Elphias knew that they were curved back and out to divert used steam and furnace exhaust away from the overhead rail and support structure.

Following the engine and coal hopper were eight train cars, their exteriors ornately decorated in dark wood panels and muted steel framings. It reminded Elphias of a larger version of his vardo, and he suddenly longed to get on the train and have a bed and walls and heat at night.

A jet of steam shot out from the *Spirit of Innovation* as its whistle blew, shrill and piercingly loud. People began to head for the train. Elphias looked at the time. 12:45. He pushed toward the clock, hoping Zediah would be there.

He wasn't.

Elphias' heart pounded and heat rose up the back of his neck. Bella was leaning against the clock base, searching the swelling crowd. She caught sight of Elphias and waved.

"Oh! There you are, Doctor Root." She smiled warmly and approached him.

Elphias stared at her stupidly. "Bella. I wasn't expecting to see you here."

"Inquisitor Oulcott wasn't sure you'd make it. I told him I thought you would, so he made me wait for you. Isn't that just like him?"

She took his arm in hers and tugged him towards the train. "Come on, we need to get on board before they close the doors." Elphias stumbled along, mind whirling. After days on the road with Cobb her perfume smelled like paradise.

"Cobb!" They'd gotten separated somewhere. Likely Cobb had stopped to admire the train as Elphias pushed on.

Bella gave him a curious look. "What was that?"

Elphias turned his head to search the dense crowd.

"Cobb, the master huntsman. He drove me here from Lancaster. I wanted to thank him." People were getting on the train or saying goodbye to those that were, others were shuffling past or waiting impatiently to watch the *Innovation* leave station. He didn't see him anywhere.

"I'm sorry, there's no time." She pulled him forward and they stepped onto the *Spirt of Innovation*. It smelled of polished wood and new carpeting, contrasting against the coal fire stink blowing in from the platform. A bell rang from somewhere and a porter ran down the line, shutting the doors and fastening them tight.

Elphias took a look around the train car, which was open except for some padded chairs strewn about. The ceiling was a painted mural of clouds, giving the impression of looking into the sky. The wall was set with large windows that took on an angle where the panes approached the floor to allow one to view below the train. Elphias determined they must be in a smoking car.

Bella released Elphias' arm. He was torn by opposing feelings once more. "This way, please," she said and began to make her way towards the rear of the train. Elphias followed, looking out the windows as he did so. He felt bad for not saying goodbye to Cobb, he'd developed a kinship with the man over the past few days. *Which is why I don't make friends*, he thought. His next thought was whether there were any medical supplies aboard the *Innovation*. They would likely have some ampules to sell.

Bella reached the rear of the observation car and opened the door. Elphias followed her through the covered vestibule and into the next train car. He noticed the sign above the door read Sleeper Car and felt an uncomfortable twinge. A memory of following Lydia into her bedroom made his eyes ache. He chastised himself for being foolish and focused on his surroundings instead. The sleeper car had a central hall running its length with rooms to each side. Some of the doors were slid open, and Elphias could see the rooms were small and consisting of two couches facing one another. There appeared to be cots hinged to the wall above the couch seats, hitched up for headroom during day travel.

They continued on through the next car, which proved to be a sleeper as well. At the far end a guardswoman was standing erect and blocking further progress. She stepped aside as Bella approached and opened the door for them. Elphias glanced at her as they started to pass through, then stopped. The guardswoman looked at him in return. Her eyes were grey and there was a small scar on the top of her left cheek.

"What is your name?"

"Alisha, sir."

"You were at the hunt, weren't you? You gave me a jug of water."

"Yes, sir."

Elphias nodded and scratched his head.

"Were you the one that also stopped me from jumping into the fire?"

She gave Elphias a small smile. "Yes, sir."

Elphias smiled in return. "Thank you, Alisha. For saving me from my own foolishness." He gave her a salute.

"Oh, I should thank you, sir," she said and returned the salute. "The inquisitor took note of my actions and personally requested me as part of his watch."

"Then he's in very capable hands."

Alisha beamed with gratitude. "Thank you for saying so, sir."

Elphias continued through the door and through the vestibule where Bella waited outside a door marked PRIVATE.

"I heard of your misfortunes," she said. "I was sorry to learn of your losses."

Elphias gave a shake of his head. "If not for Alisha it could have been worse. If I'd burned my hands…"

Bella laughed. "If you'd burned your hands you could have become an inquisitor. I heard how you questioned her."

"Now that's odd," Elphias said. "Cobb said the same on the road from Lancaster. And to think of all that time wasted on medicine."

Bella laughed. "I'm sure your patients wouldn't agree."

*Not the living ones, anyway,* Elphias thought darkly.

The shrill call of the whistle sounded again, followed by another blast.

Bella knocked on the door and it swung open. Zediah stood in the doorway, a bemused smile on his face. "Doctor Root, I see you've made it just in time. Excellent." He beckoned them into the private car as the train gave a lurch forward. Zediah gave Bella a wide grin as she passed. "I was beginning to think you would miss the train too, Miss Crevan."

"And miss a chance to be a part of history? I should think not."

"Indeed," Zediah agreed. "Come, let's all retire to the rear observation lounge for departure."

He led them through the car, which started with an office that was furnished with a sturdy wooden desk and several plush chairs for travelers. A curtained door was in the middle of the wall at the back of the office, leading to a short hallway with a bedroom to each side. Through another curtained door brought them to the rear of the private car, and the *Spirit of Innovation* as well. The rear wall was curved and set with wide windows throughout so as to nearly give the illusion of no barrier at all. The platform was sliding past to their left, and the steel track spooled away from above. Zediah motioned them to sit in chairs aligned to face rearward and they all sat to watch the scenery.

Elphias kept watch for Cobb but the faces were sliding by too fast to make them out. He thought he saw an elderly man raise a hand but then they passed out of the station and the world dropped away beneath them.

"Oh my," Bella marveled.

The stage and crowds passed below them some thirty feet, their faces upturned to watch the *Spirit of Innovation* in motion. Hands reached up in greeting and hats flew from heads in celebration. Buildings rolled by to each side and beneath, and those with flat roofs held even more people, all watching the grand sky train, the symbol of the Empire's might.

Elphias felt a chill of wonder at the grandness of it all. Cobb was right, it did feel like one was flying. He was glad Cobb had made it in time to see the *Innovation* depart and wished him well on his journey back home.

*Where will my home be, when all is said and done?* he thought. They passed over another row of buildings and then through a roil of smoke to see the tops of trees rolling beneath. *Will I want a home that doesn't move?*

A porter in a white service jacket entered the room and took their orders for drinks. He returned shortly with tea for Zediah and Bella, and coffee for Elphias. Beneath them the size of the buildings they passed over were diminishing and there were dense clusters of trees. The smog of the city still hung over the sky behind them, but to the sides the land was opening up and the skies were blue.

*I could get used to this life,* Elphias thought. *I wonder how much a private room on a train would be?* The idea was in jest, a fanciful daydream, but Elphias was content and comfortable for the first time in several days. He deserved to dream for a bit. The sky train facilitated the illusion of escape, as if ones problems were affixed to the ground below and by flying away you could leave them behind. *Maybe the higher one goes, the less ones problems have hold of you.* Elphias smiled. Since he was dreaming, why not buy an airship to live on instead?

Bella leaned forward and smiled. "Whatever are you thinking about,

Doctor? I've not seen you look so relaxed before."

Elphias shook his head and smiled guiltily. "It's foolish."

"So are a great many things," Bella said. "That doesn't make them unimportant."

Elphias gave her a lopsided grin. "Very well. I was thinking about buying an airship and living amongst the clouds. Like in one of them sky pirate books, as Cobb once told me." He glanced over at Bella and his smile vanished.

She was still looking at him but her face was pale and her smile frozen.

"Are you all right, Bella? Have I said something to give offense?"

She blinked rapidly a few times then shook her head. "I'm—yes, I'm fine, it's just…How odd, I was recently recalling such a fantasy myself."

Zediah sipped his tea. "If you've interest in airships, Doctor Root, I'll have you aboard the *Cloud Titan* the next time I make use of it."

Elphias nodded. "Thank you for the offer, I'd like to experience what that would be like. Perhaps I can hitch a ride back with you from Verdun should you choose to do so."

Zediah looked down into his tea mug. "Ah, yes, after Verdun. Hmm. Yes." He turned his head to stare out the side window.

Bella gave Elphias an amused look. "Now you've done it. You've set his mind to motion, he'll be in that state for a few moments."

Elphias bit his lip. It didn't seem like the sort of question that would provoke such inner conversation. He had a feeling it was less a question about which transportation to take home, but rather what to do with Elphias once his services were no longer required.

Elphias took a drink of his coffee and stared out the back of the train. Two seemingly innocuous things he'd said had caused unexpected reactions with his traveling companions. *Maybe I should just keep my mouth shut*, he thought dismally. *People seem to like me better that way.*


That evening they ate dinner in the observation lounge, porters bringing their meals from the dining car. Afterwards Zediah showed Elphias the bedroom they would share. One of them had two beds with full sized mattresses, while the other had four bunk cots on the side walls and a couch beneath the window.

"Miss Crevan has been kind enough to offer us the room with the larger beds," Zediah said, "as she is of smaller stature and will find the cots more comfortable than we would."

Elphias felt he should make a feeble protest but couldn't bring himself to do so. The bed looked incredibly wide and inviting after the thin bedroll of the past two nights.

"Thank you, Bella," he said and moved into the room to prepare for bed. He was completely exhausted and made plan to sleep as late as allowed.

A sudden rapping came from the front door of the car. They all entered the office area just as the door opened and the guardswoman Alisha stepped in, pushing a struggling captive in front of her. Elphias' mouth dropped open.

"Cobb?"

"Lay your hands off me, woman!" Cobb shouted at Alisha.

"The huntsman was nosing about trying to find you all," Alisha said, keeping Cobb in her grip.

Zediah nodded. "What are you doing on the train, Master Cobb?"

Cobb shook his head. "I weren't intended to be! I come aboard when twas at the station, to have a look afore you departed. Then I needed use of the toilet. They've got them on here and they flush too, imagine that! Anyway, I was taking a—" Cobb looked at the women and began to blush. "I was making use of the toilet when the *Innovation* departed. I felt it move and then so did I." He blushed again. "Forgive me, ladies, twas impolite to say."

Zediah shook his head and laughed. "It's okay, Alisha, you may return to your post. I'll speak with the conductor. Master Cobb will be staying with us." Zediah turned to Bella and gestured toward the bedroom with two beds. "Which means that room is yours by default, Miss Crevan. Us gentlemen will rough it on the cots like the brave souls we are."

Cobb sidled up to Elphias as they moved to their rooms and slapped him on the back. "Look at us, traveling like lords," he laughed and then farted. "Forgive me, tis beans on the menu in the dining car."

Elphias took a sad look at the wide and comforting beds then turned away. The stench was foul. He shut his eyes and shook his head.

*Was I really missing this man earlier?*

# CHAPTER EIGHT
## *Moonbeams and Madness*

The *Spirit of Innovation* rolled onward through the night, pushing southwesterly across Torbuld towards the Freehold of Agaria. Elphias slumbered for the most part, waking occasionally in confusion as to his surroundings before being rocked back to sleep by the motion of the train. When he did finally awaken the morning sun was high in the sky and shining through the window of their room.

He noticed that he was alone, Cobb and Zediah having risen before him. Elphias lay for a bit and enjoyed the solitude until his bladder forced him from the bunk. Each bedroom had a small closet sized area with a toilet in it and Elphias made use of theirs, thankful he didn't have to leave the room. Afterwards he dressed slowly, swaying with the motion of the train.

"Hoy, Doctor, did you sleep well?" Zediah was in the office section, sitting at his desk and examining a scatter of papers.

"Yes, indeed I did. After the last two nights of sleeping by the side of a road it was paradise."

"Ah, yes. Cobb made mention of same before he left to examine the rest of the *Spirit of Innovation*." Zediah gave Elphias a knowing smile. "Were you aware of his…curiosity with sky trains?"

Elphias laughed. "He may have mentioned a thing or two about it while we traveled together. Were you aware the *Innovation* employs an automatic feed system for the coal?"

Zediah smiled broadly and shook his head. "I see he has educated you well. So what will you do with your day? We should reach the stopover in Lacroix around 2:30 or so."

Elphias rubbed his chin. "First I think I'll examine the dining car and see what I can order for breakfast, then perhaps an exploration of the areas of the train left unseen. Tell me, is there a medic aboard?"

Zediah shook his head. "Not in any official capacity that I'm aware of. There's a conference going on along with the expo, so there's plenty of doctors aboard to be sure, but I don't think any of them are physicians."

Elphias took his leave and made his way back through the train, passing through the smoking car and into the dining section. A narrow aisle cut through the dining area with small tables to each side that sat four diners. There was a crowd in the car and from what Elphias could see, there weren't any empty tables available. He spotted waiters milling around a galley at the far end and decided to try and order something from there. He could always eat it back in the private car. In fact, the more he thought about it the better it sounded. He could sit and watch the world roll away from the observation lounge.

"Doctor Root!" Elphias recognized Bella's voice before he caught sight of her at one of the tables. Her hand was raised to get his attention and her dining companions, an elderly woman and a much younger man, turned their heads to see whom she was signaling. He stepped up to their table and Bella motioned to the vacant chair next to her. "Please join us," she said then looked across to her companions. "That won't be a trouble, will it?"

The elderly woman, dressed in a refined outfit and with an air of wealth gave Elphias an approving look and shook her head. "No, my dear, that won't be a trouble at all. Two doctors for two ladies," she said and giggled.

The man next to her in a tuxedo was dashingly handsome, with slicked back hair and deep dark eyes. A neatly trimmed goatee framed his mouth, which had only the barest hint of a smile. He gestured to the chair in a vaguely inviting manner. Elphias sat next to Bella, the confined nature of the seating placing them with arms touching. Elphias could feel the warmth from Bella's body and the smell of her perfume filled his nose. He thanked the Dualvinity that Lydia had worn a different scent.

"A friend of yours, Bella?" The handsome man gave Elphias a mischievous stare with his dark, malicious eyes. "Wait, let me guess. He must be your father."

Bella laughed. "You're being silly, Doctor Weber. This is a new acquaintance of mine, Doctor Elphias Root. He's traveling with the inquisitor as well. Doctor Root, this is Doctor Arctus Weber and Lady Danueman."

"A pleasure to meet you," Elphias said, "thank you for letting me join you."

"Oh, it's no trouble at all, young man," Lady Danueman said. "What sort of doctor are you?"

"I'm a physician." Elphias looked to Arctus. "I see you bear the title as well, Doctor Weber. What is your specialty?"

"I'm an alienist. Whereas you cure the body, I cure the mind." Weber fixed Elphias with a penetrating stare. "And how of you, Root?" He reached up his hand and tapped the side of his own head. "How are you doing up here, old boy?"

Elphias felt a sense of discomfort. "Well enough."

Lady Danueman reached across the table and patted Elphias' forearm. "Doctor Weber is a remarkable young man," she said. "Since I've come under his care I see the world much differently than I did before." There was a minor sense of detachment and vacantness in her gaze and smile. Elphias suddenly realized she was a patient of Weber's, and that she was likely suffering from some sort of derangement.

Weber touched Lady Danueman on the shoulder. "You honor me, Lady. The truth is, is that when I met you at the asylum you were without a sense of direction. I merely helped guide you through the storm, just as I continue to do today."

The Lady tittered with pleasure, entranced by the handsome Weber's kind compliment. Elphias didn't believe a word of it. He glanced at Weber. *What sort of game are you playing at?*

A harried looking waiter approached the table and delivered food to Weber and the Lady Danueman, took Elphias' order, and promised Bella that hers would be coming shortly. He dashed off as another waiter came by and filled their coffee cups.

Elphias sipped his coffee and looked at Bella. "So have you known each other long?"

"Oh, no. We just met a few minutes before you came in. The car was full and they were kind enough to invite me to sit here."

Weber smiled a dashingly handsome smile at her. "It was a natural response. I mean, there you were," he cast a glance over at Elphias, "just you, all alone, and I thought 'how cruel for such beauty to be left unattended to'."

Bella looked down at the table. "Oh, really Doctor Weber, you must stop. You are such a shameless flirt." There wasn't much protest in her words and Elphias noticed she was smiling. *Well why shouldn't she?* he thought. Weber was extraordinarily handsome and close to her own age. He bristled at the thought, however. Bella deserved someone decent. Elphias had grown up in the company of men and knew Weber for the type of man he was. *Dash you, Elphias,* he thought suddenly, *are you feeling jealous?*

"Please, call me Arctus. You're a perfectly healthy young woman. You've no need for a doctor. A man, perhaps, but certainly not a doctor." Weber punctuated the words with meaningful glances at Elphias during the key points. Elphias' distaste for the man grew immeasurably.

Bella laughed again and was joined by the Lady Danueman. "Watch yourself, dear," the Lady warned, "he's a honeyed tongue. Sometimes it's like being mesmerized when he speaks."

"You spoil me with flattery, Lady," Weber said. He cast a sly look at Elphias. "But alas ladies, we should speak of other matters perhaps. I believe we are making the doctor uncomfortable with our talk. He's only used to examining the male anatomy and may be perplexed by your feminine charms."

The ladies tittered with good nature but Elphias felt a blush rise up his neck and a tightening in his guts. It was all he could do not to cause a scene. He was wise enough to know that shouting at Weber would merely make the man's case for him.

"On the contrary," Elphias said. "I just find it unprofessional and immature to see women for their physical attributes alone. To completely disregard the beauty of their minds, is…well…frankly, I'm rather surprised an alienist such as yourself wouldn't feel the same way, Doctor Weber."

Bella laughed. "Thank you, Doctor Root. You see, Arctus? That is how a gentleman behaves in public."

Weber gave Elphias a long stare then glanced to Bella. "Forgive me, Bella. From now on let's only talk in private. My first consultation is free."

They all laughed as if nothing were wrong, all but Elphias. He knew that there was plenty wrong, and it all stemmed out of Weber.

The rest of the breakfast went better, for the alienist put on enough manners to not speak while he ate. Elphias was discomforted by Weber's frequent and penetrating gaze. Elphias knew the man was desperately trying to figure him out, to seek what was going on in Elphias' private thoughts. Weber appeared to weigh everything Elphias said while conversing with Bella and the Lady Danueman, no matter how innocuous it seemed. He was greatly relieved when Weber and the Lady took their leave and left Bella and him alone.

"I hope you will forgive him, Doctor Root," Bella said once the others had departed. "Arctus appears to be a roguish type, though I sense he's all talk."

"That's the way of alienists, I suppose." Elphias said.

Bella smiled. "Yes, that's true, isn't it? Well, I should return to the office. I've some documents that need to be telecoded back to the Academy. Will you be returning shortly?"

Elphias nodded. "I believe I will. I'd like to enjoy the observation lounge for a while."

Elphias stood when Bella did and let her exit the table. Then he sat, forcing himself not to watch her leave the dining car. Instead he looked out the window, finished his breakfast, and thought about her the entire time.


"Have you ever been followed by strangers?" the man asked Elphias. "Not, you know, the usual sort of stranger—I mean, everyone has—but what I mean is those that aren't normal strangers, but intentional ones, do you see my meaning?"

Elphias examined the man's eyes to see if either of his pupils were dilated, but they were both the same size.

"I'm sorry, but no, I don't."

Elphias had been on his way through the smoking area, back to the private car when he'd come across a group of men gathered around another man supine on the ground. Apparently he'd been exiting the car while looking over his shoulder and had run right into the side of the door, knocking himself unconscious. Elphias had identified himself as a physician and began attending to the man, who was elderly with a clean shaven face and wavy grey hair. A porter had fetched a first aid kit and provided it to Elphias. He was disappointed to see it didn't contain any ampules but knew it would have been highly irregular for it to have done so. Instead he used smelling salts to bring the man around, then cleaned and bandaged a laceration on his forehead, centered within a swelling goose egg.

"I mean," the man began again, "the sort that follow you everywhere. The sort that mean you harm."

"Were you feeling this way before you hit your head? I need to rule some things out," Elphias said.

"What? Why yes, I did. You think I'm imagining it?"

"I want to make sure you didn't sustain a brain injury, that's all. May I ask a few questions?"

The man squinted at him. "I suppose so."

Elphias held up a hand and displayed three fingers. "How many fingers am I holding up?"

The man squinted again. "Three."

"Do you remember your name?"

"Gilliam. Gilliam Watt."

"Good, good." Elphias had no idea if it was really the man's name or not. He hadn't been carrying identity papers. "Can you tell me what year it is?"

"You think I really broke my melon, don't you? It's 1867. Patero 27th to be precise."

"Good, that's correct. One more. Where are you right now?"

Watt looked around with amusement. "The smoking car. Of the *Spirt of Innovation*. Of the nation of Toravia. Of the contin—"

"Okay, okay. You're fine."

"I told you. I did, you know. It'll take more than a door to damage my noggin. Of course, that's why I walked into it, didn't I? Because they want to do more than just damage my brain. That's why they follow me. But I know it, so I keep looking. Always look over your shoulder. That's what I did, and bang!"

It suddenly reminded Elphias of Cobb's words on their journey to Lancaster. *Tis foolish to walk ever forward and never look every now and again over your shoulder. That's how you end up prey. Be it from beast of the wood or a cutpurse of the city. That's how they feed on you.*

"Why would anyone wish to follow you and do you harm?"

Watt gave Elphias a serious look. He glanced around and motioned for Elphias to lean closer. Elphias did and Watt sat forward to whisper in his ear. "Not just anyone. It's more than just a person. It's an industry." He sat back and waggled his eyebrows in a knowing manner, then pointed up.

Elphias looked up at the cloud painted ceiling.

"The...Dualvinity?"

Watt rolled his eyes and gestured again. Elphias noticed he was pointing at an overhead light fixture.

"Lux Light?"

"Shhh!" Watt leaned forward and grabbed Elphias' shoulder. "Are you mad? They could be anywhere." He sat back and shook his head. "I never should've told the Academy, I should have waited for the expo. There's a weasel in the henhouse. You'll be safe with a patent, they say, and then there they are, lurking in your footsteps, clinging like a shadow."

"Help me understand something," Elphias asked, keeping his voice low. "Why would L—" Watt's eyes started to get wide. "Why would," Elphias pointed up, "want to follow you?"

Watt's brow scrunched up. "Did you finish school at all? Weren't you listening? The patent, I said." He leaned forward and pulled Elphias close. "I invented a new type of light. One that doesn't give off harmful rays and aethers. It gets hot, but it won't kill you to sit next to it unshielded."

Elphias studied the man. If what he were saying were true, then it might well cause concern for a lighting conglomerate like Lux Light Industries, the sole source of electrically stimulated lighting.

A shadow fell over them. Watt looked up suspiciously, eyes wide with alarm.

"What are you two conspiring about?" Weber asked.

Elphias' mouth twisted. Weber laughed and clapped Elphias on the back. "Just teasing, old boy. To be rightfully honest, I really don't get the sense that you're the conspiring type at all. It takes a certain kind of intellect. An ungentlemanly intellect, but an intellect all the same."

Watt got up. "Excuse me," he said and scurried off.

Elphias stood. "I was just treating an injury, Doctor Weber. Nothing you need concern yourself with. He's of sound mind."

"Really?" Weber said. "I spoke with him earlier and detected a deep paranoia driven by a persecution complex. You didn't sense that? But then I suppose not. It takes, again, a certain kind of intellect."

Elphias had had enough. "Have I done something to give offense, Doctor Weber?"

"How so ever do you mean, old boy?"

"I detect an air of hostility from you, directed at me in particular."

"Oh dear," Weber smiled, "could we have another persecution complex aboard?"

Elphias frowned. "Are you denying it?"

"That you have a persecution complex? No, I'm not denying that at all. I'm giving it all due consideration."

"This is exactly what I'm talking about."

Weber shook his head and laughed. "Easy, old boy. There's nothing wrong with having a disorder. Everyone does, you know." His smile turned to a sneer and he gave Elphias another penetrating gaze. "And I will discover yours before this trip is done. I can promise you that, old boy." He turned and walked away without another word. Elphias watched him go, relieved by his absence. *I'll have to stay far away from that man from here on out. Far away, indeed.*

# CHAPTER NINE
## *The Heart Wants*

Bella sat in the observation lounge, teletype on her lap and fingers resting on the symbol etched keys. The etchings, glyphs of the Stenographer's Code, were a truncated way for secretaries to type dictation at the speed it was recited. A printing device paired to the teletype exported it in the same coded fashion and was distributed to another secretary for translation. The translated copy was then entered into the Bureau of Records to be archived for eternity. Only secretaries were trained in the code, which made them natural candidates to serve the Body.

Bella had been activated while still working for the paper. Following graduation from Enton she'd been assigned employment at the Herald by the Body, with the understanding that some agents would never be called to duty. While working at the paper had certainly improved her writing and observational skills, it required no spying. She was beginning to think they would never call her to action when a matron—a middle-aged woman dressed in black—had knocked at the door of her apartment.

"What will I be doing?" Bella asked the recruiter. It had never been made clear what occupation they would be employed in following activation. Bella had always imagined some glamorous career, filled with intrigue and adventure.

The matron wasn't in that giving of a mood. She blinked at Bella with cold grey eyes and deflected her with literalism. "Helping us keep the Empire in order, little bird. The Eyes are an important part of the Body. They verify that which is reported to ensure it is accurate, and watch over those whom believe themselves free of scrutiny. It is not an occupation to be taken lightly, I assure you."

It was insulting, really. That much had been made clear early in her education at Hempwick, when they were assigned as Eyes, Ears, Hands, Heart, Mouth, or Mind.

"Will it be dangerous?" If she'd known it would be the secretarial pool, she'd never have asked that laughable question.

The matron hadn't laughed however. "Danger is often a matter of perception. As long as ones loyalties remain in service of truth and the Empire, then danger is of no concern to our agents. We take care of our own, little bird. For good or ill, we take care."

Bella had been too naive to see those words for the implied threat that it was. Nor had she fully understood then the duties of a matron, those mysterious Hands of the Empire responsible for cleaning up messes and keeping the Body secret. It wasn't until some time after joining the agency that Bella wondered what would have happened to her, had she refused the matron's offer. The fact that a Hand was the recruiter made Bella suspect that she wouldn't have lived to see her leave the apartment.

But she did accept, the assassin left her to live, and four weeks later she began working at the Academy. It wasn't as glamorous as she'd imagined. Her training consisted of learning to read the subtle clues people gave off in their speech, eye direction, posture, and mannerisms. The rest of the time was spent in learning the acting arts, to better maintain a cover personality. Especially when under duress.

"Though you will walk in the light of day, you will live in a world of shadows," the acting instructor told Bella. "You must don a cloak of secrecy about you at all times and forget the person you once were. This is why they asked you to take another name during your education. The old you is gone."

It had been prior to placement testing, so forgeries of their new identities and educations could be produced for the Bureau of Records. False birth and death certificates were printed and made official. The Body had killed Ambrosia years ago, when they'd asked her to choose a new identity.

"Bella Crevan," she had said instantly, using her dead friend's given name and an invented surname. It seemed only fitting. Bella would have enjoyed being a spy.

*I do enjoy being a spy*, Bella corrected and stared out the rear window of the train. Traveling in first class comfort and aboard airships certainly beat sitting at a desk every day, but it still wasn't the adventurous trade she'd hoped it would be.

There was the typing, for one. Too many hours spent posing as a secretary and teletyping inquisition transcriptions in addition to her private reports to the Body. In many ways, she'd simply become a traveling secretary instead of one bound to a single location. When Zediah and Doctor Root had been on the hunt she was restricted to a warm, boring room at the Ellington filing reports.

Bella sighed. She did wish for more adventure. And Zediah was right, she would enjoy being an inquisitor. If not for the responsibilities. It wasn't the demands of the job she feared, but being responsible for the lives of others. The last time she'd been in charge of an adventure it had ended disastrously. She could never forgive herself for what happened that day, and was sure she didn't want to experience the like again.

"Am I interrupting you?" Elphias stood in the curtained doorway, hesitating from fully entering the observation lounge. "I can go elsewhere if you're busy."

"Not at all, Doctor Root, please sit. Save me from my rueful ruminations."

Elphias took the seat next to her. "You suffer from those as well?"

"Only when I dwell on the past."

Elphias smiled sadly. "Again you strike true. But then, I suppose everyone has some dark burden they've tried to bury."

Bella brushed a lock of hair back from her forehead. "Does it get any easier, with time?"

Elphias gave her a glance then shrugged. "For some, perhaps. Those that can forget, who can close off a memory like a door to a room." He watched the scenery roll by. "My doors won't stay shut, however."

Bella studied him, a handsome man with a woeful look to his eyes. He'd been hurt somewhere in his past, that much she could tell. *He's wounded, just like me. But I deserve it.*

"There's forgiveness," she said. "Some have that capacity."

Elphias gave her a smile. "My self forgiveness must have escaped out one of my open doors." He laughed in spite of himself. "Fleeing for better opportunities elsewhere."

So he blamed himself for whatever haunted his soul. Bella felt a bond of kinship. Although burdened, he was still a kind and decent man. *If only he were younger,* she thought with sudden surprise.

"My own forgiveness is fickle as well," Bella said. "Perhaps they are off together having as wonderful an adventure as we are."

Elphias smirked. "Do I detect a degree of sarcasm, Bella?"

"I'm not sure, have you a thermometer that measures such a thing?"

Elphias laughed. "Degree. Thermometer. You've a witty mind. I like that." He averted his gaze to look out the side window.

"Thank you, Doctor Root." Bella smiled. "There, you see? I've talked to you for a bit and I'm already feeling less melancholy."

"I'm pleased to hear that."

"And how of you? Is there anything that placates your mind?"

Elphias fell into thought. "I have found…certain medications to be effective. But only short term. It does nothing to cure the underlying cause." He smiled. "If there were a way to excise bad memories and experiences, I'd likely find a brisk and profitable trade to engage my time instead of introspection."

"But," Bella sat forward, "don't you find that we are shaped by our experiences? That they make us who we are?"

"I suppose that's true, though one may argue whether it's for better or worse."

"But don't you think it helps guide ones actions? I see it as a reminder—an unpleasant one, but a reminder nonetheless—of what not to do or what to do differently the next time something arises in the future."

"So you're saying you wouldn't wish to forget whatever it is from your past that troubles you?"

Bella placed her fingers to her chin, then shook her head. "The event, yes, I suppose I would. But not the person it's related to. I would never want to forget her."

Elphias nodded. "I see your point and find I'm in agreement." He gave Bella an odd sort of look, that wounded glance he cast her way sometimes. "I'd like to forget the pain and keep just the good, but I'm afraid it's all tangled together. But as far as remembrance, her face is still fresh in my mind."

Bella laughed. "Oh what joyful company we are, picking old wounds open. I think we need a change of view." She set the teletype down on the floor and stood up, straightening her twirl skirt. "In fact, I think perhaps we should be at the front of the train looking forwards instead of watching where we've come from."

# The Spirit of Innovation

Elphias gave her a surprised look. "A philosopher as well? Intriguing." He laughed and nodded his head. "Very well, what do you suggest?"

"Have you been beyond the dining car? That's as far forward as I've gone and I'm suddenly struck with curiosity to see what's beyond. Would you care to join me?"

Elphias gave a nod and stood. "Your logic is sound, Bella. Yes, let's explore this wondrous train. We shall stride forward as agents of optimism instead of pessimism."

Bella laughed. "That's the spirit, Doctor!"

"The *Spirit of Innovation*, I believe," he said and they both laughed as they exited through the curtained doorway.


They moved their way forward toward the front of the train, Elphias in the lead and Bella tagging behind. His mind swirled with questions and possibilities. Was he falling in love with this woman? No, that would be foolish and unfair to Bella. It was primarily an imprinting of the affection he'd had for Lydia. Wasn't it? Certainly there was the similarity of appearance, but he found himself drawn by her wit and intellect too. He'd been too long wandering alone, running from companionship. The past few days had reminded him the pleasures of conversation, the value of friendship. And it troubled him greatly. What good would it all bring? After whatever purpose Zediah needed him for was completed he'd likely never see the inquisitor or Bella again. And Cobb would probably die of old age before Elphias crossed his path again.

Elphias felt like he were at a fork in the road; hexed if he did and cursed if he didn't, as the old saying went. To entangle himself in emotion would open himself up to pain. But to live without emotion wasn't really living at all. He cursed himself for his turn of thoughts. Why couldn't he just enjoy Bella's company without diving into inner turmoil? Couldn't he just think of her as a friend without causing himself torment? *If only she were older*, he thought.

They passed into the dining area and made their way back toward the galley. No one was in sight which was a relief to Elphias. He'd been sure they'd be accosted by Weber before reaching their destination. A narrow hall cut around the kitchen area and continued forward.

"Into the unknown," Elphias said and opened the door exiting the dining car.

"Lead onward, brave sir."

Elphias crossed the vestibule and pointed to the sign above the next door. Baggage.

"Weren't we trying to avoid that?"

Bella laughed. "I guess we'll have to discover what lays beyond it then."

Elphias pushed through the door and they entered the baggage car. Luggage and assorted crates were stacked against the walls, leaving the center of the car open. An oblong hatch was set into the floor, bordered by a safety railing. Closed now, Elphias imagined that when the hatch was open it allowed the baggage to be loaded from below. A pulley system attached to the ceiling above the area confirmed his suspicions. The metal hatch doors rattled with the train's vibration.

"Watch your step," Bella said jokingly. They passed around the hatch and approached the door out.

Elphias stopped. "Oh dear," he said and pointed to a sign mounted on the door itself. NO ACCESS / TRAIN STAFF ONLY. "I don't suppose you work for TransRail, do you?"

"No, I'm just a lowly passenger, I'm afraid."

"There's nothing lowly about you," Elphias said before he could stop himself. He turned to leave and there she was, standing close and looking at him. Their eyes locked and there was a vacuum, a compression of time and reality as if nothing else existed. Peripherally Elphias was aware of the baggage car but the center of the universe was Bella. He found himself leaning towards her, heart pounding. And she was leaning forward to meet his lips.

The door to the staff area wrenched open. Startled, Elphias and Bella stepped apart, casting their eyes guiltily away from each other.

"Hoy," Cobb said with a sly smile. "What are you two up to, then?"

"Just touring the train," Elphias said rather quickly. "And what of you, Cobb? Found a new career?"

Cobb looked at the sign on the door. "Oh, don't I wish. Nay, Doctor, just talking the ears off the driver and the firekeeper. They're a decent pair, they let me drive the throttle for a spell."

"That's wonderful, Master Cobb," Bella said. "It's good to know there's a relief available should something happen to the driver."

Cobb cackled with delight. "Thankee, Miss. I wish no ill to Mister Halbert there, but I must admit I wouldn't mind the opportunity."

"Well let's hope there isn't," Elphias said. "I've no doubt of your driving capabilities, Cobb, I've just had enough travel related adventures to last me for a time."

"Then it may suit you to know we're almost halfway to Verdun, Doctor. Next stop, Lacroix."

They began to head for the door to the dining car.

"Have either of you gentlemen ever been to Lacroix?"

"I've passed through when traveling between the provinces," Elphias said. "But I haven't stopped to enjoy its ambiance for many years."

"Tis nay for me, Miss. Never saw much want of leaving the Union for the foolish ways of the Freehold."

"How of you, Bella? Been to the Freehold before?" asked Elphias.

She was silent for a moment. "Not Lacroix, though I've always wanted to go. They say everyone should see Lacroix before they die."

"Then tis good I'm being forced to go now," Cobb said with a bitter little laugh.

As they made their way back, an announcement came over speakers recessed into the ceiling of all the cars. From somewhere in the train the conductor told the passengers of their next stopover.

"We will be arriving in Lacroix station at 2:45 to restock and water the *Spirit of Innovation*, as well as take on additional passengers. We will depart at midnight, and encourage you to enjoy the cultural attractions offered by the city while you wait." There was a pause and the sound of a paper rattling, then the conductor continued. "I will be selling tickets shortly in the smoking car for theatrical performances, sporting events, museum entries, and other attractions. A list will be made available with the specifics, prices, and times of all available entertainments. Come see me if you wish to make a purchase."

"What say you, gentlemen?" Bella said. "Should we see if Inquisitor Oulcott is up for the 'available entertainments'?"

"I'm afraid I must visit the apothecary, I've no supplies at all. Perhaps I'll seek you out later."

"I hope you do, Doctor Root. And how of you, Master Cobb? Will you be joining us?"

Cobb scratched his chin. "Mayhap I will," he nodded. "At least to serve as an escort while you walk through the city, Miss. I've heard tell of the wild ways that people of the Freehold engage in. I've heard some mate in the streets like animals, forgive me for saying, Miss. Tis no place for a woman to walk unmolested, from what I hear."

"Their customs are different," Elphias admitted, "but they are far removed from that, Cobb. They are a gregarious people to be sure, but they still maintain social morality."

Cobb waved his hand irritatedly. "Well, tis only what I heard. I'll discover for myself, right enough." He nodded his head. "But I do know one thing. It'll not compare to the wonder of the Union. No Agarian tongue wagger will convince me of otherwise."

They reached the private car fifteen minutes before arrival and made preparations to depart. Bella and Zediah went to see what attractions were available while Cobb used the men's cabin bathroom. Elphias sat in the observation lounge, watching the landscape pass. To his right the land flattened out as it progressed to the distant Southern Sea, contrasting with the rising foothills of the mighty Cragback mountain range to his left. The wide and raging Dragon River still marked the traditional border between the provinces of Torbuld and Ostravia this far south, but soon ended against a massive upthrust of granite which defiantly split it into the Twins. The Twins roared onward to the distant ocean while also defining the Freehold's borders.

Lacroix was built atop the granite outcropping, serving as the Agarian capital and its most northerly city. It was little wonder that TransRail had negotiated a stop there. The Freehold begins in Lacroix it is said, and the rest is all scenery.

Elphias' eyes barely acknowledged any of the scenery. His mind was on Bella and their near kiss in the baggage car. Had it really been as he remembered? Had there been an actual spark or was he just losing his mind? He felt thrilled by the adrenaline of attraction, but also deeply ashamed, as if his age was an impression of taking advantage of her. He had been fifteen the year she was born—nearly out of boarding school and taking the placement tests which would determine his career. He graduated from the University of Kulbreg the year she moved to boarding school. She was just a girl.

*She's not a girl any longer,* he thought from somewhere below awareness, as if an intruder had whispered in his ear. *She's a grown woman with a mind and a will of her own.*

There was a truth in that line of reasoning, and also a great danger. Elphias could sense his world spinning, slipping away like the landscape outside. His heart screamed opposition, yearning for both freedom and isolation, abandonment and security. The pain of the past, his dead lover and their stillborn child, still burned deeply and viciously and unforgivingly. His forgiveness hadn't run away, it had been murdered and dumped in a bog of regret. He had become a doctor to save lives, and the lives he loved the most had been the ones he'd been unable to save. It was a bitter cruelty in a world without remorse, a world that just was, for good or ill. The hidden order of the world creaked on, and sometimes lives got caught up in the cogs. Lives which got mangled or crushed to bits.

Elphias knew then that he would not be joining the others later in the evening. He was going to the apothecary and buying as many ampules of Blue Oasis that they had. And then he would ride a brief oblivion and let his heart and mind know some peace. A part of him, the intellectual doctor part, feebly protested that it was perhaps time to stop medicating his pain away, that some wounds needed to be lanced and drained instead of covered and ignored. But as the *Spirit of Innovation* crossed over the raging East Twin River and the vast city of Lacroix rolled into view, that voice quietly acquiesced to silence. He was infected, after all. Infected by a potentially heart scarring condition that caused a befuddlement of ones senses. Yes, it was an infection right enough. And infections needed to be treated.

He stood and went to Zediah's office just as Bella and the inquisitor returned with theater tickets.

"May I have a word, Zediah?"

"Certainly, Doctor Root. Will you excuse us, Bella?"

"I need to change anyway," she said and passed into the bedrooms. She didn't meet Elphias' eye and his heart floundered with pity. The perfect reason to drown this madness.

"What can I do for you?" Zediah asked.

"I need an advancement, if it's possible. For medical supplies and tonics."

"Ah, yes, of course. How much will you require?"

"One hundred should suffice, if you can spare it. I'm assuming there will be the proper tools for an autopsy at our destination, so I only need a few necessities."

Zediah pulled out a wallet and removed a $100 bill. "You're sure it will be enough? I could give you a Duchess if you'd like."

"If you could share further details of what I may expect in Verdun, I could better assess what—"

Zediah shook his head. "I'm sorry, I cannot say at the moment. I know that's unhelpful, but all will be clear after we arrive in Verdun, Doctor, I assure you."

Elphias took the money with a sense of bemusement. *I should be used to waiting on answers by now,* he thought and then began to prepare for departure.

The train station was built in the northern part of Lacroix, close to the entertainment district and off the broad central avenue running the north-south length of the city. Although the elevated train station and sky rail towers hadn't been there the last time Elphias had visited, the rest was refreshingly familiar. The smell of spiced food and soups filled his nose as he left the station. He wasn't surprised to see the food vendor stalls had spread down Liberty Avenue from Border Cross, the intersecting street that turned to bridge in each direction, west to Ostravia and east to Torbuld. It was a heavily traveled stretch of road and the businesses within the Cross Point area of Lacroix did brisk and profitable trade.

Elphias turned south instead, then shirked the well traveled thoroughfare to sidle down a narrow alley and into a secluded courtyard. Only the apothecary fronted the enclosure, the other walls were the featureless backs of other businesses. Besides the standard windowless first floor, the apothecary of Lacroix could not have been more different than the one in Lancaster. The building itself was built of masonry, looking more like an ancient temple than a modern structure. A real human skull looked down from a niche above the sturdy black door, and when Elphias gave greeting to the speaking tube he was answered immediately. When the door was unbarred, Elphias entered into a dimly lit foyer of alternating black and white tiles. Curtains hung from the wall, disguising any exit, and at the far end a dark suited man waited stoically next to a medical school skeleton. Elphias walked forward and approached the skeleton hanging from its stand.

"Hail, brother," he said and shook the skeleton's hand.

The man beside the skeleton cleared his throat. "You have passed through Death's door and greeted his visage. Come now into the land of light." Following the standard greeting he stepped off a few paces and swept back the curtain to reveal the hidden door.

Elphias passed through and into a short hallway, with doors to either side and stairs up at the end. The door to his left led to the reading room, so Elphias headed right to seek the pharmacist.

A stern-looking Agarian woman tended the counter.

Elphias decided to get right to the point. "Do you have ampules in stock?"

"This sister does. What does the brother need?"

Elphias let out a sigh of relief. Then he told her exactly what he wanted.

# CHAPTER TEN
## *Stopover*

Liberty Avenue swarmed with pedestrians, each one as colorful and lively as the next. The road was closed to horse and carriage traffic, so it was just people walking as far as the eye could see. Bella had never seen anything like it, and had to remind herself to blink on occasion so her eyes wouldn't dry out. She walked with Zediah and Cobb on each side, all of them taking in the sights.

"Be prepared to avert your eyes, Miss," Cobb had advised as they'd left the station. "I'll guide you till tis safe." Instead she noted that Cobb was as wide eyed with wonder as she was. But how could anyone resist the assault of ones senses by a city as wondrous as Lacroix?

Store front vendors and food stall operators called for peoples attention as they passed by, shouting in the bouncy sort of way that Agarian's spoke in. Entertainers took up post along the avenue, singing songs, juggling, and performing sleight of hand illusions. And all the people, tanned skin men and women walking arm in arm, some with children in tow. It was a curious custom of the Freehold, a civil institution called marriage. It was similar to a Cohabitation Partnership in the Empire, but it was a primarily verbal agreement. There was a simple license, to be sure, stating who, where and when. But that was all, there were no contracts stating assets, obligations, or rules of conduct. Nor were there Permits of Procreation, nor a limit to the number of offspring allowed each individual. It had somehow seemed immoral when she'd studied about the Agarian culture, but now that she saw it for herself it seemed like a natural form of life.

The people were enjoyable to watch as well. The men wore colorful, open throated shirts without jackets and the women wore blouses scooped to below the collar bone. They also sported comfortable looking flat heeled boots which poked out from beneath their skirts as they walked. Bella envied those boots, wondering why tight laced high heels had become the fashion of the Empire. She made a decision that perhaps she would be the first to change that trend, and began scanning the stores and services they passed. A sign in the shape of a shoe was further up the street, hopefully they carried boots for women. She was about to tell Zediah of her desire to stop there when another sign caught her eye, a small purple circle marked Spiritualist. An arrow pointed down and as they passed the location Bella noted a set of stairs descending to a lower level of the building. She caught sight of a door and window, upon which a poster was displayed.

### Madame Renault
Speaker to the Dead
*Speak With Your Lost Ones Once More!*

A chill ran up Bella's spine followed with an almost claustrophobic dread. Such things were forbidden in Toravia, too close in nature to the forces defeated by the Purge. But that wasn't why she'd reacted the way she did. It was the thought of communicating with her lost one once more. There was a sense of unease, a fear of discovering what the dead thought about your role in their demise. But there was also a longing, a desire to put things right and explain ones actions.

*Perhaps I should tell Elphias about this, see if he would accompany me to put past pains to rest.* His name triggered an association of feelings and thoughts. They'd nearly kissed! She was still confused about it, unsure what had happened, unsure exactly what had ignited that momentary spark between them. She had been willing then, but in retrospect it seemed so foolish and illogical. Elphias obviously was accustomed to being on his own, traveling the land at the whim of his heart. What relationship could they have with her at the call of the Academy and him ever roaming? And there was the age difference. Of course he'd been attracted to her, experience had suggested most men were attracted to younger women. Except perhaps for Zediah, who seemed altogether focused on his career. But Elphias was obviously hurt and there she was, toying with his affections, drawing him into something he didn't want.

Why was she behaving this way?

Bella blinked and realized they'd passed the shoe store. She touched Zediah on the arm. "Excuse me, Zediah. If we've the time I'd like to see if I can purchase a pair of those boots." She pointed down at the passing women's footwear.

He consulted his pocket watch. "Ah, let's see. We've only got…three hours before the show starts. I don't suppose that's long enough?" His eyes twinkled with mirth.

Bella smirked and shook her head. "And to think, I gave up an opportunity with Inquisitor Martel for this."

Zediah burst into a laugh and waved her in the direction of the shoe store.

The inside of the store smelled of leather and wood, and had shelves lined with footwear. The boot Bella was searching for was prominently displayed amongst the offerings for women. They were similar to riding boots now that she could see them fully, but ended mid-calf.

The Freehold of Agaria used a different system of measurement than the Empire, so she had to try on two pair before finding a proper fit.

"Would the woman like these delivered to the sky train?" the clerk inquired.

Bella nodded. "I suppose I must. I wish to wear them now, but then I'll have to carry my old boots."

"If the woman pays the delivery fee, this one will see her old boots are delivered instead. It makes no difference what goes in the box if the sale is made."

And so Bella left the shoe store with a new pair of boots and the slightly disorienting perspective of seeing things two inches lower.

"You've shrunk," Zediah said. "I thought you were going to buy boots, not get hexed."

Bella laughed but Cobb scowled without humor. "No joke, that. They have them hereabouts, the witch folk. Tis foolish to indulge their occupations." He pointed across the avenue where a dark blue sign hung over an arched doorway. *Futures Told Here* proclaimed a scrolling font beneath an illustrated staring eye. "There as an example. What good could come of that? Tis not for man to know his morrow, only the deeds of his lasterdays."

Bella's eyebrows rose with surprise. "That's poetic, Master Cobb. I see all your years have granted you much talent and wisdom."

Cobb blinked then looked down at the ground. "Tis not as many years as may seem."

"I'm sorry, Master Cobb. Have I given offense? I meant no disrespect to your age."

Cobb blushed a bit and shook his head. "Nay, Miss, tis…tis hard to explain."

"What Master Cobb is trying to say," Zediah said, "is that he's younger than he appears. Much younger than you could possibly imagine."

Cobb gave Zediah a startled stare. "Did he tell you, then?"

Bella looked between the two men. "I don't understand."

Zediah shook his head. "If you're talking about Doctor Root, or anyone else for that matter, the answer is no. I figured it out on my own."

Cobb squinted at him. "How?"

Zediah sighed. "Ah, well it was the dead fireman. Benson, I believe. He had similar age lines and an unusual elasticity to the look of his flesh, just as you do. I noticed the similarity, but it was only an educated guess. Until I reexamined your file. I'd used it to draw up our contract, to acquire your name and residency status. But who ever really looks at the birth year? Until you need to know it."

"Know what?" Bella asked with exasperation.

Cobb gave her a shrug. "I was hexed in the Purge. I'm all of thirty-seven years."

Bella gasped. "I'm so sorry, Master Cobb. I had no idea."

Cobb shook his head. "Nay, Miss, tis no offense. I should'a expected Inquisitor Oulcott to find my truth. 'Never a secret from an inquisitor shall ye keep'. The first line of the Order of Inquisition, and the only one everyone remembers. Except me." Cobb laughed. "Tis a funny, funny world, this."

They ate at an outdoor restaurant to pass time, eating deep fried rabbit from wooden skewers. The waiter pushed them to order some wine. "Would the people like to try some Agarian Red? Yes, this one thinks they would. It is an excellent vintage from the southern vineyards. The people will try some, yes?"

So in the spirit of enjoying local customs they ordered a bottle and began to enjoy its fragrant bouquet. The alcohol warmed their insides and flushed their faces, and they fell into a contented silence, observing people stroll by the restaurant. A few recognizable faces came and went, fellow travelers from the *Spirit of Innovation*.

Bella found herself looking for Arctus, wondering where he'd been hiding of late. No doubt tending to his charge, Lady Danueman. Before Elphias had joined them, Arctus had intimated that the Lady was a suicide risk and that he was using the excitement of travel and a change of air to rectify her melancholy. She'd later overheard him asking the porter if any windows on the train could be opened, so she supposed he must be on constant vigilance to keep the Lady from self harm.

There was a warm flushing from elsewhere on her body as she thought of how compassionate he was to do such a thing. He gave off an air of smug confidence but really he must have a tender heart beneath his cavalier, bad boy facade. *That perfectly handsome facade,* she corrected and felt more warm flushes. Now there was a more sensible choice for a relationship, certainly for breeding. His children would be dazzling, she was sure. He was of similar age and maintained a steady profession within an asylum. *If only I'd catch him alone in the baggage car.*

She felt suddenly ashamed, as if she'd said something unkind about Elphias behind his back. Such conflicting emotions, Elphias was safe but unavailable and Arctus was the opposite. Elphias was a decent man after all. They could be friends, but could they ever be more? Likely not. For he was always on the move, but never really moving forward. Arctus on the other hand…well, maybe she'd have to speak with him and see where his feelings lay. He was an alienist after all, who better to know their own personality?

Elphias slumbered in a twilight sleep, barely hearing the activities occurring within the apothecary. He'd gone straight from the pharmacy counter to the men's washroom and downed an ampule of Blue Oasis. Then he'd found the most comfortable looking high back chair in the reading room and settled into it. He also motioned for a valet and instructed the man to wake him around 10 at night to ensure he'd make it back to the *Spirit of Innovation.* Then he'd eased back and closed his eyes, letting the drug eat his doubts, fears, and miseries. He dived deep and darkly but gradually a voice began to trouble his dreamless void. It was far away and not directed at him, but it troubled some untapped part of himself nonetheless. His consciousness surfaced to grey awareness, like a leviathan rolling just beneath the surface to dive deep once again. The click of footsteps approached his chair and eventually a hand shook his shoulder.

"Root," the voice said.

Elphias' eyelids fluttered. He felt heavy. Was it really 10 already? "Is it time?"

The voice laughed, thin and cruel. Elphias recognized it at once. "It is. It is indeed, old boy."

He cracked his eyes briefly to make sure he wasn't just hallucinating. No such luck. "Go away."

Arctus laughed again. "Come now, old boy. Don't bear a grudge. It was all my fault, isn't that what you'd like to hear? I wasn't treating you as a fellow professional. Let me make it up to you."

Elphias fully opened his eyes to witness Arctus tucking an ampule case within the jacket of his tuxedo. Elphias felt his own coat and relaxed when he felt his case where it should be. "You can make it up to me by leaving me in peace," he said.

Arctus gave him that penetrating gaze. His eyes went wide and he laughed mischievously. "You're smacked to the gills, I'd recognize that pupil dilation anywhere." He grabbed hold of Elphias' arm and started to drag him up from the seat. "I'm afraid I won't take no for an answer, old boy. It's a professional courtesy to keep you in my company while you're under the influence of medications."

If Elphias had possessed more awareness he'd have shrugged off Arctus' hands, told him to leave or left himself. But he was still deep under the influence of Blue Oasis, which when used by those who remain awake casts them into a strange, dreamlike state where they have little resistance from the influence of others.

"Where are we off to?" he asked Arctus. "Back to the train?"

Arctus laughed. "Not in the least, old boy. We're going to have an adventure, you and I. I've tickets to something special and am curious to gauge your reaction."

Arctus led him from the apothecary and then though a system of alleys. Elphias' short term memory ebbed and flowed along with his awareness. They crossed a busy intersection and a blink later were waiting in line with several other men.

*Where has he taken me?* Elphias wondered. He looked blearily around and noticed they all stood outside a massive building with Lacroix Sporting Arena painted above the front doors. A cloth banner hung next to the doors, bearing the illustrated figure of a mustached man wearing a bowler. He was also shirtless and seemed to be one huge muscle to Elphias' drugged vision.

Printed on the banner he could make out the words LUX LIGHT CHAMPION PUGILIST above the muscleman and MILLARD MULD / THE GENTLEMAN BEAST below.

Elphias gestured weakly toward the banner. "Who does he fight?"

"Whomever he wants," Arctus said and laughed.

Elphias disliked the sound of his mirth, there was nothing benign in his humor. Did the man never stop with his wicked laughter?

The front doors to the arena opened from within and a cheer erupted from the men gathered outside. To Elphias' ears they sounded mostly drunk, but then who was he to judge? The men shuffled forward and Arctus tugged at his arm, guiding toward the wide doorway. To Elphias it looked like the open mouth of a giant. He made a feeble effort to turn away but Arctus' grip tightened and he hurried them forward. The mouth of the giant grew wide and swelled around them and then it swallowed them whole.

The belly of the giant smelled of sawdust and sweat. Elphias returned to awareness seated next to Arctus on a rough wooden bench. They were set slightly above a row of men in front of them and Elphias noted the same design of seating behind them and surrounding the square boxing ring in the center of the room. A lux light strung high above the ring cast a spot of light down, illuminating the illustrated muscleman made incarnate. He looked less like a muscle and more like a man sculpted from flesh, the sort of man you wouldn't want to trifle with. Muld's eyes were dark and unkind above a thick curled mustache which disguised the foul set of his mouth. There appeared to be a great deal of anger coiled within his tall, chiseled stature.

"Muld, Muld, Muld, Muld," the crowd chanted his name and the bare chested giant acknowledged them with a tip of his bowler.

"They say his father was a bull," Arctus whispered hotly in Elphias' ear, as if Muld could possibly hear him above the noise and distance.

"What do they say of your father?" Elphias asked.

Arctus shot him a cold look. "Asking me a personal question? Why I didn't know you cared, old boy." Then he laughed, but the coldness never left his eyes. It was the same angry stare that Muld possessed, and Elphias suddenly realized that Arctus was just as much a tormenter as the brute in the boxing ring. How many fellow students did both of these men terrorize and bully during their boarding school years? How many tears and nightmares, how many future phobias did they scar upon any children unfortunate enough to have crossed their predatory sights?

*And now Weber has me in his sights,* Elphias thought with alarm. He felt another wave of oblivion washing over him and he tried to fight it, he needed to get free of this cruel man beside him. And then he was sucked under, drawn deep below the surface to the multitude's fevered chant of "Muld, Muld, Muld…"

The Lacroix Opera House was a tall and ornate building fronting on a wide open plaza that joined numerous streets of the city. Gargoyles stared down from atop the opera house and from niches between the tall columned entrance. Some, Bella noted, had been sculpted holding opera glasses to their eyes, to look as though they were observing the audience streaming into the building.

The lobby was wide and vast, its columned walls covered with gold leaf designs that rose upwards to the distant ceiling. A red carpet led across the intricately tiled floor to a broad central staircase leading up to the mezzanine. Zediah steered them to the stairs, passing through the people conversing in the lobby. Bella tried to understand what they were saying but their voices mingled in an indistinct babble that echoed off the hard surfaces of the room. They climbed the stairs to the mezzanine and then headed right to the far end where another set of stairs led upwards to more balcony seating. They headed down a hallway at the first landing, passing a few curtained openings until Zediah matched his tickets to the label beside the door.

"Here we are," he said and led them into the theater box.

Bella set eyes on the theater. "It's beautiful." The lower floor sloped down toward the orchestra pit and front of the house, where ornate designs and flourishes bordered each side of the proscenium rising up to the distant ceiling. Box seating dotted the walls to each side, and two balconies rose above the mezzanine level. A large lux stone chandelier hung above, casting a warm glow to the faces of the audience, turned expectantly to the curtained stage and awaiting entertainment. She sat and turned to address Cobb.

"What think you, Master Cobb?"

His head was rotating, taking in all the details of the vast room. "I've not see'd the like," he admitted. "Are there theaters like this in Austra?"

Bella nodded. "Yes, but not as ornate or as grand. There is a beauty and sensibility to Toravian design, but it can also be a little sterile if you understand my meaning."

Cobb scratched his chin. "Aye, I do, I think. Tis like the buildings we passed to get here. They look similar to those of the Union, but there's more color and fanciness on the outside."

Zediah grinned. "Ah, yes, they do seem to have a love of ornamentation here."

"Tis a little too much for the eyes to take."

An eerie warm swell of notes swirled up from the orchestra pit as the musicians checked their tunings, then the music faded away an instrument at a time. The muffled murmuring from the audience silenced and the lux chandelier dimmed.

"Thank the Dualvinity," Cobb whispered to Bella. "Now I can get some shuteye."

A lux spot glowed to life, focused on center stage as the thick red curtains parted and swept from sight. A man stood in the spotlight's beam, dressed in a tuxedo. He tilted his head to the middle of the house.

"The people are gathered, the tale will be told," he said, voice ringing clear and loud. "For this is the story of Ramos the Bold." The man stepped swiftly from the spotlight to the accompaniment of scattered applause.

The band struck up a martial tune and the stage lights flared up to reveal a cloth backdrop painted to resemble a wall bearing a Toravian flag upon it.

"I like this already," Cobb whispered.

An actor and actress entered from opposite wings and met center stage. The woman was dressed like a Toravian, with heeled boots while the man was dressed in a military uniform of the Royal Guard.

"That's the style I wore," Cobb noted.

The woman looked at the soldier and clasped her hands to her breast. "Oh, sweet Ramos, you've returned to me from the Purge!"

"Indeed I have, my love," said Ramos, "but only for a spell. I must return shortly to continue the fight."

Ramos's love swooned comically. "Oh, how I wish to hold you once more, but I haven't got the proper permit."

The audience roared with laughter.

"Not to worry, Dorrie," Ramos said pulling a folded paper from his uniform. "I've a permit of another kind."

More laughter erupted. Dorrie shook her head. "If only we could, dear Ramos, but I popped out my twain while you were away." She stepped forward toward Ramos. "Perhaps we could pretend I didn't."

Ramos unfolded the paper. "I'm not sure if that's covered, Dorrie."

The audience howled and Bella joined them.

A bugle sounded from off stage and Ramos snapped alert. "Alas, I must return but fear not sweet Dorrie, you shall be protected as always." Two actors dressed as soldiers wheeled in a large golden birdcage with a bed, desk, and stack of books inside.

One of the soldiers opened the cage door and the other helped Dorrie climb inside. Ramos stepped forward and closed the cage. "There you are, fair species, safe at last." He snapped off a salute then turned to one of the soldiers. "Guard her well. I'm off!" Then Ramos and the other guard exited the stage to laughter and applause.

The remaining guard waited a moment before unbuttoning his uniform jacket and removing it to reveal the colorful open throated shirt of an Agarian. He opened the cage door and stepped inside.

Dorrie gave him an intrigued look. "Why sir, where is your permit?"

The Agarian took her boldly in his arms. "Permit? This one needs no permit."

They bent together and froze in the prelude to a kiss. Bella suddenly thought of Elphias and wondered where he was.

The curtains swept closed and the audience roared approval.

Bella shook her head, laughing. "How amusing."

Zediah joined her. "A cutting satire," he said.

Cobb scowled and shrugged. "Seems foul intentioned to me."

The next act began shortly, with the band sounding a military cadence. The curtains rolled away to reveal Ramos and other soldiers taking small, slow steps across the stage. The backdrop was painted to resemble a forest, and tall grasses to each side blocked views of the stage exits.

Ramos raised his hand and the soldiers stopped moving. "Captain Ramos," one of the actors said, "what should we expect to engage?"

Ramos tilted his jaw up bravely. The musical cadence segued into a moody melody. "The most afeared menace to walk the face of Betha."

"Dragons?" an actor queried, voice quaking with mock fear.

"If only," Ramos sneered.

"Griffins protecting a nest of basilisks?"

Ramos shook his head. "I wish it would be so easy."

The soldiers all reacted and spoke as one. "You don't mean—"

Ramos nodded. "Yes, lads. Wood nymphs."

The actors shrieked with fright and huddled together.

"There's naught funny about that," Cobb said, but it was drown beneath the laughter of the audience.

"Come together, lads," Ramos commanded. "There's nothing to fear. We've the might of the Empire on our side. We are men, and we were created to die."

A flute gave a quick high pitched melody from the orchestra pit and the soldiers screamed with fright. The stage grass began to waver with motion.

"Ready yourselves, lads!" Ramos shouted. "The evil is nearly upon us!"

The soldiers raised their prop rifles and formed a haphazard firing line. Their knees quaked and their rifles bobbed up and down with fear.

With a sudden shriek of joy, actresses playing wood nymphs bound from the grasses. They were petite and slender, with grass skirts and a crown of twigs upon their upswept hair. Brown makeup covered their bodies and tiny bared breasts.

The soldiers screamed with fear and broke formation. They ran in a silly manner, each chased by a wood nymph. Some soldiers ran into each other while others would see each another, then scream and run in opposite directions. The wood nymphs merely skipped after them, tossing handfuls of flower petals from baskets slung over their arm.

Ramos meanwhile stood center stage, frowning with displeasure. "You must stop this nonsense!" he shouted. "There is no authorization for this behavior!"

The audience howled. Bella had tears in her eyes. She turned to see Zediah wracked with laughter, hands over his face. The entire theater was laughing. All except Cobb. Bella's laughter dried up.

Cobb's seat was empty. He was gone.


Elphias returned to consciousness looking down at his bloodstained hands. He was kneeling over a man laying supine upon a ground of sawdust, the man's face swollen and blood spattered. A roar of men filled the air.

*What have I done?* he thought. Then he realized his hands didn't hurt, and that his knuckles were blood covered but showing no sign of damage.

"Oi!" a booming voice called out over the rabble. "Keep those hands to yourself, you grey suited bastard. I didn't give you permission to fix him."

Elphias looked up and noticed he was at the end of an aisle between two sections of bleachers. He glanced over his shoulder to see he was close to the boxing ring, and that Muld stood at the ropes like a bull at a fence, his dark, merciless eyes focused on Elphias.

"I'm a doctor," Elphias said, feeling he should say something. He glanced around and noticed Arctus sitting on the opposite side of the ring. Elphias had wandered around it without any recollection.

"Doctor? Is that what you said?"

Elphias nodded. Perhaps Muld could be reasoned with after all.

Muld rubbed his mustache. "Sounds like a fighting name to me. Is that your fighting name? Are you challenging me?"

Elphias shook his head quickly. "No."

Muld looked to the crowd. "What do you say, boys? Was he challenging me?"

The men screamed a response. Elphias thought he heard one or two voices in his defense but it was hard to understand anything, the words were lost in a roar. Muld of course took it how he wanted to take it.

"The truth is revealed. You want to fight me."

Elphias shook his head no.

"You don't want to fight me?"

Elphias continued shaking his head no.

"So you say no, you don't not want to fight me?"

Elphias stopped shaking his head.

Muld grinned. It was cold and cruel and radiated raw power. "Bring him in, boys."

Elphias tried to stand but hands fell upon his arms and torso and he was quickly hauled to his feet. He struggled to break free, but his assailants dragged him toward Muld. The man increased in size as they approached and Elphias knew he had to do anything but get in that ring. He sought out Arctus in the crowd.

"Arctus! Stop them!"

Arctus laughed, then cupped his hand to his ear and shook his head.

The men brought Elphias to the ropes and Muld grabbed hold of his shoulders and lifted him clear of the barrier before tossing him into the ring. Elphias hit the canvas and rolled to the other side. *It's a good thing my body's loose or that may have hurt more*, he thought, trying to catch his breath.

Muld faced him, rolling his neck and stretching his triceps. He grinned and motioned for Elphias to stand. Elphias got to his feet and held up his hands in surrender, palms facing Muld.

Muld roared with laughter. "Are you going to slap me?"

Elphias shook his head. "I can't fight you. I'm a doctor."

"So you're a passive fist?"

Elphias shook his head. He wasn't a fan of violence, he'd seen its aftermath. But he would have no problem giving this man a taste of his own medicine. It was just physically impossible. He'd need a sledgehammer to hurt that stocky face.

"No. I can't damage my hands."

"Your hands?" Muld laughed and turned to the crowd. "I guess you'll just have to use your head and feet."

Elphias felt a rage building and an inspiration from Muld's words. He had one shot, otherwise this cruel beast was going to beat him for no other reason but personal enjoyment.

Muld turned back to Elphias, setting his fists up to fight. Elphias' foot lashed out, driving the tip of his boot hard into Muld's crotch. There was a stopped moment of time, a terrifying moment when Elphias realized the strike had no effect, that it was only a fuel to facilitate a greater beating. And then Muld's face screwed up upon itself and he dropped to the mat, curled in a ball.

The crowd exploded into cheers and jeers, divided by the tactic of Elphias' victory. He had no illusion how Muld would see the outcome. He needed to get clear of this place, to get away while he could.

He crawled through the ropes and dropped to the floor, aware that men were beginning to fight in the stands. Legs charged at him and he rose up, ready to meet his attacker.

Arctus grabbed hold of his shoulders, laughing wickedly. "Let's go, old boy." He pulled Elphias along and started to dash for the exit as men tussled and punched each other around them. "You are a treasure," Arctus giggled. "Too precious to waste! That was more fun than I'd imagined, even more than watching Muld pound you to a pile of meat. What would your lady love say then?"

"Leave Lydia out of this," Elphias mumbled.

They rushed through the doors and back into the spicy hot scent of Lacroix.

Arctus' eyes glittered maliciously. "Lydia, is it? Who is she, some secret love?"

"None of your business, Weber."

Arctus led him briskly along an unfamiliar road, not a surprise considering Elphias had been in a fugue state for most of the journey to the arena. Arctus stopped suddenly, halfway across a short bridge over a lazy canal.

"Oh, it is my business, don't you understand? My specialty is prying beneath the pretense to find the psychosis and perversions under the mask. We all wear one, don't deny it. And this Lydia you speak of is dear to whatever lurks beneath your mask, old boy. Tell me, does Bella know of your Lydia? I suspect not. It might sour your chances to ruin her virtue. Can't say as I blame you, she is a tender, sweet piece of flesh, hot and—"

Elphias' fist flashed out, streaking like the *Spirit of Innovation* as it collided with Arctus' face. Weber gave a startled cry of pain and staggered back. The back of his legs hit the lip of the bridge and he tumbled over and out of sight, followed by a splash. Elphias wandered over to the edge. He wasn't sure how he'd feel if Arctus was dead.

Instead the alienist was treading water and staring daggers. Arctus clutched the side of his face where Elphias' fist had made connection.

"You really are an over sensitive arsehole, aren't you?" Arctus stated.

Elphias looked down on him. "Leave me alone, Weber. And leave Bella alone, you vile, twisted snake. If I see you talking to her I'll throw you off the train myself."

He turned and staggered away, shaking his right hand. The knuckles throbbed and were reddened. He'd feel it more once the last bits of Blue Oasis exited his bloodstream. Elphias began to seek familiar signs and landmarks, but wasn't too concerned. Lacroix wasn't that big of a city. Eventually he'd find his way back to the *Innovation*. He moved onward, taking no note of Arctus, who stood dripping on the bridge and watching him go. Arctus' eyes were flat and dark and still, a sharp contrast to the chaos which swirled within his fevered head.

# CHAPTER ELEVEN
## *Revelations*

Cobb stalked the streets of Lacroix, following a trail of angry thoughts rather than any external navigation. He clenched his fists and wanted to punch something. The playwright, for starters. The play was an outrage! Cobb had told the man in the box office so when he'd stormed out of the theater. He told him off for allowing such a show that was obviously an Agarian intent to slander the goodness of Toravia. The man in the box office had listened patiently then sadly shaken his head. "The man is entitled to his opinions, yes," he had said, "but perhaps they are misdirected." He then pointed to a line of text near the bottom of the playbill posted in the lobby. It stated the play and theater company were on tour, hailing from Toravia.

Cobb slapped his thigh and let out a huff of disgust. To think his taxes helped pay for such misguided rubbish, and to produce it to entertain the dogs of the Freehold was too much. The fools in the audience had laughed, but would they have laughed if real wood nymphs had taken the stage? Would they have giggled once they'd seen for themselves, seen the reality as opposed to bare titted stage wenches? No, there would have been no such laughter, only screams of fear and pain as the idiots made haste for the exits. And the wood nymphs would have slaughtered them all and afterwards crafted instruments from the bones of musicians and patrons alike. It was too much, it was really just too much.

He turned blindly down an alley, wandering without purpose. A scrawny cat came slinking out from behind some cans of rubbish, blinking at Cobb with yellow green eyes. It meowed a scratchy greeting and padded toward him with tail raised and crooked at the tip.

"Get away from me!" Cobb lashed out his foot to kick it, but the cat easily dodged his clumsy attempt. It trotted further up the alley then turned and looked back at Cobb with a slow blink. It sat and proceeded to lick its paws, clearly unimpressed and not afraid of the slow moving man. Cobb stooped and picked up an empty bottle, then threw it at the taunting animal. The bottle missed but caught the cat by surprise anyway. It leapt into the air as the bottle shattered on the cobblestones behind it, then ran off down the alley like it was on fire. It brought no satisfaction to Cobb, he could take no pleasure in the misfortune of some stupid animal. His dark rage could not be absolved so easily. The play had ignited the fire, but the kindling and fuel had been laid long before.

He stormed onward through the alley, lost in his anger. The sounds of stifled conversation drew him to a dim tavern housed in the sublevel of a building and accessible by a short set of steps leading to its chipped wooden door. He pushed into the smoky interior, dingy and smelling of sweat, ale, and hopelessness. Filthy straw was scattered across the dirt floor, hardpacked by years of drunken, tromping feet. Cobb ordered an ale from the barkeep, then found an unoccupied corner in an alcove to settle down and drink.

The ale was warm and had a bitter aftertaste but Cobb was beyond caring about such complaints. He stared down into the dark liquid and sighed. He'd organized the hunt because he feared that the locals were becoming too complacent. But it was far worse than that. The apathy, the indifference was coming from the duumvirate as well. Almost from the start, really. It had almost been like a spigot had been turned off; one day the Purge was the only thing that mattered, the next day it was over and everyone was ordered home. He shook his head. It really made no sense. Did they really not understand the victory they'd won and what was at stake if they turned a blind eye toward a defense from the same dangers? He lifted his head and looked around at the other patrons. Did any of them not appreciate the sacrifices made? Would any of them trade modern safety for the days of old? If so, they were fools.

Cobb finished his ale and left the filthy bar, determined to return to the *Spirit of Innovation* as quickly as possible. *I should'a stayed aboard*, he thought bitterly. Now that his anger had subsided enough for other thoughts, he was sorry to have left the inquisitor and young woman the way he did, but they seemed kind and forgiving so there would likely be no ill feelings toward him.

And after all, what did they expect his reaction would be when confronted by such garbage as that treasonous play?

Cobb reached the sky train station twenty minutes after leaving the bar, his mood still foul. He stalked up the stairs and across the passenger platform with eyes forward, refusing to see anything more of Lacroix. *I'll never come back here*, he fumed. *Of course you won't, you old fool*, he amended. *You'll be dead of old age afore you know it.*

Cobb shook his head at his own anger, knowing it was bordering on irrational. He decided it was best to avoid his traveling companions until he'd calmed down, so when he entered the *Spirit of Innovation* he made straight for the engine. He needed to distract himself with some train talk. As he entered the dining car he was peripherally aware of a man seated at one of the tables. The man looked at Cobb and did a double take.

"Pup? Is that truly you, then?"

Cobb stopped and turned to face the man, who was now standing to embrace him. Recognition suddenly gave name to the familiar face.

"Nelson?"

Nelson nodded and they embraced each other with friendly pats on the back. Nelson took a step back and gave Cobb a look of amazement that suddenly shifted to serious.

"What are you doing on this train?" Nelson asked him.

"I could ask the same of you, Nelson. Sit with me?"

Nelson nodded and gestured to the table he'd been drinking a beer at, then sat down. Cobb pulled out a chair across from his former squadmate and slumped into it. Nelson's joyous surprise had evaporated and he now looked dismal.

"The fates are cruel sometimes," he said.

Cobb squinted at him. "What are you going on about?"

Nelson's brow wrinkled and the bags under his eyes seemed to deepen. "Oh, Pup. Where to begin? Where to begin, indeed."

"How about after we mustered out."

Nelson nodded. "Aye, good a place as any I guess." He took a long drink of beer then motioned a waiter for another. "After the Purge, we joined the men's guard, me and Charlie, Mack, and Vic."

"I remember how we used to say we'd do that," Cobb murmured.

"Aye, until what they did to you…" Nelson's face darkened a moment and his brows pinched together. He closed his eyes and let his features relax. "So after the Purge, the rest of the goon squad did just that." He stared down at his hands. "Sometimes I wish I'd have found work in a foundry or manufactory, but…well, those ain't the cards I dealt myself."

The waiter brought another beer for Nelson and took an order from Cobb for an ale. Nelson waited until they departed before continuing.

"So Charlie, Mack and me, we get assigned to the Academy, right? Vic, on the other hand…well, that's another story. But three of the goons were together and we made the most of it." Nelson shook his head and sighed. "So about four years ago, we were assigned a simple task. The Academy was expanding the Bureau of Records and there were several boxes of old files which needed to be disposed of. It was late in the day and the furnace was cold, so we was ordered to guard the stack of boxes until the next morning, when the stoker would come in and fire the furnace to temperature. We got the order from some prig in administration who acted like he was a grand inquisitor. He gave the order and asked if there were any questions. You should have seen the look on his face when I raised my hand, Pup, it was a sight to remember."

Nelson shook his head and rubbed his nose. "I asked why they were burning files, didn't the Academy pride itself on possessing all knowledge? It just didn't make sense."

"The prig seemed to take it personal, he made a big scene out of that not being necessary information for us. Then the prig ordered us not to look at the files and sauntered off like the dandy little shite that he was."

The waiter brought Cobb his ale and asked if they wanted anything else. Cobb shook his head and wondered where Nelson was headed with all this. Once the waiter left Nelson continued.

"Now, you know well enough, Pup. Remember how boring it was between engagements, how awful the waiting for something to happen was?"

Cobb nodded.

Nelson smiled grimly. "Well it's worse when there's no danger of monsters attacking at any moment. It gives a whole new meaning to the word 'boring'."

"How long did it take you?"

Nelson swallowed. "To read some of the files? Not much. Not much time at all." He closed his eyes. "There's been many a night I wished we hadn't, though." He fell into silence.

Cobb cleared his throat. "What did they say?"

Nelson shrugged. "I can't say for sure, not all of them. But we found one box, one that…I almost still can't believe it." He ran a hand through his greying hair.

"Tell me," Cobb prodded.

Nelson raised his head to meet Cobb's eyes. "They caused it," he said. "The whole blazed thing. It was a plan, a conspiracy right from the start."

"What are you talking about?"

Nelson licked his lips. "The Purge, Pup, the Purge. They caused it to happen. They brought it down upon us all."

"You're mad," Cobb said. "Bah! The volcano caused the creatures to encroach our territory, not people of the Union! You must have read something wrong. "

Nelson shook his head. "Many a night I wished that were true." He rubbed his forehead. "But it were all right there. The details, the supplies, even the names of those that done the deed. Five platoons of firefighters, it was. Five platoons went to the north and ignited the forests up there, burned them to drive the foul down our way."

Cobb shook his head dismissively. "It doesn't make sense. Why would they do that?"

Nelson gave him a look. "Doesn't it? Or do you just not want to see it. Think on it, Pup. You were too young to remember how it was before then. The Union was young and unsteady, nearly torn apart by factional divisions and territorial rivalries. Then the creatures came pouring out of the north and men went back to the old ways, working alongside one another for the sake of survival."

Nelson shook his head and clenched his hand into a fist. "And it worked, Pup, worked only too well. Nationalism and progress surged, industry and commerce churned great profits. So they kept it going. For money and power, they left us to fight what should never have been."

"You're daft," Cobb said quickly. He didn't like this conversation. He didn't like how Nelson's lie had a tiny ring of truth to it. "The Purge lasted because of the need for improved firearms, which were remedied after the jacketed ammo came out, you remember. Besides, dragon powder is a rare substance, there's only a limited supply."

Nelson grinned but there was no humor in it. "Which is where Vic comes in. He'd been assigned to guard the cave where Morgrum and Daughters mined the powder, where it's said to contain fossilized droppings from the dead beasts of old."

"And…?"

Nelson chugged his beer, draining the glass with a large gulp. He set the glass down and smacked his lips. "Have you ever seen an animal work a mine, Pup? Seen a cow, swine, or sheep heft a pickaxe and start swinging?"

Cobb shook his head, irritated at the frivolity of the question. "Nay, tis a foolish thing to ask."

Nelson nodded. "I agree. But good old Vic swore that was what was being sent down into the caves, large numbers of livestock every week. No one was allowed into the caves without proper gear, they said, there were dangerous aethers. But Vic noted none of them livestock were wearing anything. No protection at all."

"Are you suggesting there's a dragon in the cave, then?" Cobb laughed dryly. It couldn't be true.

Nelson shrugged. "So says Vic, and he weren't one to have a vivid imagination if you remember. He also heard roars. They sounded far away and deep underground, but that's what he claims to have heard. Roars. Emphasis on there being more than one. He was going to investigate further. I told him to be careful, but you know Vic." Nelson sighed, deep and distressed. "I never heard from him again. They said he'd been transferred, but no one could say where."

They fell into silence. Cobb's mind wheeled. Was any of it true? Could the Purge have been ended afore he'd even joined? Was his curse, his sacrifice for the nation he loved just a lie? The black rage that flamed during the play threatened now to burn him to cinders. "So what then?" he said, his voice sounding tight and distant.

Nelson shrugged. "We left. One by one. I couldn't do it no more, I had no faith. Everything I thought was true was a lie. Ended up here with others that disagree with what was done. The way things are." He shook his head. "It's all gone bad, Pup, the Empire has. But we're going to make a statement, we're going to make the people of Toravia open their eyes."

"How do you plan to do that?"

Nelson looked down at his hands again. "We've a plan. It's why I'm here, partly." He lifted his empty glass, noticed it was dry then set it down again. "I drew the short straw, so I'm drinking for courage. I was praying for a sign, to see if it were the right course." Nelson looked up, eyes shining. "And then in walked you, Pup. Once I saw you—remembered what they did to you and all the others—I knew it was right. They need to pay. They need to pay for all they killed and maimed for profit and power."

Cobb sat back, mouth dry and heart pained by betrayal. His country had lied to him. Sacrificed countless men for ulterior motives. It didn't seem right. "I'm not sure what to say, Nelson. How do you plan to make them pay?"

Nelson looked furtively around the dining car as if searching for someone amongst the scattered diners. "Not here, Pup. I don't know who's who."

"Who's who?" Cobb scowled at his former squadmate. "What are you on about? Part of this 'we've a plan, they need to pay' mystery?"

Nelson gave a barely perceptible nod of his head. "Let's go to my berth. I'll explain it there."

"I'm not sure I want to know now," Cobb said bitterly, but he stood when Nelson did and followed him toward the dining car exit without hesitation. *What's this fool got his self into?* he wondered. Nelson hadn't been the sharpest blade of the goon squad, but he'd had a good heart. This didn't seem much like him. The conspiracy had obviously affected him, had drove him to this foul nation to become embroiled in some scheme.

They crossed the vestibule and into the smoking car, which was filled with passengers standing around something or someone, murmuring with excitement. Nelson turned suddenly, as if inspired by a notion. "You should bunk with me, Pup. There's a spare berth in my room. We can catch up on the past few years. I haven't even heard how you came to be aboard the *Innovation.*"

"Aye," Cobb said. "Tis a grand adventure, that. Good folk I travel with too, but t'would be nice to bunk together once again."

Nelson looked relieved. "Good. Good," he said quietly.

Cobb wondered which of the two of them he was speaking to. A sudden chill ran down his spine. *My adventure ain't done yet I suppose.*

He wasn't sure how to feel about that.

# CHAPTER TWELVE
## *Full Steam*

Oren Halbert stretched his back and yawned. Soon it would be time for the *Spirit of Innovation* to get moving once more, making the final leg from Lacroix to the city of Verdun. It was as easy a run as ever, a special premiere express route. After this inaugural journey more stops would be added between Beltram, Lacroix, and Verdun, but for now it was just a straight shot.

Even though it wasn't his job Halbert double-checked the pressure gauges and the water level sight glass to make sure the engine was in good running order. As driver, he felt a certain sense of ownership over the train and wanted to make sure it was working as smoothly as possible. Besides, there was nothing else to do but wait. The *Innovation* wasn't set to depart for an hour and his partner in the cab, Stan Motts, was in the sleeping compartment behind the tender, talking with the relief driver and firekeeper.

A loud clunk sounded from beneath the train as Halbert felt a momentary vibration under his feet. A frown crossed his face. He couldn't think of anything that would have caused such a sound. Nothing good anyway. He turned and crouched over a circular door set into the floor. Opening it revealed a small shaft leading down and out of the bottom of the train that served as an emergency exit for the cab. He leaned forward to take a look but could see nothing but the loading room floor some thirty feet below. He'd need to unspool the rope ladder and crawl down the hatch to inspect for any underside damage. Perhaps a baggage lift had clipped it somehow.

The ladder was rolled up and stored in a box behind the floor port. Halbert reached to extract it when the cab door opened. Two men stepped in and gave him a flat, sullen look. They were dressed in rail clothes, but something seemed a little off about them.

"Who the blazes are you two?"

"We're the relief," one of them said.

"I've got relief. What happened to Biff and Rollie? Where's Stan?"

Halbert realized then what was off about the men. The dirt on their faces looked like it had been placed there, not the random result of working in a dirty environment. And also their hands. It looked like smeared blood on their hands.

The men reached into their jackets and pulled daggers from their sheathes. They fell upon Halbert, stabbing and slashing. The shock kept him from feeling the pain but there was no hiding the spraying of his blood. Halbert tried to back away but the floor wasn't there to meet his foot. He fell back, hit the side of the open hatch and plunged out of sight with a surprised cry.

The assassins looked down through the port, watching from overhead as men working a lift beneath the engine approached the body sprawled in an expanding puddle of blood. One of them turned his face up to meet their eyes and gave a wave. The killers nodded and motioned for their accomplices to deliver the remainder of their device. They would wait to dump the other bodies until after they were in motion once more. There were plenty of deep crevasses to pass over once they climbed into the Cragbacks.

The men smiled at one another. Everything was going according to plan.


Elphias returned to the *Spirit of Innovation* and went immediately to the private car, relieved to find it empty. He changed to a nightshirt and then crawled into his bunk. Sleep eluded him. When he shut his eyes he either pictured Bella tilting up for a kiss or his fist slamming into Arctus' smug face. Both carried a twinge of regret and a great deal of pleasure. The near kiss, just the thought of it, was more pleasurable than the sucker punch, but the latter certainly had its own advantages. Arctus would likely leave Elphias alone now, and Bella as well. This suited Elphias fine, he had no intention of running afoul of Arctus' observational attitudes during the next half of the trip. And if the young brat still hadn't learned his lesson, well then Elphias would teach him once again.

He still couldn't believe how close he'd come to being beaten senseless by the menacing fighter Muld. Just another in his series of misadventures since his vardo had burned. His vardo! It seemed like months ago that it had been destroyed instead of merely days. *I'm still falling,* he thought, *still untethered and drifting to who knows where.*

From the office came sounds of voices, Zediah and Bella had returned. Drowsiness was tugging at his consciousness so Elphias lay where he was, reaching for sleep.

The curtain to their room parted and Zediah entered, then turned around and walked out. Elphias could hear him from the other room.

"Doctor Root is here, but there's no sign of Cobb. I'll speak with the porter immediately and make a search of the train."

"I do hope he's all right," Bella said.

Something had happened with Cobb? Elphias got out of his cot and slipped on his trousers, pulling the suspenders over his nightshirt.

Bella was in the office area. She turned as he entered. "Elphias."

"Has something happened with Cobb?"

Bella brushed a lock of her hair back. "We hope not. We were watching the performance of a play. It was a silly thing really, satire and pratfalls. But Master Cobb seemed to take offense and left us before we noticed. Is that much like him?"

Elphias shrugged. "I've no idea. I've only known him but a short while."

"Really? I'd assumed you two were friends for some time now."

Elphias shook his head. "We traveled together, so…There's a certain bond that forms when you do that."

A heavy silence fell for a moment as the implications of his last statement worked through their minds.

"Is it lonely," Bella asked quietly, "wandering as you do?"

Elphias opened his mouth to tell her. *Where to begin?*

The door to the car banged open and Cobb walked in tailed by Zediah.

"Tis naught to do with that, Inquisitor."

"Are you certain? It seems strangely timed."

Cobb waved a hand at him. "Nay, I'm fine." He stopped. "Hoy, Doctor. Miss Bella." Cobb lowered his eyes. "Forgive me for leaving you, Miss. I…"

"There's no need to explain, Master Cobb. I understand. Or at least I believe I do."

Cobb gave a small smile, his gaze still to the floor.

"Thankee, Miss. Twas fate, I think. I came across an old squaddie of mine that boarded in Verdun. I'm going to bunk with him for the remainder."

Elphias blinked. "What? Are you sure?"

"Aye, Doctor," Cobb said and gave a little laugh. "You'll finally be free of my night stink." He scratched the back of his head. "You're a good man. You were decent to travel with."

Elphias studied him. Cobb seemed off somehow, a certain spark missing from his eyes when they actually looked up. "Thank you, Cobb. You as well, and…This isn't a goodbye is it?"

Cobb blinked. "Oh, no, naught like that. Just in case we don't see each other afore the end of the trip. The cars are all crowded with folk goggling at the great celebrity in our midst."

Zediah rolled his eyes. "The smoking car is an obstacle of fawning masculinity. I was prepared to lose myself within it in search of Cobb when he found me instead."

Bella laughed. "Who is this new mystery passenger?"

"Some big lug of a fighter," Cobb said. Elphias' blood ran cold. "Never heard of him. Supposed to be doing some fight at the expo for the Lux."

"Muld?" Elphias' mouth was dry.

Cobb nodded. "Aye, tis the name sure enough." He squinted at Elphias. "I never took you for having an interest in pugilism, Doctor Root."

Elphias shook his head. "And you'd be right. But I…became acquainted with him in Lacroix. I remember his banner called him the Gentleman Beast."

"Tis what some star-struck man told me. Said Muld was undefeated." Cobb waved his hands. "But another said no, it had happened tonight, and the other said impossible and so on."

Elphias felt like his lungs were compressed. *Breathe, you fool!*

Cobb coughed. "All I know is that this Muld fella looked angry and dangerous, like a horse about to kick. Mayhap he did get beat tonight. He was walking with a little limp and was awful curious to find someone."

"Who?" Elphias barely recognized the sound of his own voice. Was Muld after him? If so, how had he known where Elphias would be? He instantly thought of Arctus, then reconsidered. Considering his drugged state of mind, it was just as likely he'd told Muld himself and given him a map to the train.

Cobb shook his head. "Won't say who, or at least I didn't hear him say."

Elphias' heart pounded. Thankfully he was in a private car, protected by a rotating shift of guardswomen. He'd just stay behind their protection until they arrived at Verdun. He nodded. It would do. Nothing short of a catastrophe would move him otherwise.

The *Spirit of Innovation* pulled from the station shorty after Cobb had gathered his things and moved out. It steamed over the rooftops of Lacroix and then lanced out over the West Twin River, headed for the mighty Cragback Mountains. A large metal housing was now attached to the bottom of the engine, clamped tight with a magnetic grip. The bomb within slumbered patiently, waiting for a trigger catalyst to awaken it in a display of sound and fury.

The track began a gradual incline, guiding the massive sky train up into the rocky terrain. The *Innovation*'s new driver clenched his hand on the throttle, fingers, palms, and knuckles stained with the gore of the former man who held that position. The irony was not lost on the anarchist. In fact it seemed like justice of the Dualvinity. Many revolutions began with the blood of the common man. And revolution was coming. He grinned madly, heart filled with righteous hatred, and opened the throttle to maximum. The steam driven mechanical stoker increased speed, feeding more coal to the fire. The *Spirit of Innovation* roared its way up toward the snow covered treachery of the Cragback's steep mountainous peaks.

"How's the pressure?"

The anarchist serving as firekeeper examined the gauges, careful not to lean upon the triggering device mounted next to them upon the boiler backhead. "It'll hold." He gave a dark laugh. "This beast was made to run full chisel."

The driver picked up a sledgehammer they'd brought aboard. He hefted it up. "And that's how it will die," he said and swung the sledge sideways across the throttle handle. The handle bent, twisting the hinge point and locking it in position. The driver hit it a few more times to be sure. There was no going back. There would be no stopping now.

"So what's this great mystery then?" Cobb sat on his bunk, arms folded and a frown on his face. Nelson had refused to talk more about it until the *Spirit of Innovation* was in motion once more.

Nelson sat on the bunk opposite, a morose expression on his long face. He leaned forward and exhaled a nervous breath with his mouth. "I'm taking a great risk telling you this," he said and from his tone Cobb didn't doubt Nelson believed it.

"You risk me dying of age if you keep dawdling on. Get to the matter, Nelson."

Nelson nodded with sudden determination. "We're going to blow it up," he said firmly.

"Blow what up?"

"The *Spirit of Innovation*. That's why I'm aboard. I'm the triggerman, Pup. I'm going to sacrifice my life and blow this blazed train up."

"No," Cobb said, stunned by Nelson's plot. "Tis madness, what are you thinking? Why would you consider such a foul thing?"

"The eyes of the nation are upon her, Pup. It's a symbol of the vanity and pride of the corruptions that stain the Empire. Do you know how many men died during construction of the transcontinental rail?"

Cobb shook his head.

"Over a hundred," Nelson said, "but you'll never hear their names during the grand speeches about the greatness of the deed. Nor the names of the men who die in the manufactories, nor in the mills every year, nor even those which died by our side during the Purge. It's the working man who pays the price of progress, who pays the cost of a company's profits."

Cobb put his head in his hands. "What has become of you? Tis traitorous to talk of such a thing."

"Is it?" Nelson tapped his hand on his leg. "We swore allegiance to protect the Union from evil influences, from 'the Foul Creatures which endanger Our lives', didn't we?"

"By killing innocent people?" Cobb shook his head. "I can't let you do it, Nelson. I have friends on this train."

"It's beyond stopping now." Nelson looked at him sadly. "Sorry, Pup, I truly am. The operation is already in progress. Alternative plans are in place. Do you understand? If I don't do it someone else will, and they won't be as merciful."

"Merciful? By the Dualvinity, how can you even say that?"

"There are other forces at work here. Others that hate the Empire, despise it to the point that they want to destroy the *Innovation* when it arrives at Verdun station so as to kill the most amount of people." Nelson shook his head with dismay. "I don't want that, not at all. I'm going to blow it up *before* it reaches Verdun. That way the explosion will be heard and witnessed by the city, yet sparing them from the alternative horror."

"Yet killing those aboard."

"Not if I can help it," Nelson said. "I want to destroy the train, not murder innocents. I plan on forcing the train to stop so that everyone can get off before I blow it up. It's a deviation that may get me killed before I can do it, but I've already drawn the short straw anyway."

"There are more accomplices?"

"More than you could imagine, Pup. Not even I know who is involved. I just know the role I'm supposed to fulfill and what will happen if I fail."

Cobb stared at his former squadmate, remembering the horrors and sacrifices they'd gone through to secure the nation for prosperity. During this time the wealthy had stayed sheltered within their cities, earning vast profits on the misery of the frontline. And all of them served the soulless entity of their government, where they were categorized, filed, analyzed and regulated to the point of needing a license to know the comforts of a woman's private passions. A part of Cobb suddenly understood the mockery of the play, the illusion of freedom that permeated Toravian culture. Even so, this was too much.

"I can't be part of this," Cobb said. "And neither should you." Cobb held up a hand as Nelson opened his mouth to protest. "There's no need for you to die. Or anyone else. I'm traveling with an inquisitor. He's a smart fella, and can probably figure out a solution to this mess. What say you, Nelson? Will you turn away from this madness?"

Nelson looked at him for a bit, silent and face unreadable. Gradually he nodded his head ever so slight.

"Good," Cobb said with relief and began to stand. "Let's go see him now."

Nelson grabbed hold of his arm, expression grim.

"We should inform the driver first. The bomb's attached to the bottom of the engine."


Cobb and Nelson entered the staff car beyond the baggage hold. No one was in sight, which eased Cobb's stress only marginally. They passed through an area with a table and chairs and past some sleeper bunks set into the wall. Some had their privacy curtains closed, and a light snoring sounded from behind one of them. Cobb put his finger to lips and they crept silently forward. They couldn't afford to be delayed or detained by anyone that might not believe their story. They rounded a small galley and exited the car. The air in the vestibule was cold and the wind whistled through gaps in the canopy.

The door ahead was bolted closed from the other side. The sign on it read ENGINEERS ONLY. They'd made an exception for Cobb when he'd toured the *Innovation*. He hoped they'd still be as accommodating.

Cobb rapped his knuckles on the door. "Oi. Biff. Rollie. Tis Cobb. Open up."

They waited, swaying with the motion. Cobb gave Nelson a look then knocked a little louder. "Oi! Open up, lads."

The bolt sounded from the other side and the door was wrenched open.

A foul looking man with stringy hair and angry eyes scowled at them. "What the fek do you want?"

"Where are the lads?" Cobb said. "I've never see'd you afore."

The man scowled further. He snatched out his hand fast and grabbed Cobb's collar, then yanked him through the door and slammed him against the metal wall. They were in a small cot space tucked at the rear of the tender. The man pushed Cobb up against the hard surface and held a dagger to his eye. "How bout you see never again, Pappy, eh?"

Cobb recognized the look in his assailant's eyes. He'd witnessed it when men had gone into a battle frenzy during the Purge. There was no reasoning, only blood lust. And the small room reeked of blood. The poor lads. If the relief boys were dead it was likely true of Halbert and Stan too. Cobb closed his eyes. They'd been a good bunch.

Nelson cleared his throat. "It's a steady hand that extinguishes the light."

The man gave Nelson a dirty look, then scowled at Cobb. "You're both part of the scheme? Why the fek didn't you say so." He lowered his blade and shoved Cobb away.

Cobb scanned the room. There were no bodies but the walls and cot were tacky with dried blood.

Nelson gestured at Cobb. "My associate here knew the original crew. He was hoping to persuade them to our cause."

The foul man grinned, lips twisted with wicked glee. He held up his dagger. "Oh, they been persuaded all right."

Cobb had a desire to snatch the dagger away and bury it in the man's throat. He'd had battle frenzy himself. It had helped bleed some of the rage from the hex.

"Who's up front?" Nelson asked.

The man stared at Nelson with contempt. "Do I look like a secretary, you simpering dolt?" He flung his hand in the direction of a narrow passage leading forward to the engine cab. "Go and find out for yourselves."

The passage to the engine was narrow and confined, tucked beneath the coal filled tender. Cobb and Nelson moved forward in single file, the hall filled by the sound of the mechanical stoker grinding its payload to the fire. Halfway down Cobb turned to face Nelson.

"What's the idea with this?" he whispered harshly.

"Saving your life, Pup. Play along, for your own sake. Please."

Cobb shook his head with bitterness and moved forward once more.

The door to the engine was closed but unlocked. Nelson opened it and they stepped into the cab.

The air was hot and smelled of coal smoke and dried blood. The driver and firekeeper turned to face them, pulling daggers from their jackets.

"What are you two on about?" the driver said in a flat tone.

Nelson raised his hands. "Just checking to make sure everything is going to plan."

The driver gestured with the tip of his knife toward Cobb. "Who's this one, then?"

"A new recruit to our cause."

"I've not seen him before," the driver said.

"Nor me," added the firekeeper.

"Nor I as well," said the stringy haired man from the doorway. "Mister Torvo didn't say naught about another."

Cobb and Nelson looked over their shoulders. Stringy hair had slipped up behind them without notice, leaning in the door frame with a nasty sneer on his face. They were trapped.

Sweat trickled down Cobb's brow. The only way to deal with monsters was to think like they did. "I'm the backup triggerman," he said. "Unless one of you wants to volunteer."

The other men looked between one another. The driver laughed. "Nay, elder father, you two may have the honors. We've still some things to accomplish afore the revolution is complete." He motioned to the broken throttle handle next to the foul looking trigger device. "We've set the controls for you already."

Cobb's heart sank. The handle was savagely bent and nearly broken. He doubted they'd be able to repair it enough to slow the *Innovation,* let alone stop it. His mind reeled. What to do now? How could he save his friends from certain destruction? He'd have to tell the inquisitor. The inquisitor would know what to do.

"Looks like you lads have it in control," Cobb said and turned to the door.

The stringy haired man still blocked their way. "Where the fek do you think you're going?"

Cobb scowled. "Back to the train, where else?"

Stringy hair shook his head. "Nah, no one is going anywhere. We're all a happy group now, like lads at boarding school."

Nelson frowned. "What's the purpose for this?"

Stringy hair pointed his dagger at them. "Mister Torvo didn't say naught about another triggerman. It ain't part of the plan, eh? Now you may trust him, but I don't. I don't know this old turd from nobody."

Cobb's face darkened. "We can't all stay here!"

Stringy hair pointed his dagger toward the floor hatch. "You can take the quick way out if you'd like. But you sure as shite ain't getting past me."

A stifling silence filled the cab, despite the roar of the fire behind the boiler backplate, the ceaseless grind of the mechanical stoker, and the wind shrieking past the cab windows. Outside the night was dark and without stars. They swayed with the rock of the engine, waiting for something to happen. Steam hissed through the pipes.

Cobb cleared his throat. "Can I sit down at least?"

# CHAPTER THIRTEEN
## *Without a Trace*

The next morning Elphias took breakfast in the private car, eating from a tray as he sat in the observation lounge. They were fully in the mountains now, rigid peaks and snow swept gorges passed by outside the windows. Frost decorated the panes and the glass felt cold to the touch. Occasional phantoms of snow swirled in the wake of the *Spirit of Innovation*'s passing, whirling away and scattering to the wind. Elphias understood how it felt. How had he allowed himself to get this way? What life had he allowed himself to live in the aftermath of his flight from pain? To continually live in the shadow of a trauma? Running from that pain had only fed it more energy, like coal to the furnace, growing stronger until it had become some great fiery giant, one burning step from crushing Elphias into oblivion.

The deaths he'd been fleeing had happened so long ago. But he'd never moved on. He'd been living in a graveyard for far longer than that penultimate night in his vardo. Would Lydia have wanted that for him? How had he not seen this before?

"Are you unwell, Elphias?"

Bella stood in the doorway, looking at him kindly.

"Mm? No, I'm fine."

"Not dwelling on your past, are you?"

Elphias gave her a lopsided smile. "I thought that was the purpose of this section." He turned and stared out the back of the train again. "But now I see that it's to cast the past off. To leave it behind where it belongs."

"Sounds like you've had an insight. Is this a recent revelation or a souvenir from Lacroix?"

Elphias laughed. "More like a slow dawning."

"Then congratulations, good sir."

"Thank you, m'lady. And how of you, what are your thoughts of late?"

"I'm…trying to be realistic about the future."

A swirl of snow cascaded down from a support tower as they passed through.

"You asked me before, if I ever got lonely," Elphias said. "I never had a chance to answer."

There was a pause. The wind rushed past the windows.

"And do you?"

"I—" Elphias shook his head and gave a small laugh. "I didn't think so. For years I've thought that, but…" He gave Bella a glance. "Recent events have made me reexamine that notion."

Bella smiled, a light flush to her cheeks. "And, is this a good thing? This reexamination?"

Elphias looked at her again and this time he did not drop his gaze. "Yes, I believe it is."

Bella lowered her eyes, still smiling. "I'm glad to hear of this, Elphias."

"I was hoping you would."

Bella looked at him. "Truly?"

His heart thudded heavily in his chest. *Tell her, you fool! Tell her the truth!*

Elphias nodded. "Yes. I do not say those words lightly. You intrigue me. I would wish to know you better when time permits."

Bella cast her eyes down. "I…we should speak of this further, at the end of the journey. I need to focus on my duties. I've fallen a bit behind on my transcriptions." She smiled. "But you've given me much to think about. Thank you for your honesty." She laughed nervously. "I'm hungry, would you care to join me in the dining car for breakfast?"

Elphias lifted his tray and smiled. "Just finished, sorry." It was easier than telling her he was hiding from Muld.

"In that case I will bother someone else." Her eyes sparkled. "Perhaps I will encounter Master Cobb and he can relate all the sordid secrets he learned about you during your travels."

Elphias laughed. "In that case drink plenty of coffee. It'll be hard to stay awake."

Bella found herself sitting in the dining car without remembering much of the walk there. She was alone at a table with a cup of coffee and a waiter was waiting patiently for her to order.

"I need a moment," she said.

"Of course, Miss," the waiter said and headed back to the galley. Bella looked down at the menu laying open in front of her. None of it made any sense. The words were plain enough but it was as if they were jumbled, the letters mixed up. All she was thinking about was Elphias and what he had said. Once again there was a hidden fork in her life revealed at last, a surprise turn in the road that led up and over a hill. The last detour from her life had led to being a secretary spy. What could this alternate route lead to?

It was just so unexpected. Elphias had been the least likely of men to capture her heart and so she'd let him get close. And now what? She'd have to tell him at some point. Whether she was allowed to or not, she wasn't sure, but if she fell madly for him she would anyway. What would he say then? What would he say when she told him the real Bella was dead and had been for decades? More importantly, what would he say if he discovered she was a murderer?

*You don't deserve to be loved,* she mused. It had been a long time since she'd had that thought. *I must care for him more than I know.*

The heart, she suddenly realized, was a dark and dangerous place.

Bella ate her breakfast to the distraction of her thoughts. She was rewarded for her efforts afterwards by noticing she'd dribbled egg yolk on the front of her blouse. *This will make an attractive impression when I return,* she thought wryly before realizing she could get a spare blouse from her trunk in the baggage car. The thought of the baggage car reminded her of the near kiss and a string of Elphias related thoughts. She made her way through the dining car and around the galley, moving through the vestibule and into the baggage car.

The air was frigid and fresh smelling, the sound of the wind roaring loudly. The floor hatch was open and Arctus stood at the rail, staring down at the landscape rushing past far below. For a moment Bella thought he was about to jump but then noticed the broad grin on his face. She'd not seen this smile on his face before. The others had been forced, or as punctuation to statements of flirtation or cruelty. But this was a natural look. *I'm seeing the real him,* she thought.

As if sensing her, Arctus looked up. His dark eyes were unreadable but the smile faded.

"How long have you been watching me?" he said.

Bella had learned that it paid to be vague. "Long enough," she said. She motioned toward the open hatch. "Enjoying yourself?"

Arctus smiled. "Curiosity. It's one of the remarkable traits I love about women. Did you know that?"

"I know that you enjoy speaking flattery," she said.

Arctus laughed. His face was flushed with the cold wind and a sense of joy. "An engaging wit is another one." He motioned her to join him. "Please, come enjoy the view and I shall tell you more of my secrets."

Bella approached him with a smirk. *This ought to be entertaining.* She suspected Arctus was getting fresh air because he'd been hitting the bottle. That would explain his unguarded behavior.

The cold air rushed in, clearing her mind and flitting the loose hairs around her face. She looked down at the ground below. They passed over a deep gorge, sheer and glittering with snow.

"Beautiful, isn't it?" Arctus said. "And beauty is another thing I love about women."

He shifted over closer to her. *He's making his move,* she thought with amusement but didn't move away.

"And I love how our culture has idolized you women, setting up our society to protect you all from harm."

*He's laying it on thick. Watch yourself Bella.* She smiled. *I'll resist him,* she thought. *I will.*

Arctus was next to her now, turning to face her. His impossibly handsome features were almost impossibly irresistible.

*I will turn him away if he tries,* she promised herself. *I will give it my best.*

"But you know the thing I love the most? The thing I absolutely love the most about women?" He leaned forward to whisper his secret in her ear.

*He's a smooth one,* she thought. *Smooth as a snake.* "No," Bella said, "what is it?"

"Killing them," he said, and then shoved her over the rail.

Bella clung to the *Spirit of Innovation*, hanging from a support strut beneath the baggage hatch. Her legs dangled freely from the underside of the train, swaying in the chilling wind. Far below her feet sharp rocks poked up through the snow.

Arctus stared down at her with a passively curious expression upon his face. "You should really just let go," he said matter of factly.

"Arctus, please!" she pleaded. "Pull me up! Have mercy!"

Arctus shook his head slowly. "I'm afraid I don't have the capacity. Empathy, mercy and sympathy are just words to me, you see. I know how the average person reacts from these emotions but I've never had those particular weaknesses within myself."

He blinked at her. "So you may as well just let go."

"No!" The air howled around her, rushing past cold and fast. Her hands were numbing.

"Very well," Arctus said and turned away. He returned a moment later with a small luggage case, then threw it down at her. It missed and bounced off a strut next to her, then spun away into the frigid sky and was gone.

"Stop! Please, I beg of you!"

Arctus hefted another small suitcase and placed it on the safety rail. "Look, if you're not going to let go then at least have the decency to tell me which bags are yours. There's no need to inconvenience someone else."

"You're mad!"

Arctus shrugged and dumped the suitcase. It bounced off the wall next to her shoulder and fell away. Her luck would change eventually. She had to think of something.

"Why are you doing this?"

"It's nothing personal," Arctus said and then paused. "Actually, it is personal. Not so much you, though. No, not so much you. I will enjoy watching Root's reaction when he learns of your death." Arctus laughed. "I may even offer him free consultation should he find himself too mentally distraught."

Bella screamed. "Help!"

Arctus scowled. "Stop that, someone will hear you!"

The door to the baggage car opened from the dining car side and a man appeared in the doorway.

"This just isn't my day," Arctus said quietly. Then he squinted. "Muld? I say, Muld. Everything's all right. You can return to the dining car."

Muld glanced at Arctus then stepped into the baggage car, shutting the door behind him. He moved to the rail and looked down at Bella.

Her eyes were wide with fear. "Help me, please! He pushed me!"

"She's hysterical," Arctus said. "She jumped and I was trying to save her."

Muld squatted down above where Bella was. He gave Arctus a warning glare and then leaned forward and extended his meaty left hand to Bella.

"Take my hand," he said.

She released one hand and grabbed hold of his. He clutched her tightly and began to haul her up without much effort. Bella let go with her other hand and clasped it to his for support.

"Thank you, sir," Bella said, "I thought for sure—"

Muld's right fist came fast, she barely recognized the block of flesh for what it was. There was a glint of gold on one finger and then it impacted with the side of her face, jarring her teeth and making her grunt with pain.

"All women are useless cunts, my mother taught me that," Muld said and released her hand. She offered little resistance. Stars filled her head and she was suddenly tumbling through the sky, air rushing past her limp body. Little made sense but that her face was a wide bubble of pain. *What's happened?* she thought, and then a merciful unconsciousness washed everything away, fading her vision to black as she plunged toward the mountainous terrain racing to meet her.


Arctus stood rigidly, watching Muld stand. "That was…unexpected."

"That's how you throw someone from a train, is what it was," Muld said and adjusted his bowler. He crossed his arms and stared at Arctus.

Arctus' eye twitched. "So, what now?"

Muld smiled. "I reckon my little lesson was worth a Duchess. If you have a problem with that I can demonstrate once more on you instead, so you may truly appreciate the artistry involved. Or you could let me bugger that ass of yours. If it's as pretty as your face…"

Arctus shook his head and reached for his coin purse. "I can appreciate the value of a good lesson. However, I'd rather employ you instead. I've plans for the future, and we seem to have a mutual interest." He cast a glance through the open hatch, sharp rocks rushing by far below.

Muld's face remained passive. "I already have an employer. Lux Light Industries. Maybe you've heard of them?"

Arctus pulled a gold coin from his wallet. "No need for sarcasm. I'm aware of your sponsor, I just thought you might enjoy doing something more fulfilling than simply boxing."

Muld smiled a lazy, confident smile. "I do more than just box. They pay me to handle problems too." He cracked his knuckles.

Arctus proffered the Duchess and Muld took it with his massive hand. He tucked it into his trouser pocket. "To tell the truth," Muld said, "I'm handling a problem now."

"And what problem is that?" Arctus asked. *What else does this brute do besides box?* he wondered.

Muld began to groom his thick mustache. "I'm looking for an inventor, a man who invented something he shouldn't have."

Arctus raised his eyebrows. Of course. Gilliam Watt. The paranoid fellow who thought strangers were after him. Arctus nearly laughed at the absurdity of it all. Not only was Watt right, he was also being shadowed by the most dangerous stranger he could ever hope to avoid. Arctus smiled. "I believe I met the man of whom you speak. Does this…illuminate…things for you?"

Muld's brow clenched and he stepped forward. "Where is he?"

Arctus shook his head. "I'm afraid I don't know. Not at the moment, anyway. I met him in the smoking car, but he's been laying low since." Arctus smiled. "However, I can help you find someone else. Someone you might be very interested in meeting face to face. Someone you've met recently."

Muld scowled and flexed his fists. He didn't like guessing games. "Who?"

Elphias drank coffee in the observation lounge and wondered where Bella was. She'd been gone for at least two hours and he was hoping he hadn't given her that much to think about. *I know I've improvements to make,* Elphias thought wryly, *but I don't think I'm a lost cause yet. There's still hope.*

Hope. There was a funny, rarely used word in his vocabulary. He'd never put much faith in it following Lydia and the baby's deaths. They had been his whole and entire hope, and when their bodies had stilled so had his optimism. But now it was returned. Bella had shown him that. Whether she wanted a further relationship with him or not he'd seen the possibility of living with a sense of hope, even if it were just a dream. Because either way, it sure beat living with fear.

He laughed to himself. Very brave to sit there thinking of living a fear free life when the whole reason he was there in the first place was a fear of being beaten by Muld. But at least he had a refuge. He would remain in the private car the rest of the way to Verdun.

"Doctor Root? Could you come into the office, please?" Zediah called.

Elphias got up from his chair and took a last glance back at the wide, cold mountains. The peaks were diminishing, the slopes less angry. Soon they'd be out of the Cragbacks for good. He passed through the curtains, marveling at the transcontinental rail line. Modern technology was a wondrous thing. Now man could pass safely through the mountains without fear of death.

Elphias passed into the office. Zediah stood in the center of the room, a sheaf of papers in his hand.

"Yes, Zediah?"

"Alisha just informed me that two gentlemen were trying to gain access to the car. Said they were friends of yours."

A chill went up Elphias' back. "Besides the people within our party, I have no friends aboard this train," he said.

Zediah nodded. "So Alisha suspected and drove them away. She detected a menacing air from the men. She's actually quite gifted at reading people's intent."

"I don't doubt it," Elphias said. "And she's quite correct about this too. If it's the two men I'm thinking of, they have no intentions of friendship." He then gave Zediah a brief version of events from the previous day and evening in Lacroix, including his woundings of Muld and Arctus. He left out the threat about leaving Bella alone, however. Zediah didn't need to know everything.

Zediah rubbed his chin once Elphias had finished. "Ah, well that explains Muld's limp then," he said and then laughed heartily. "I wish I'd have seen that great oaf curled to the mat. I've had my fill of brick-hearts and bullies. They infest the Academy as well." He shook his head. "The alienist is troubling though. To think of such a cruel man tinkering with the fragile state of an unbalanced mind is disturbing."

There was a knock, and before Zediah could reach the door it opened and the conductor stepped into the car.

"Forgive me to disturb you, Inquisitor," he said. He was of Kavan ancestry, dark-skinned and with hair cropped short beneath his red uniform cap.

"No trouble whatsoever. What may I do for you?"

The conductor blinked uncomfortably and shifted back and forth. "It's just that, well, you're the last, sir. I've run the train up to here and all's accounted for."

Zediah frowned slightly. "What are you talking about?"

"Is the lady with you, the one you travel with?"

Zediah tilted his head toward the bedrooms. "Bella?"

"She went to the dining car," Elphias said. "She was going to eat breakfast."

The conductor blinked with unease and continued to shift his weight back and forth. He removed his cap and fingered the brim.

"It was an ice crew, sir. Why we were alerted so quick. They work the towers, you see. Inspect the rail and keep it free of ice. It's dangerous work."

"Where's Bella?" Elphias asked, his voice sounding far away and strangely pitched. The room seemed to be growing larger, the walls receding away.

The conductor looked to the floor, clutching his cap in front of him. He wiped his brow with the sleeve of his red jacket.

"They called the Trans, and the Trans called me." He looked up, discomfort etched in his expression. "They found a body, you see. A female body. Beneath the track, sir. Nearly a hundred miles back."

"She went to eat breakfast," Elphias said again, wondering who was speaking. "She was going to the dining car."

"What makes you sure that it was my secretary?" Zediah asked, his face pale.

The conductor looked at Zediah sympathetically. "All else is accounted for, sir. I checked the passenger manifest to here. You're the last car left. And only your one is missing, none other." He shook his head. "As I said, all else is accounted for."

Zediah took a step backward. Elphias felt as if a great vacuum surrounded him and that he might implode at any moment.

"What," Zediah began and then licked his lips. "What does the body look like? What was the description given by the ice crew?"

The conductor twisted the cap in his hands, mouth twitchy. "It's unpleasant to say, but…I mean, you are an inquisitor…"

"Out with it, blast you!" Zediah shouted suddenly.

The conductor startled at his outburst. "Forgive me, Inquisitor, it's just that…They couldn't say, you see? Much beyond it were a woman's body, they really couldn't say. She were dashed to death upon the rocks. The boys were traumatized right enough. There weren't much left to describe."

Elphias turned sluggishly and headed through the curtains. They felt strange and heavy and his hand looked like it was small and pale. He wanted to get out of sight. He didn't want the others to see his response. Tears welled in his eyes and he stifled a sob. It couldn't be true. It couldn't! He had just seen her a few hours ago, and she'd been bright and charming and alive. It had to be a mistake!

He heard Zediah curse and tell the conductor he'd search the train himself, and then the outer door had slammed shut. Good. If anyone would get to the truth of the matter, it would be Zediah. Zediah wouldn't rest until he'd discovered the truth.

*Look at yourself,* he thought bitterly, *look how useless you've become. Because you opened your heart again. Because you opened your heart she's dead!*

Elphias fell heavily into his chair in the observation lounge and fumbled the ampule tin from his jacket. He opened it with shaky hands and looked at the display of colors within. His fingers touched the Black Poppy, then trailed across the other ampules to a Blue Oasis. He pulled it free and snapped the top off, then drained it down his throat. He hurled the empty ampule to the floor and heard it shatter against the wall. It was a travesty, a cruel joke by a cruel world. He crushed his palms to his face and rocked forward. *Let it be a mistake,* he raged, *let me awaken to find her laughing at my foolishness. Laughing with air in her lungs and the smell of coffee upon her breath. Please, let it be a mistake.*

He staggered to his feet. He did not want to slide under in this room, this room where they had last spoken. The train rocked unsteadily and he slid along the wall to the door of his bedroom. He stumbled in and crawled into his cot with his clothes on. He turned to the wall, burying his face in the pillow. *Let it be a mistake.*

The darkness was welling up, like black water flooding up from the ground, and Elphias turned and fled deep within it. Kicking and swimming, diving for oblivion, his thoughts growing tiny and floating away like little bubbles.

*Let it be a mistake…*

# CHAPTER FOURTEEN
## *Dreams of the Dead*

Death was cold, and grey, and muffled. She could not feel her body, she was merely a conscious extension of the ceaseless cold in which she found herself. There were no endless fields. There was no golden city. The scant light available was muted and without detail, leaving her in a dim grey void. She could hear the wind on occasion, but it sounded flat and dull, like a thick blanket hung between her and wherever the winds were blowing. A veil between the worlds.

She could not remember her name, but she did vaguely remember living a life once. Images from it flitted up from her tattered memories, incidents and faces without name or meaning. An older man with a trimmed beard, kind face, and sad eyes; a younger man, handsome and cruel; another man, with a bearded face, glasses, and a warm smile. Flashes of them came and went but she could make no sense of the who or what. Then an image of a young girl with long golden hair splashing her bare feet in a river.

Bella. The girl's name was Bella. And they had been friends once. Bella wore a school uniform, so it must have been long ago. A throbbing pain lanced up through the memory. Something bad had happened then, something that had formed the path of the life she'd led before the cold, grey void of being dead.

*Is this all we're left with? An emptiness without end, with only broken memories for entertainment? Memories which we can gather together or cast to eternity? And what then?*

If there was nothing to do but exist in this endless twilight then she may as well discover the truth of who she'd been. Weigh the measure of her worth.

She allowed the image of the girl to fill her attention, letting it swallow her so that she might discover its hidden lesson.

"Come on, Bella!" She was standing on a hump of dirt, looking back at Bella parting through a tall mass of cattails.

Bella grinned at her. "Are we there yet, Commander?"

She shook her head. "Don't be silly, we have to cross the river." She turned and pushed onward.

The water she splashed through was brackish and glittered in the sunlight. This close to the coast the mighty East Twin spread out to become a sluggish estuary. Gulls lifted and dipped from the mud flats, or bobbed on the surface of the distant sea, shrieking with piping tones.

She ran through the shallow water, mud squishing beneath her toes. The water felt cold and refreshing.

"Ambrosia, wait!"

Ambrosia. Something lurched in her mind. *My name was once Ambrosia!*

Ambrosia turned, waiting as Bella sloshed in her direction. It was just the two of them that day, their other friends were serving detention for some minor offense and remained back at the school.

Bella gave her a sly look. "Let's cross together. Sneaky as sky pirates."

Ambrosia nodded in agreement. "We will cross at the wreckage of our airship," she said, "and seek that which our enemies have tried to deny us!"

She held out her hand as Bella came close and then they ran, laughing and screaming the rest of the way, hands locked together. Near the edge of the estuary were the remains of a ruined structure, perhaps an old pier though Ambrosia couldn't think of who would build one there or why. Only a few weathered pylons remained, thrusting up from the muddy ground like the rib bones of some ancient beast. To Ambrosia and her friends it was the remains of their airship, downed by the evil sky pirates from the Castle of Clouds. It was also a convenient landmark to let them know how close they were to the border. Five yards beyond the pylons and across another shallow stream lay the Freehold of Agaria. The land looked no different, there were no lines marked upon the ground to denote the border, but it was there anyway—an invisible division which allowed certain actions to be legal on one side of it but not the other. Ambrosia had always considered such things foolish, the foolish games that adults played. It was really no different than their make-believe airship when she had taken time to think on it. But such thoughts were far from her mind that day. They were going to cross into an imaginary enemy's territory, these brave young women, who—unlike their feminine counterparts—were allowed to fight and endanger their lives as men did.

"Forward!" Ambrosia cried and they dashed from the wreckage of their airship and across the silly invisible line.

As often happened, these adventurous forays turned to simply playing in the environment. Ambrosia was digging flat pebbles from the mud to skip across the water while Bella stood shin deep in a tiny stream, working her feet into its sediment up to her ankles. The sun was high and bright, and the sky blue with promise. It was a beautiful day, the kind where nothing could go wrong.

But of course it did go wrong. Horribly, terribly wrong. Because that was when the man showed up. He was filthy, his clothes were ragged, and he sported a dark beard that was thick and unkempt. He appeared from a thicket of cattails across the stream from Bella, a yellowed grin breaking the dirty thatch of his beard. Ambrosia would later wonder if he had been watching them for some time, or merely chanced upon them in some perverted twist of fate. But at that moment, all she could think of was the warnings they'd been given at the boarding school about how most men were noble but some were anything but. They had monster hearts, and you needed to keep away from them.

"Now don't you two smell awfully sweet," the man said, in a feeble attempt to disguise his intentions through flattery. Then he reached behind his back and pulled a rusted knife from his waistband. "Treat me nice and I'll treat you nice too," he leered and stepped toward them.

"Run!" Ambrosia screamed, and they did. Ambrosia in the lead, dashing through the mud, brackish water splashing into her face, legs pumping toward a sheltering clump of cattails. They plunged into it, turning and twisting a random trail before dropping to a squat. Hiding there, breath flaring and heart pumping.

Ambrosia listened for the stranger's footsteps. Instead she heard a girl's distant shriek. It quickly cut off. "Bella?" Ambrosia whirled to look around. She'd sworn Bella had been right behind her but hadn't checked, she'd been too afraid. Too afraid the dirty faced man would be reaching to grab her shoulder or stab her in the back. And then she remembered that Bella's feet had been sunk in the mud. She wouldn't have been able to run until she'd got them free.

Time expanded. Seconds seemed like hours. She had two options, run back to Hempwick or try and help her friend. Running back to the village would take too long. Bella could be gone by then. Strangers took children sometimes. Bad strangers took them and they were never seen again. It might already be too late.

She headed back toward Bella, screening herself with the cattails as much as she could. Eventually she had to leave their shelter and slink toward the tilted pylons poking up from the mud. They looked different now. Sinister. Part of her knew that even if Bella was okay, they would never come here again. Their private playground would be forever tainted by this darkness, by this monster hearted stranger.

She entered the perimeter of pylons and picked up a flat stone barely wide enough to stand on. Ambrosia had always stood on it to issue her proclamations and orders to the crew. She called it her power stone. Holding it now gave her a sense of courage, a tiny measure of protection and luck. Ambrosia shuffled forward, angling toward another crop of cattails to shield her crossing of the border. She crept into them, heart pounding as she made her way to a point where she could finally peek through their stalks.

Her heart broke. The man was atop Bella, his back to Ambrosia. She couldn't see her friend, only her legs angled carelessly to each side of the man's thrusting body. His pants were down and Ambrosia could see his pale buttocks, shockingly white compared to his tanned back. It was if they had never seen the sun before.

A deep, dark anger filled her then, the sort she'd always pretended to experience when fighting illusionary sky pirates. But this man was real, and so was her rage. How dare he assault Bella! How dare he ruin everything!

She found herself moving toward him, holding her protective power stone. Step by step, part of her terrified he'd turn at any moment. She kept to his back, hoping to grab his knife but she couldn't see it anywhere. She figured he must still be holding it in his hands, keeping Bella complacent during his rape.

Ambrosia raised the rock over her head and advanced quietly. She was two steps behind him when she sloshed enough water for him to hear. He whipped his head in her direction, an evil glint to his glassy eyes.

"There you are," he said.

Ambrosia tried to tell him to leave, to get off her friend but nothing came out of her mouth but a dry creak.

The man glared angrily. "Put that rock down. If you're good I'll be nice and only do you in the arse."

She lowered the rock and stepped forward.

"That's good," he said. "Now—"

She raised the rock and brought it down on his head with a speed and strength she didn't even know she had, aiming for those baneful eyes. They went wide before she lost sight of them beneath her power stone. It cracked hard into the side of his face, shearing the top of his ear off and crushing his temple. He flopped to one side, screaming something and waving his hands in erratic motions. Ambrosia jumped on his back and brought the rock down twice more, then stood and dropped it on his ruined head as she staggered away from the body.

"Bella," she said turning, "are you all—"

But she wasn't. Bella wasn't all right. Her eyes stared up at the sky and her mouth was open, teeth stained by the blood that had fled the deep gash in her neck.

Ambrosia fell to her knees, screaming and crying. Begging forgiveness. But there could be no penance from running away. There could be no redemption from blind cowardice. Later Ambrosia would trade names, trying to give Bella a life that had never existed, sacrificing her own identity in a desperate and pathetic act of atonement. But it was as false as sky pirates. The fact was plain and always had been. Bella was dead.


A wracking sob for her long dead namesake escaped Bella, and an explosion of agonizing pain shot through her, giving a defining border to the extension of cold. She gasped from the pain and a chilling wetness filled her mouth. Bella flailed out with her arms. She wanted to escape this grey void of death. She wanted to live!

Bella sat up, wincing from the painful protest of her muscles. A vast panorama of snow sloped down and away from her before continuing on to a series of jagged peaks dominating the horizon. An unfocused blot of white obscured her vision and she lifted a hand to brush it away. As she flicked away the snow she brushed the left side of her face. An explosion of pain made her cry out and watered her eyes. And then she remembered everything. Names aligned with faces and facts and she suddenly recalled the how and why of how she'd been thrown from the *Spirit of Innovation*.

A wide brick tower thrust out of the snowy expanse further down the slope, supporting the heavy rail system passing over where she sat. She turned her head to look behind her, neck stiff and painful. A vaguely humanoid shape was imprinted into the snow further up the slope and a wavy disruption of the powder made its way down to her. A few yards from where she had impacted another support tower clung to the side of a shear rock face, passing the rail safely over the obstruction.

*I'm lucky to be alive,* Bella thought. *Very lucky.* She shivered. *I'm not free of it yet. I could still freeze to death.*

Bella cautiously examined her body, expecting to discover broken bones. Her body ached and felt like it'd been beaten along the length of her back, but nothing seemed out of place or bent at unnatural angles. She huffed with pain and forced herself to stand, then assessed her condition once more. She felt lightheaded and the side of her face throbbed where Muld had struck her, but that seemed the worst of it.

Muld. She would see him pay for his assault, along with Arctus. That was incentive enough to get going, to live and see them suffer. *If only I were a Hand. I'd make them beg for the noose,* she thought with uncharacteristic malice. Bella pushed it from her mind. Vengeance could wait. She needed to survive first.

Bella assessed her surroundings and was grateful for the sky rail system to aid with navigation. Following it one way or another would lead to civilization. She regarded the tower behind her. The rock face split off from a large peak and then trailed along to end at a chasm. The only way past it would be to climb the tower. Steel rungs were spaced up the side but Bella didn't trust her strength to make it to the top. Still, perhaps there was an outpost just over the ridge. She needed to try.

The loose snow made walking upslope difficult. Bella was thankful she'd purchased the flat soled Agarian boots in Lacroix, her old heeled footwear would be useless. She struggled for twenty minutes to reach the cold tower of brick, then had to lean against it and catch her breath. Vapor formed from her exhalations, a phenomena she'd never seen before. It would be fascinating if it didn't signify an environment where exposure was deadly. Sweat was beginning to freeze on her brow. She had to get moving.

Bella put her hand on a rung. The metal felt like ice, chilling her already frigid hands. Her teeth chattered. *Move!* She put her foot on the lowest rung and began to climb. The pain was intense and her face ached, but it was the quaking of her muscles that dispirited her the most. Bella looked up. The ledge she needed to reach was still thirty feet above. She might make it halfway, but there was no way she'd climb that far and have enough strength to transfer over from the tower.

Tears formed in her eyes and she angrily rubbed them away. This was not the time for pity. She wasn't finished yet. She could still walk and the sky rail offered another direction to go. *I'll walk all the way back to Lacroix,* she boasted to herself, *I'll walk the entire way if I have to.* Bella started forward, the passage down the slope much easier. She lost her footing and slid a few yards once, but she was still making forward progress. She couldn't really walk all the way to Lacroix, it had to be over a hundred miles or more from her current position. She needed to find someplace closer. The outpost of Istas was located in the mountains but she had no idea where. Her only option lay overhead. The rail would lead her somewhere. All she had to do was follow it.

Bella trudged through the snow, navigating by rail as best she could. At one point she tripped over something and went sprawling into the snow with a cry of pain and surprise. Her irritation turned to gratitude when she discovered it to be one of the luggage pieces Arctus had thrown at her. Bella thanked the Dualvinity and opened the case, then she thanked them again. The case contained clothes for a man, large enough to slip a shirt, vest, and lounge jacket over her own, along with a pair of pants to wear beneath her skirt. She tucked the pantlegs into her boots, wrapped another pair of pants around her head to cover her ears, then slipped a pair of thick woolen socks over her hands. Although she was warmer, the reality of freezing to death remained. Bella left the pilfered suitcase and followed the rail once more.

An hour later she encountered a ravine, the rail passing easily over the hazard while she was left panting with exhaustion and trying to think of an alternative. There had to be a way across somewhere, the workers who'd built the rail system made their way through the mountains at some point. Bella wrote articles on the logistics of its construction when she had worked for the paper. Part of those logistics required TransRail to build temporary towns for workers to shelter, eat, and produce materials in. It also required rope bridges to cross obstacles. Despite those cautions, more lives were lost in the

Cragbacks than any other section of the rail. *I'll be one of those lives too if I don't reach the other side,* she thought and then surveyed her surroundings.

An impassable peak still blocked progress to her right, so she headed the other direction to seek a crossing point. Ten minutes later she found it, a narrow rope bridge traversing the ravine where both of its treacherous sides were relatively close to one other. Bella congratulated herself on discovering the bridge, then had to nerve herself up to cross over. The support ropes swayed as she inched her way step by step, teeth chattering with fear and cold. A wind howled down through the ravine, tugging her hair and skirt. Bella waited for the bridge to give way, to snap loose and plummet her into the deep chasm below, but it held and soon she was across and kneeling on the other side, hunched over and trying to catch her breath. *Get up. Get up before you can't!*

She staggered to her feet and pushed forward, angling back toward the guiding trail of rail towers. The sun was sinking behind the unforgiving peaks, casting mighty shadows and turning the snow a light shade of blue beneath the fading light. Bella had received enough wilderness survival lessons during her training to know what her fate would be if she didn't find shelter and find it soon. Night was falling.

# CHAPTER FIFTEEN
## *Plans and Plots*

"Elphias. Elphias!" A voice was calling through the darkness, stirring consciousness to life. There was also a distant feeling of motion, a hand shaking his shoulder. "Doctor Root!"

Elphias cracked his eyes open, trying to focus. A hazy shape leaned over him, features golden from a slanting sunlight streaming in through the window. "Elphias, I need your help. Something's amiss."

"Zediah?" Elphias leaned up on one elbow and clutched his head. Thoughts began to emerge from the murk of his drug induced slumber. He looked at Zediah suddenly. "Is it Bella? Have you—"

Zediah shook his head. "No. But I refuse to accept that conclusion until I have exhausted all other possibilities."

Elphias' heart sunk. He had no such optimism. He knew how the score of his own life went.

"Zediah..."

Zediah shook his head again. "Listen to me. They've found another body."

"What?"

"A man's body this time. Only fifty miles back, just outside of a town called Gervon."

Elphias sat up, rubbing his face. "I'm familiar with it. I think I have money in the bank there," he shook his head. What a long, strange road this had been so far. "Have they identified the body?"

Zediah looked out the window. "No, but the conductor is checking the passenger manifest as we speak. I've already vouched for you being aboard."

"Thank you."

Zediah turned back from the window, a serious look to his face. "Here's the thing. Turns out the conductor also had taken a verbal confirmation of passenger wellness when assessing Bella's fate."

"What are you talking about?"

"There's a female passenger, a Lady from what I understand. She's under attendance of your morally corrupt alienist, Doctor—"

"Weber." Elphias' heart thudded dully in his chest. "I dined with Bella at their table…" his brow creased, "lasterday morning?" He shook his head. "It seems like forever ago. Nevertheless, I met his patient, the Lady Danueman. She seems a delightful woman, despite the company she keeps."

Zediah nodded as Elphias spoke. "Ah, so you've seen her then. As it turns out, when the conductor was checking for a missing female passenger, Doctor Weber said the Lady was in her cabin but was too ill to see anyone. The conductor had no reason to doubt him and moved on. No one has seen the Lady outside of her cabin since then either. From what you told me of your adventures with this fellow, I question his integrity."

Elphias sneered with disgust. "You are right to do so. He is a lowly, pathetic man." A sudden stabbing thought thrust through Elphias' heart. He looked up at Zediah, eyes intense. "Do you think he had something to do with Bella being thrown from the train?"

Zediah frowned. "I hope not, for his sake. My concern is for the Lady Danueman. I placed a televox call to the Academy. Seems this Doctor Arctus Weber has amassed a small fortune by treating mentally unstable women. Women of wealth, strangely enough. As part of his contract of treatment, Weber gains executive power over their finances."

"The man is a charlatan. Putting money over the value of a life! I suppose the treatments last indefinitely." Elphias' fists clenched. The knuckles of his right hand were still sore and red from punching Arctus in the face. It had been worth it.

"Ah, well, not exactly. They last until his patients commit suicide. As this is a breach of their contract, this wretched fellow gets forty percent of the estate before it is subject to any wills, rights of inheritance, or donations."

A hollow black point of horror filled Elphias' mind. He'd known Arctus to be a disgusting worm, but this was something else. This was a calculating, moral evil, a man who would be unrestrained by empathy and compassion. A man without heart.

"Zediah," Elphias said, "there's more you should know. He—this man had…interest in Bella. An unhealthy interest, I sensed. So I, when I hit him, I told him to leave her alone. I told him to stay away. He may have killed her to get back at me. He—"

Zediah held up a hand. "Let's take this one step at a time. If this man did touch Bella I will put him in the black robes myself. But until then I need your help with something delicate."

Elphias nodded his head and shrugged. "I'm not sure how I can help, but I'll do whatever is necessary."

"Good. Excellent. This foul fellow has me in a legal loophole. As you are well aware, constitutional mandate allows me broad legal power to summon, question, and temporarily detain whomever I choose to get the answers I seek. However it also prohibits me from entering private residences without warrant, nor can I bypass caretakers of incapacitated individuals. To her misfortune, Doctor Weber acts as the Lady Danueman's representation. I cannot go to her, and I cannot make her come to me. Only Doctor Weber will show up. So this is what we will do."

Zediah sat down on the cot opposite Elphias, then leaned forward in a conspiratorial manner.

"I will summon Doctor Weber to my office and compel him to answer whatever questions I choose. I doubt I will get honest answers, but that is not the goal of the interrogation."

Elphias shrugged. "Which is?"

"While he is engaged, you will enter the Lady Danueman's cabin to see how she fares. As a physician, you have every right to be concerned for her physical well being, something Weber is unqualified to address."

"And what do you expect me to find?"

"An empty cabin. If my theory is correct, Doctor Weber brought the Lady aboard this train for her 'suicide'. He was asking porters if any windows opened on the train. For her 'safety' of course. I think his intentions were otherwise."

A dark thought began to form beneath Elphias' consciousness. Something was gathering to conclusion. Suddenly it became important to know the detail. "And do they? Do they open?"

Zediah blinked. "Not that I'm aware, so the matter of—"

"The baggage car. There's a floor hatch in the baggage car. It's right next to the…"

The dark thought bubbled to the surface. Elphias stood suddenly fist clenched.

"The dining car. The bastard probably had breakfast with the Lady and Bella then took them to the baggage car and—" He clenched his fists to his head, eyes squeezed shut.

Zediah stood and placed a hand on Elphias' shoulder. "They only found one body. Bella may still be aboard. I haven't checked the staff car nor the engine. She could be desperately trying to escape a lesson on trains from Master Cobb."

Elphias snorted an attempt at a laugh but didn't think it likely. He opened his eyes, all sense of humor gone.

"The other body, the man. Have you seen Cobb lately? I've not left our car, but he was acting strangely when he last left us."

Zediah took in a breath. "I hadn't considered that. Mercy, I hope not. That would be foul indeed."

Elphias closed his eyes and shook his head. When would this nightmare end? Had he really once been fishing in a river on a beautiful day with nothing to do but breathe? He let out a shaky sigh. "Yes, it would. Sweet Dualvinity, could this journey possibly get any worse?"

The *Spirit of Innovation* steamed onward, rolling over the foothills of Ostravia as the sun sank on the horizon. Steam jetted from the twin exhaust pipes and dissipated into the darkening sky. Wind rushed over the housing of the bomb, an unwelcome addition which broke up the streamlined design of the train. Night lay ahead and beyond it the sparkling gem of Verdun waiting to greet them as the sun rode high once more. It was rumored both duumvirs would be in attendance to see the historical event, to see the marvel of the Empire arrive at the station. And when the *Spirit of Innovation* did arrive, roaring into Verdun at full chisel and unable to stop, the bomb would deliver the bright light of sun to the assembled masses, consuming them in its fiery birth. A new dawn would bloom then in the Empire of Light, a deep and violent, blood red dawn.

It was dark, and cold, and she walked with the dead. Sometimes it was Bella, the real Bella, other times it was the rapist, sometimes both at once. They didn't speak to her. How could they? One with a gashed neck and the other with a crushed head. They made poor conversation and even less desirable traveling companions. Time had lost meaning, a word without concept. She mostly looked down at her legs pushing through the snow, powder scattering with each torturous step forward. Everything ached, everything was chilled, but she plowed onward. She knew if she stopped, if she fell again, she would not be able to continue. It would be the end. And she wasn't finished yet. No, not yet.

"An admirable quality. Do you know how many dead people have thought that same thing?" Someone else walked beside her now, some shadowy thing at the corner of her eye that had the ability to speak with her own voice.

"Shut up," Bella said. Her throat hurt too, it felt raw. She may have been screaming at one point, or maybe that was somebody else. Her footsteps were faltering, her thoughts sluggish. A strange warmth was beginning to take hold of her body, though there was no reason for it. She looked up to make sure she was still following the sky rail. It was there, a thin void in the vast canopy of stars high above.

"It's a beautiful place to die, really," the shadow thing said. "You could lay on your back and watch the stars as your eyes turned to ice."

Bella pressed her lips together. They felt frozen and cracked. There was a temptation lurking, a hollow boned idea swimming beneath the surface. A temptation to listen to the voice, to lay down and rest. Just for a bit. She reached up and touched the swollen side of her face. Pain ignited a jolt to her thoughts and her eyes watered. *They're not ice yet*, she thought victoriously. The pain also chased the shadowy thing away. It likely wouldn't last. She was running out of energy. If she didn't make shelter soon there would be nothing left.

The rail line began a gentle curve, passing over a cluster of square shapes at the base of a slope. A tendril of smoke curled up from one of the shapes. Bella blinked her eyes. She'd had hallucinations earlier. A castle in the clouds and an airship resting in the snow. A cold wind brought the smell of a wood fire to her nose. Could this possibly be real? Her pace quickened, churning her way through the snow, frozen legs pumping their last toward the buildings. It didn't matter whether they were real or not, there wasn't much longer left. There was still several hundred yards to go and she was growing faint. How cruel to fall this close to salvation.

"Hoy!" she screamed, but her voice was too raw to give it much strength. Her dead companions and shadowy nemesis were with her once more, she sensed them at the corner of her sight. They had come to watch her fail, to see the tragedy come to an end. The curtain closes and she is sad Master Cobb has left the theater. Elphias leans in for a kiss. She tries to kiss him, his lips look so warm.

"I told you this would happen," the shadowy thing gloats. She catches sight of a grey phantom drifting towards her through the snow, a wispy shape with pale skin and wide eyes.

"Are you sister or sinner?" the phantom asks in a female voice. Death has come for her at last.

"I'm sorry," Bella says as her knees buckle. She tries to stop the fall but it's inevitable, her muscles have spent their last. The snow softens her collapse, muffling the world in cold and grey. The last thing she feels before darkness swallows everything is cold icy hands grabbing hold of her and a sensation of movement. *Here I go,* she thinks, and then there was no more.

Elphias hid in a narrow linen closet at the end of the sleeper car, watching through a crack in the door for Arctus to pass by on his way to meet with Zediah. He waited in semi-darkness, his thoughts in a similar state. Zediah held out hope for Bella's safety but Elphias was not so inclined. He knew what the score was, death was eager to take what it could. He only hoped that her death had been quick and painless. He also wondered if she'd thought of him at all before the end, then felt shamed for doing so.

Alisha stood guard outside the vestibule door with a clear line of sight to the other end of the car. "He's here," she said softly and without moving her lips. Elphias closed the door to the closet. He wasn't sure he'd be able to control his emotions is he saw Arctus' smug face. Zediah needed him to investigate the wellbeing of the Lady Danueman on his behalf and it was helpful to only focus on that.

Alisha's muffled voice came from beyond the door. "The inquisitor is expecting you."

"That's why I'm here, isn't it? Tell me, is the coward with him?"

Elphias' fists clenched. He fought an urge to wrench the door open. *Yes, lunging from your hiding spot in the closet would be a wonderful way to prove how uncowardly you seem.*

"Not yet," Alisha replied. "You need only cross the vestibule." Elphias' admiration for the guardswoman grew. No wonder Zediah had chosen her for his inquisition party.

"Charming. Never learned how to address one's superiors, I see."

"Indeed I have, sir. However, there is nothing superior about you except your own opinion of yourself."

Elphias wished he could see the look on Arctus' face right now. He waited to hear a response but there was nothing but the creaking of the train. A gentle knock sounded at the door.

"It's clear, Doctor."

He cracked open the door and slipped out. "Thank you, Alisha. I must admit I enjoyed your verbal sparring with Doctor Weber."

Alisha smiled. "I appreciate that. It's a trait I've had to develop over the years. The Guard is a very competitive environment, so I've had plenty of practice at lancing overly inflated egos."

Elphias grinned. "Then I shall be mindful to always remain humble around you."

She gave him a curious stare. "May I speak freely to you, sir?"

"Yes, of course you can."

Alisha nodded. "You're a kind man, Doctor Root. But I sense there is a wound within you, one you've carried for a long time."

"Zediah said you had a gift of reading people."

She shrugged. "I have plenty of time to observe and think in my position. I just wanted to say that everyone has some misfortune or regret in their past. Sometimes many. At least for me I have found that it isn't what has happened, but how one deals with the event that matters. Dark events are usually short in occurrence, but the aftermath can exist forever if we let it."

Elphias smiled with admiration. "I've not heard it put that way before. That's a very succinct observation, Alisha. You've given me much to think on." He chuckled. "You should be an alienist instead of Doctor Weber."

Alisha smiled but shook her head. "I'm content to serve as I do. I just know that if I were to be wounded, you would treat me and give me the proper guidance to be healed. I just wanted to return the service."

Elphias felt the warm bond of human contact blooming and knew he'd been a fool to avoid it all these years. "Thank you, again, Alisha. For this and all you've done."

"You're welcome." She winked. "Now go find whatever it is you need to find. The inquisitor and I have this rascal under control."

The Lady Danueman's room was contained within a larger suite that Arctus had booked. The suite was in the middle of the forward sleeping car, and Elphias made it in little time. He knocked softly at the outer door.

"Lady Danueman?" Elphias waited a brief moment then opened the door and stepped into the suite. He found himself in a tastefully appointed sitting room, with dark wood paneling and a deep red carpet. Sliding doors to each side of the room led to the sleeping chambers, but Elphias had no idea which door was the Lady's. The door to his left was slightly opened, so he stepped to it first and looked through the gap, then slid it open completely.

A tuxedo hung from a brass hook on the wall and a decanter of brandy sat on a small stand next to the cot. The window shade was closed to the outside. Elphias turned out of the room and approached the other door. He listened outside of it for a moment and thought he heard movement.

He rapped his knuckles on the surface. "Lady Danueman? It's Doctor Root," he began to slide the door open, "we met at breakfast the other morning. I—"

Muld stood on the other side of the door, a tight smile beneath his thick mustache. His fist was fast, blazingly fast, and struck Elphias hard in the gut.

The breath drove from Elphias' body and he sagged forward with a grunt of pain. Muld's meaty palm grabbed hold of his collar and kept him from dropping to his knees.

"Hoy, boyo, I was hoping to find you earlier," he said in a casual tone, then flung Elphias against the far wall. Elphias hit the paneling hard and slid to the floor, still gasping for breath. Muld loomed over him and yanked him quickly to his feet.

Muld leaned in close. "That was unsporting the other night, wouldn't you say?" His breath was hot and stunk of halitosis.

Elphias opened his mouth to speak and Muld drove a fist into his guts again.

"I'll take that as a yes," Muld said. He threw an arm around Elphias' shoulder then locked his neck in a viselike grip. "Let's celebrate our joyous reunion with a walk."

Muld wrenched open the door and dragged Elphias from the room. He turned and headed toward the smoking car. As they approached the vestibule

Muld leaned his head to Elphias.

"We're mates on our way to the dining car, got it? I only want to show you something, but cause a disturbance and I'll snap your neck like a chicken." Muld's arm around Elphias' neck tightened and his vision began to grey. "Understand?"

Elphias nodded. There was no way of speaking a reply. His heart pounded in his chest. What did this beast have in store for him? Elphias' mind raced to think of what knives or burning surfaces were in the dining car galley that Muld would want to 'show' him.

"Good," said Muld and released his grip slightly. Then he moved them through the vestibule and into the smoking car. The hour was growing late and not many people were gathered in the car. Those that glanced their direction quickly looked away. Elphias figured they'd already encountered Muld's intimidating personality and had no desire for further interaction. He knew how they felt but was dragged along anyway. Muld set a quick pace and many times his pounding footsteps were the only ones on the floor, Elphias being lifted and bustled forward, his boots dangling.

They passed through the next vestibule and into the dining car. Elphias was hoping someone would be there to intervene but it was after service and the car was deserted. The tables were made for the next days breakfast and he eyed the place settings as Muld dragged him along the aisle. He tried to reach for a fork but his fingers weren't more than a few inches when Muld yanked him back and laughed in his ear.

"That wouldn't be sporting either, now would it? You're not very honorable, are you?" Again his arm clamped tight, squeezing off any possibility that Elphias could say otherwise. "No," Muld said, "I didn't think so."

He kept the arm clamped shut and Elphias began to grey out again. He was aware that they passed through the next vestibule from the smell of the air and the increase in noise. Then they were in the baggage car and he found himself flying though the air. The floor impacted with his body and Elphias rolled to a stop against a stack of luggage. He struggled to rise but was still disoriented from the oxygen deprivation. Muld stepped up quick and delivered a punch to the side of Elphias' face. He fell back to the floor, dazed and nearly unconscious.

"Stay down," Muld said and paced towards a turn crank protruding from a control panel. He gripped the crank and began to rotate it. A small grinding noise vibrated through the floor and air began to whistle in from a gap where the hatch was slowly opening.

*He's going to kill me,* Elphias realized. His hand dug into his frock coat, seeking his case. *If I take a painkiller I may have enough strength to get away,* he thought desperately. The sound of the outside grew in intensity as the hatch door retracted. Elphias pulled out the case and fumbled it open. The glass entombed colors reached his eyes and an idea quickly formed. He would likely still die, but it would certainly be better than doing nothing.

Muld stopped cranking. "Good enough." He walked toward Elphias, slow and sure. There could be only one outcome in his mind. "I'll do you like the inventor."

It suddenly clicked into place. Of course. The man's body they'd found. Gilliam Watt. Lux Light really did have it out for him.

Elphias remained slumped, ampules hidden in his hands. He desperately tried to think of how to pull off the administration, but knew there would only be one chance when it came. He could try smashing his forehead into Muld's nose, but that would cause the man to raise his hands, covering his mouth. No, that wouldn't do at all.

Muld grabbed his shoulders and lifted him up. He grinned at Elphias, his bully nature fully engaged. "You should pick your friends more carefully," he said with delight. "I wouldn't of even known you were on this train if it weren't for Mister Weber."

Elphias grimaced with anger. "That bastard is no friend of mine," he said.

Muld's eyebrows rose with mock surprise. His eyes still remained hateful and cruel. How many people had they terrorized? Muld laughed. "Truly? But he knows so much about you."

Elphias snapped off the tops of the Blue Oasis ampules and palmed them. *Laugh again,* he thought.

"Like how devastated you'd be when you discovered we'd killed your love," he grinned then, eyes glinting and evil.

A dark coil roiled up from somewhere deep in Elphias, fueled by an anger long since festering. His hand lashed out without him being aware, driving the tip of an ampule into Muld's right eye. Muld screamed and Elphias threw the two ampules into his open mouth.

Muld shoved him away, hands clamped to his eye and throat, gagging and coughing on the glass at the back of his mouth. He dropped to his knees and gagged one of the ampules out into his palm, then flung it away in a rage.

Muld roared with anger and got to his feet, advancing toward Elphias with his fists clenched. His steps faltered and he swayed, remaining eye unfocused.

"Unsporting bastard!" Muld shouted and dropped to one knee.

*Fall asleep,* Elphias thought desperately, *then wake to wear the black robe.*

Muld swung out his fist at nothing, hitting only empty air. Then he tumbled over backwards and rolled out the open hatch.

Elphias lunged forward, arms out to prevent Muld from falling but he was too far away. The weight of Muld would have pulled him out anyway. He collapsed to his knees and clamped his hands to his head, the revelation still burning hot.

They had killed Bella.

# CHAPTER SIXTEEN
## *Lost and Found*

Consciousness returned slowly, like the sun claiming back the sky in the morning. Bella sensed she was lying on her back on a bed of some sort and that she was sheltered from the elements. *I'm alive,* she thought dimly. *I must have found safety.*

Someone rustled past her, she could feel the breeze of their wake.

"I see your thoughts swimming like a little fish, and hear their tiny tails going swish, swish, swish," said a female voice in a childlike fashion.

Bella cracked open her eyes to find a thin, pale woman staring down at her. The woman's long and unkempt hair was whiter than Cobb's, though she appeared to be around Bella's age, and was blended into the ragged layers of clothes and robes she wore. They were in a small shack. A fire burned in a central pit, its smoke vented though a pipe and out of the roof. There were a table and chairs, all roughly built and ridiculously sturdy in construction. She must be in one of shelter towns built for the TransRail workers. Bella tried to sit up but found herself bound tight to the cot.

"Why am I restrained?"

The woman tilted her head, examining Bella with curiosity. She had bulbous, pale green eyes that gave her an otherworldly appearance. "I don't know you at all, do I? No, I don't at all. Are you sister or sinner? Loser or winner? Friend or dinner? Well, I really don't know. You could be any of those things or all of them. So you see, tying you to the cot was the sensible choice instead of…well, I'm trying to be kinder. I truly am."

"Please, I need help. I was thrown from the sky train and I—"

The woman stepped forward and squatted by the side of the cot, putting her face almost level to Bella's. "Is that where you got this?" She pressed a finger against the spot where Muld had hit her. Bella gave a cry of pain and glared at the woman.

"Don't touch me!"

"Well I really can't help it, can I? I mean, I did touch you to get you here, didn't I? Yes, it was me that did that. I'm kinder now, you see? Kinder than I've been treated and far kinder than…well, I shouldn't speak of them. Shouldn't, wouldn't, couldn't. No need to speak about such terrible, awful people. Not people really, but they still look like them all right."

Bella felt a sense of dread. This woman wasn't in her right mind and Bella needed her trust if there was any chance of being freed. She gave the woman a kind smile, practiced in front of a mirror during her training. "Forgive me, you're right. I didn't mean to offend. Thank you for saving me. You are very kind indeed."

The woman nodded, eyes wide. "I am, aren't I? Yes. You said it, I said it, we all said it. Words are wonderful, aren't they? Words make everything true." Her dirty face cracked into a smile. "I am Deirdre the Kind. Not Deirdre the Weird, nor Deirdre the Dumb. You said it, I said it, we all said it. Deirdre the Kind." She reached out with index finger extended and placed it on Bella's forehead. "But who, who, and who, are you, you, and you?"

Bella swallowed. "My name is Bella Crevan, a pleasure to meet—"

Deirdre removed her finger and leaned in, gently touching their foreheads together and angling her head to stare into Bella's confused gaze. "Oh, that's not entirely true, is it? No, not at all. There's more than one you wearing these clothes, wearing this face, wearing those thoughts that race, race, race." Deirdre closed her eyes and sat back, tilting her head to the ceiling. "Ammm… Amber…" Her eyes popped open wide. "Ambrosia! Ambrosia Trent!"

Bella's heart pounded with surprise. "No," she said, her voice dry. "She's dead." She shook her head and shut her eyes. "Ambrosia's dead."

"Only because you killed her. With words. The words of your name, you changed the words and made a new truth. Words make everything true, don't they? Yes. Yes, I think they do."

Bella opened her eyes and glared at her. "How do you know these things?" As soon as the words left her mouth she suddenly understood. "You're a witch."

Deirdre stood up and paced away. "I prefer gifted, yes, don't I? Yes. Witch sounds so...well, you know what they say about them, don't you? What happens to them?" She whirled around, eyes wide and burning with emotion. "But not me! Never me! Isn't that right? Isn't it?!"

"Yes, you're right. Never you. Because you're Deirdre the Kind." Bella shifted against the rope, subtly testing the bonds, but it was secured tight.

Deirdre's expression softened and she laughed. "I am, aren't I? And kind people can't be...oh, I can't even say it, it chills me so. But you!" She approached Bella and stood next to the cot, an expression of joy on her face. "You, you, you! You are kind as well, I hope. I wonder. I wish."

"I try to be," Bella said.

"Well, we will see, won't we? But because you are being kind now I will also do you a kindness." She hiked up her skirt to facilitate crawling onto the cot atop Bella.

Bella's heart began to race. "Please, you don't have to...I'm not of that—"

"Shhh," Deirdre said, putting a cold finger to Bella's lips. "Nor am I, pet. I've already known the flesh of a man," she made subtle thrusting movements and shook her head. "Not of my choosing, was it? No, it wasn't. Some men are crueler than the rest, aren't they? They follow not laws but the whims of their little skin swords and the blood rage of their evil minds. It almost makes you want to crush their head in with a sea stone." She looked down at Bella and grinned, a slow, luxurious grin as if they shared a deep secret.

Bella's eyes went wide but she dared not speak, the witch still had her finger upon Bella's lips.

"In my case," Deirdre whispered, "I burned him up. When the beast turned me from green to red the symbols all changed up in my mind, didn't they? It was what I focused on, while he...well, I focused on these new shapes and one really stood out, didn't it? Yes, it did. Bright bloody red burning blood bright shape, inside out snake and a bone blistering blight. Words are unable to describe, but it is true. Yes, it is still true, and I thought the shape and touched his sweaty foul flesh and he screamed, louder and higher than I had, he screamed. Til smoke came from his mouth and an orange glow was visible at the back of his throat, coming up from his burning guts, his heart hot coal, his stomach boiling oil. He kicked and danced and twisted and rolled and I watched until he was naught but ashes on the wind."

Deirdre stared off at the wall, lost in her vengeful memories. Her finger drifted from Bella's lips as her hand fell slack upon Bella's sternum.

"He deserved it," Bella said softly.

Deirdre looked down suddenly, returning to the present. Then her brows knit and tears began to spill from her eyes. "My dear little pet, you are kind. You truly are, aren't you? He did deserve it. And you," she reached her hand up and caressed Bella's forehead, "you deserve something special too." She closed her eyes. "A special shape all your own."

Bella opened her mouth to decline, to say anything to stop her but Deirdre's hand did a gentle twitch and then white hot purple fire exploded in Bella's mind, snuffing all words, crushing all thoughts, and once again her consciousness was taken from her.

# CHAPTER SEVENTEEN
### *The Painful Truth*

Elphias probed his tender midsection by touch, thankful nothing appeared to have been ruptured internally. Muld's fist had felt like a sledgehammer and he'd feared suffering severe trauma to his organs. He'd still need to keep an eye out for blood in his daily excretions to be certain.

Elphias had returned to the private car after leaving the baggage area, beaten and disheveled. Upon sight, Alisha had ushered him through immediately. Zediah had been behind his desk with Arctus sitting arrogantly before him. They still maintained those positions as Elphias stood near the window conducting his self diagnosis.

"I've no idea what he's talking about," Arctus told Zediah.

"It seems relatively clear to me," Zediah said, and adjusted his glasses. "Especially given the nature of your interactions with Doctor Root in Lacroix."

Arctus shrugged with indifference. His attitude had been much this way since meeting with the inquisitor. "This alleged allegation is based on hearsay from a man who is now conveniently deceased. For all we know, Doctor Root invented the tale. It's certainly rather suspicious, perhaps he is the murderer you seek."

Elphias' face twisted with anger. "You dare accuse *me* of the deed? You reprehensible little—"

Zediah held up a hand, keeping his grayish green eyes on Arctus. "I have no illusions about responsibility in this matter. I have traveled with Doctor Root and know him well enough to make a credible judgement of character." He leaned forward in his chair. "You however...let's just say your record is troubling."

Arctus' eye twitched. "My record? Why are you accessing my records?"

"What has happened to Lady Danueman?"

"She was asleep in her chamber when I was made to come here. If she's not there now then this Muld character or Root would be the likely—"

"No!" Zediah slapped his hand loudly on the desk and stood up.

Arctus leaned back, eyes wide at the unexpected aggression. "What do—"

"You will stop with the deflections, the false innocence, and the bull wash. I've no patience for continuing this charade. You have been playing a dangerous game for some time now, but now you've made a catastrophic mistake, an incalculable error."

Arctus blinked, and gave a subtle shrug. "Which is?"

Zediah stalked around his desk to glare down on Arctus. "You've involved people I care about in your machinations, perhaps even fatally so. I hope not, for your sake. You'll wear the black either way, it's just a matter of the subsequent elevation of your feet from the ground. Walk or hang, the sentence will be determined upon what you have done."

Arctus stared at him passively then shook his head. "I will do neither of those things, Inquisitor Oulcott, because I am innocent of your paranoid imaginings. You've proof of nothing, and until you prove to me that the Lady Danueman is not asleep in her chamber or elsewhere aboard this train then we've nothing to be gained by further inquiry."

Elphias clenched his fists and clamped his mouth shut tight. Arctus' arrogance irritated him and it was all he could do not to punch him in that smug face once more.

Zediah's face darkened. "Fine. We will play your little pretense to its inevitable conclusion. And then you will answer my questions. One way or another, you will answer them all."

Arctus smiled and gestured towards the door. "Shall we then?"

They made their way to the suite, Arctus in the front and Zediah behind. Elphias followed them both, wanting to see how it all played out. An ampule of Red Rose had taken the edge off his pained abdominal region and made the walk easier to endure.

Arctus stopped outside the door of his suite. "Wait here for a moment, I will go in first; she is of delicate mind and the shock of—"

"We will go in together," Zediah said in an unamused tone.

Arctus smiled. "Very well," he said and opened the door. "Lady Danueman? I've returned with some company." He stepped into the suite and approached her open door. "Lady? Are you well? I shall never forgive myself if you've caused harm to yourself."

Elphias rolled his eyes. "He should have charged for this performance."

Zediah shook his head. "I wouldn't have paid. I only enjoy good theater."

Arctus ducked his head into the Lady's room then looked at Zediah with surprise. "She's not in there!"

Zediah put his hands on his hips. "You're joking. Wherever could she be?"

"I really don't appreciate the sarcasm, Inquisitor."

Elphias smiled. "I find it rather entertaining."

Arctus scowled. "I don't care what you think, Root. Why are you even here?"

"I was assaulted in this room by your associate. He was hiding in here." Elphias managed a look into the Lady's room. A woman's dress lay out upon the cot and a man's bowler hat upon the pillow. Elphias grinned. "Is that the Lady's hat? I don't remember seeing her in that before. Although it does look familiar…"

"You must have planted it there when you did harm to my patient. Where is she, Root? What have you done with her?"

Elphias shook his head. "This again?"

"I've heard enough," Zediah said, "let's go find the conductor."

"Allow me one more indulgence," Arctus said, crossing the small room and looking into his suite. "The Lady may have left…yes, there it is. She's left me a note. This will explain all." Arctus disappeared into the room.

Elphias looked at Zediah. "There was no note earlier."

Zediah sighed. "Nor is there now I suspect." He walked towards Arctus' room. "Come now, Doctor Weber, let's not devolve into cheap theatrics." He paced through the door with Elphias following.

Arctus stood near his cot, back to them and head down. *Pretending to read a note*, thought Elphias as he stood in the doorway. *This man knows no shame.*

Zediah reached out and touched Arctus' shoulder. "Time to g—"

Arctus whirled about suddenly, dashing the side of Zediah's head with the decanter of brandy from his bed stand. Zediah grunted with pain and fell heavily against the wall, then crumpled to the floor and lay motionless.

Elphias' eyes grew wide with shock and met Arctus' cold gaze.

"So," Arctus began.

Elphias launched himself at Arctus, filled by a dark rage. Whatever the alienist had thought would happen, it wasn't this. He yelped with surprise and raised the decanter above his head. Elphias hit his midsection with a tackle, arms locked around his torso and smashing Arctus into the wall. Elphias kept his head low and to the side, beneath Arctus' right arm and out of range of the decanter.

"Let go of me!" Arctus said with a vicious tone, then brought the decanter down on Elphias' back. It registered dully somewhere at the rear of Elphias' mind. *Without the Red Rose I'd really have felt that,* he thought through the rage burning in his mind.

Arctus brought the decanter down again, centered on Elphias' spine.

*He's trying to paralyze me,* Elphias thought with dim alarm. The rage within him suddenly turned over, pushed aside by a deeper and darker fury; unleashed from the pit of every injustice and terror ever experienced. *He murdered Bella!* Elphias screamed with primal outrage and lifted Arctus up. Then he fell, turning their bodies as they dropped, smashing Arctus against the floor and driving all Elphias' weight atop him.

Arctus grunted with pain and the decanter flew from his hands, crashing against the wall and landing on the floor on its side. Brandy drizzled out of the open spout, filling the room with its thick fruity tang.

Elphias took the opportunity of Arctus being dazed to pull down his arms and enclose them in a bear hug.

Zediah began to groan and his legs stirred.

"Zediah!" Elphias shouted. "Inquisitor Oulcott! Can you hear me?"

Arctus squirmed in Elphias' grip. "I can hear you fine, old boy. Now kindly release me from your lustful embrace. I find you wholly unattractive and your smell offends me."

Zediah struggled to sit.

"Zediah, it's Elphias. Can you hear me?"

"Un—yes," Zediah said and managed to rise off the floor. He sagged back against the cot, clutching a hand to the side of his head. Blood trickled down the side of his face. "What…where?" he mumbled, trying to focus his vision. His glasses were askew, the lens cracked and temple support bent where Arctus had struck him. Elphias deduced the spectacles had taken the brunt of the damage and likely saved Zediah's life.

"We're on the *Spirit of Innovation*. You were struck on the head by this man I'm holding. Do you understand what I'm saying?"

"Lies," sneered Arctus. "This man assaulted you and then attacked me. I fear he means to do me harm."

Zediah leaned back against the cot, removed his damaged glasses, and shook his head. "No. No, he won't." He opened his eyes and sat forward, his motion unsteady. "But I will. I will put the noose around your treacherous neck myself."

There was a commotion from outside the room and a shape appeared in the door. The conductor looked in on the scene with mouth agape. He shook his head with bewilderment, eyes wide with disbelief. "This train has gone mad. Absolutely mad!"

"Conductor," Zediah said, motioning with his hand. "I was coming to find you."

The conductor pulled off his cap and ran a hand across his scalp, then clamped the cap back on. He nodded and looked somehow relieved.

"So you know, then, praise the Dualvinity, you know."

"Know what?"

"They've taken the train, sir," the conductor said with dismay. "Anarchists have taken the train."

# CHAPTER EIGHTEEN
## *Explosive*

Sweat trickled down Cobb's brow and back, the heat from the furnace nearly unbearable. Distant pounding sounded from the barricaded door to the staff car.

"So, that's that, then," Stringy hair said, nervously fingering his dagger. "Time to bail off and let you lads do your business."

Cobb smirked. "Tis noble of you, that. Stepping aside so other men can die."

Stringy hair sneered. "I've done my part. Just make sure you do yours."

"How about I do it now?"

Stringy hair and the other anarchists all froze and gave him a startled look.

"Don't be joking around, elder father," Stringy hair said flatly.

"Then mayhap you and the rest of you cowards should 'bail off' immediately as you say." Cobb scratched his chin, beard damp with sweat. "Because I'm not much the joker."

The anarchists sprang into action, opening the emergency hatch and unspooling the rope ladder, which they quickly fed down through the mouth. The wind roared in, cooling the sweat on Cobb's body.

The driver stared down through the opening. "We're not over the lakes yet," he said. "That's a twenty foot drop off the end there at the least!"

Cobb shrugged. "Aye, tis a chance. But you're the fools who set the speed. Think you'll survive the blast instead?"

The driver cursed and began to clamber down the ladder. Once his head dipped below the floor the firekeeper followed. Stringy hair waited his turn, then started down, giving Cobb an untrusting glance as he descended.

Cobb cleared his throat. "Don't suppose you'd leave a dagger so that we can defend ourselves 'til tis time to detonate?"

Stringy shook his head. "You'll have to make do." He grinned. "To the revolution," he said and then ducked out of sight.

Cobb got unsteadily to his feet.

Nelson watched him. "You all right, Pup?"

Cobb nodded and opened a small cupboard mounted to the back of the cab. "Just sat too long," he said and removed a fire axe.

"What—" Nelson began and then Cobb brought the axe down on one side of the ladder. The rope snapped easily and whipped from sight. Shouts of alarm sounded up through the hatch.

Cobb brought the axe down again, severing the remaining rope. It ripped down through the hatch accompanied by high pitched screams that quickly faded away. Cobb tossed the axe to the floor and began exit the cab.

"What are you doing?" Nelson asked.

Cobb stopped and pointed to the damaged controls. "We need to stop this runaway afore any other folks die."

"Gods, what have I done?" Nelson ran a hand through his hair then nodded, face ashen. "Do what you can, Pup."


Elphias and the conductor stood in the tender car vestibule, trying to kick its door open. Zediah watched from behind, his head bandaged by Elphias and his pain assuaged by Red Rose. He clutched his shock gun and stood centered to the door, ready to fire upon anyone who appeared. Alisha and her relief were guarding Weber back in their sleeper cabin. Cobb was missing. It was up to the three of them now.

"I told you it's useless," the conductor panted. "It's iron bolted through both frame and floor."

"We'll get it open," Zediah said. He reached up and adjusted his bent glasses.

The conductor gave him a doubtful look. "I pray that's true, Inquisitor. It's either that or coins for the corpse at this point."

Zediah's face remained firm. "I'll blast it if I need to."

The sound of a bolt retracting came from the door.

"That may not be necessary," Elphias said.

Zediah motioned for them to get out of the way. Elphias and the conductor stood wide of the door as the final bolt snapped loose. It opened swiftly and Cobb blinked out at them.

"Master Cobb? What is the meaning of this?" Zediah demanded.

"There's a bomb aboard this train."

Elphias swallowed. "Did you say bomb?"

"Aye, I did, Doctor Root."

The conductor wiped his brow and muttered to himself. "Madness. Madness!"

Elphias looked to Zediah. "Is this sort of thing usual for you?"

Zediah shook his head. "I was going to ask you the same."

"There's naught time to explain," Cobb said, "but the thin of the matter is this. Anarchists attached a bomb to the engine and plan to detonate it in Verdun."

"Then we have to stop the train," Elphias said. "Are the anarchists at the controls?"

Cobb shook his head. "Nay, they've taken their leave. You'll find their treacherous bodies back a ways, in one shape or an other. Tis only my squaddie and I left. They killed the original crew."

Zediah stepped forward. "Then let's stop the *Innovation* while there's time."

"We'd a done so if we could, Inquisitor Oulcott. Aye, we'd already be stopped, but the controls are damaged full open. There's no way to slow her, and no way to remove the bomb. It'll blow when she crashes in Verdun. We've but one choice as I see it."

"Which is?"

"Uncouple the engine from the rest of the train. Then, when tis a safe distance, detonate the bomb."

Elphias stared at Cobb. "You have the ability to detonate it?"

Cobb nodded. "Aye. Tis hands on and already primed to go. No harmonium trigger, that."

Zediah rubbed his bandaged forehead. "Are you involved in this conspiracy, Cobb?"

Cobb shrugged. "I walked in at the end. Enough to get caught up in the thick of it. Didn't know about the bomb til after we parted. Either way, there's naught to do about it now. We're trying to save innocent lives here."

Zediah nodded. "How do we disconnect the cars?"

Cobb pointed to the shifting metal plates beneath their feet. "The couplers are under the flooring"

The conductor nodded. "It's as he says. There's two pins to be pulled, one per side. It's a failsafe, so it takes two people to do it." He rubbed his face. "What's more, the staff car is fitted with an emergency brake system. Once the steam connections are severed and the pressure drops they'll engage. The rest of the train will stop fairly quick once they do."

Elphias tried to make sense of it all. "Would they be enough to stop the engine if we simply severed the steam connectors now?"

"No," the conductor said. "They'd slow us for a bit, but eventually they'd heat hot enough to set the staff car ceiling afire."

"Time's wasting," Cobb said to the conductor. "I know enough to get them uncoupled. You should ready the passengers for the stop. Tis going to be a rude surprise otherwise."

"Yes, yes you're right," the conductor said, and dashed into the staff car.

"I can get this side. One of you will need to do the other."

Elphias nodded. "I'll do it, Cobb." He turned to Zediah. "You should ready yourself, someplace clear of any loose items that could do further injury to your head."

Zediah stood for a moment and then nodded. "Good luck to you both," he said and turned to go.

Cobb lifted the floor plate on his side. The outside air rushed in. He looked up suddenly. "Inquisitor. There was a name they mentioned, them anarchists did. Some fellow named Torvo was the plotter behind this."

Zediah nodded. "That may be useful. Thank you, Cobb. I'm sorry you got mixed up in this evil thing."

"There's evil in the Empire of Light too, don't kid yourself that." Cobb shook his head. "They caused the Purge for nationalism and sustained it for profit."

"That's insane," Elphias muttered.

"Aye, tis that and worse, Doctor Root. The Academy done burned the records, but my squaddie saw them first. Aye to his end he regrets it, but that he did."

"What is his name?" Zediah asked.

"Nelson," Nelson said from behind Cobb. "Harris Nelson. And all Pup said is true."

Zediah blinked. "Pup?"

"They served together, before Cobb was aged," Elphias said.

"Ah, yes." Zediah looked at Nelson. "Can you verify this tale beyond your own accusation?"

Nelson shrugged. "I reckon so, but what's the point? I'm soon to die. I left one evil to find another."

"No," Cobb said and lowered the plate. "Help secure the inquisitor and answer his questions, then we'll do this. Be quick. I'll give you ten minutes. Do some good afore the end!"

"Dash it," Nelson swore and moved across the vestibule. "I'll answer what I can but we must hurry."

"Of course," Zediah said. They entered the staff car and closed the door.

Cobb raised his floor plate. Air stirred his long grey hair to motion. "You must do the same, Doctor Root."

Elphias squatted and looked at Cobb. "He'll never forgive you for doing this."

Cobb shook his head. "Mayhap, but he don't want to die. They short strawed him into it, them evil ones he fell in with. They tricked him cause he's a good hearted lad, he ain't like them. He's a veteran like us. Help him if you can, Doctor Root."

Elphias lifted his floor plate. More air roared in through the opening, creating a vortex in the vestibule. The coupling was mounted between spring cushioned bumpers, a thick metal strut linking the cars by large pins at each end. The world raced by far below, fields and pastures a blur. "I don't know what I can do, but if he needs aid I'll render what I can."

Cobb reached down and grasped the pin's hand grip. "I know you will. You're a good friend, Elphias."

Elphias smiled sadly. "And you as well, Brogan. I'm honored to have met you. Truly." He reached down and grabbed hold of the pin handle. "Are you sure this is what you want?"

Cobb nodded. "Aye. Tis a good death, I think. Saving lives. And aboard the *Spirit of Innovation* to boot. Shame I'm the one to destroy her though. Tis a funny, funny world, this." He laughed at the irony and then glanced at Elphias. "You should do yours first, Doctor, then get inside afore the brakes engage."

Elphias nodded and pulled up on the pin. It slowly eased upward, then popped loose. Elphias stood and saluted Cobb. "Dualvinity be with you, my friend."

Cobb returned the salute, face proud. "And you as well, Elphias. You as well."

Elphias turned and entered the staff car. He glanced back through the window to witness Cobb remove the remaining pin. Elphias ducked into a vacant staff cot and waited. His heart pounded and he blinked back tears. There was a dull thunk followed by a popping hiss.

A sudden shrieking came from above, vibrating the entire car. Elphias slid forward, his heels slapping against the bulkhead to the accompaniment of items falling and banging from elsewhere. Muffled shouts came from behind his head, accompanied by a heavy thump.

Seconds dragged on as the cars shuddered to a stop. Elphias rolled from the bunk as soon as possible and dashed to the door. He wrenched it open and stuck his head out, watching the *Spirit of Innovation* roaring away, free of the weight it had pulled for so long.

Steam billowed from the twin stacks and coiled behind as it passed through a support tower and entered a long curve.

A commotion sounded from behind Elphias.

"What's he done? What's that fool Pup done?"

Elphias opened his mouth to answer.

A bright flash appeared beneath the *Spirit of Innovation* and then it exploded in a torrent of fire, steam, and twisted metal. The rail and support girders above it snapped apart and the remaining chunks of shattered chassis rolled loose, tumbling to the ground amidst a cloud of scalding water and burning coal.

The boom reached Elphias' ears followed by the shock wave. He gasped at the horror of it.

"Cobb."

He closed his eyes and sagged against the wall. *I hope there truly is a golden city that the god folk speak of,* he thought. *And if there is, I hope you find peace there, Cobb. You and all the others I have loved.*

# CHAPTER NINETEEN
## *Cold Fire*

Bella awoke to the sound of voices in her head. They were distant and indistinct, as if from another room where she could hear the pattern of the speech but not the clarity of its content. She opened her eyes to find herself still in the cabin, still bound to the cot. She was alone, a rarity, and the voices had also ceased. *Curious,* she thought and shut her eyes again.

Gradually the voices returned. They were male to be sure, murmuring in low tones. She tried to focus more on what they said, reaching out with her senses. An image began forming in her mind, wispy and dreamlike at first, then increasing in clarity. Five men in thick jackets walking single file through the snow and pulling a supply sled. Packs and rifles were strapped to their backs and steam puffed from their mouths when they talked.

"…and smelled like griffin shite. But he still went back for seconds."

The men laughed, save for one who merely grinned and shrugged. "I was hungry. You'd have done the same."

She floated somewhere above the men and could see everything at once, them below, the sky rail above, and the surrounding Cragback Mountains. The men were walking up a gentle slope and the sun shone in the sky.

*What has the witch done to me?*

As if summoned by the thought, Bella heard a rustling next to her and the touch of a cold hand upon her forehead. Her eyes snapped open and the image faded from sight.

Deirdre stood over her, half-lidded and glassy eyed. "What do you dream when you dream of a dream that can dream like a dream of your youth?"

"I don't think I understand."

Deirdre blinked and looked down at Bella, as if suddenly realizing she were there. "A man called me mad, once. I turned his insides to bugs. I didn't do that to you, did I?"

Bella shook her head, unsure of how to answer. Best to remain neutral. "I don't think so," she said.

"Oh, you would know," Deirdre said seriously. "He did. He screamed and they started to pour from his mouth. The rest ate their way out." She rubbed both hands on her belly.

Bella tried to push the image of such a death away. She had to win Deirdre's confidence somehow. It was her only chance of getting free.

"Absolutely not then. I'm not sure what you did, but it certainly wasn't that. You've only been kind to me."

Deirdre smiled. "I have, haven't I? Been kind? Yes, I have. Very kind, indeed. Deirdre the Kind, if you remember. But then you did, didn't you? Yes, you did, I did, we all did, so thank you." She hunkered down and sat cross legged on the floor, facing Bella. "I don't know what they do, you see? What I did to you. Not always. They come to me, the patterns, the special shapes that only I can see. Like words, but these aren't words, are they? No. They come to me from somewhere, and I know not how or why. But sometimes they go back too, and I can't see them anymore. And my special shape for you, yes, you and you and you was that way, and I only remember the taste of purple and it was gone. Then we slept for a bit. Me less than you, yes, but that's how it's always been, since…well, who needs more than three hours of sleep anyway?" She giggled and rocked gently back and forth.

Bella closed her eyes, seeing if she could sense anything coming from Deirdre. The witch had mentioned Bella's thoughts being like little fish. Did Deirdre have such fish of her own? She opened herself up for reception but only heard the sound of boots crunching through the snow. They broke step at the sudden intrusion of an intermittent buzzing sound. Bella recognized it immediately as the incoming call notice of a televox unit. She followed the noise to its source, a squared satchel slung over one of the men's shoulders.

He was working the leather covering open while the others stood around observing.

"This can't be good," one of the men said quietly. "They must've found another one."

"You don't know that for sure," the one with the vox said, but he didn't sound entirely convinced about his statement. He opened the satchel, removed a head set and put it to his ear, then toggled a switch.

"Ahoy," he said into the speaker. "This be Crew Fifteen. Go ahead." He listened for a moment, then shook his head with disbelief. "Say again? I hope I misheard you," he asked in a pitched voice. His face turned ashen at the response. "Sweet Dualvinity, how could things have gone so wrong?" He ended the call and stared wide eyed at his companions. "No other way to tell it, lads. Anarchists have struck. They've blown up the *Spirit of Innovation*."

Bella's eyes popped open and her heart raced. The *Innovation* had been blown up? She cursed herself for breaking the link and shut her eyes. The vision seemed long in coming but they still stood facing one another, shaking their heads at the terrible news.

"...to dispatch airships for survivors, I suppose," said the one with the televox and then sighed.

*There were survivors? Please let them be all right*, she wished, but knowing Zediah, Elphias, and Cobb they were right in the heart of the matter.

"It was cursed from the start," said one with thick sideburns. He made a circular motion around his heart. "Too many people ignore the Dualvinity these days, there were bound to be a reckoning."

"Shut your mouth, Murphy," a burly fellow said. "Wasn't gods that did this but cowardly traitors." He clenched his fists. "I'd like to wring their necks."

"So what now, Foreman?" the one with the questionable appetite asked.

The man with the televox scratched his face. "What do you mean? We've still the job to do. Pylons, suspension, and rail still need inspection, now more than ever, eh?"

"Aye," the others answered halfheartedly.

"Come now, lads," the foreman said, "let's double march to the next pylon. I won't be surprised to see a short-liner or two stuffed full of troops from Istas rolling over before we know it."

The men fell back into formation and began hustling their way toward a tower at the top of a rise.

Bella turned her thoughts to Zediah and Elphias, trying to force her mystic vision in their direction. The running men faded away but nothing replaced the muffled sound of their movement.

*Who are they?* she wondered. *Why am I affixed upon these strangers?*

She opened her eyes and looked for Deirdre but the red witch was nowhere in sight. Bella could hear her talking from somewhere outside the hut and had a brief hope that someone may have arrived that could rescue her. But then it became apparent it was just Deirdre talking to herself in her singsongy cadence of rambling thought and word play. *She's fixated on language. How can I use that to my advantage?*

She closed her eyes, deciding to investigate her personal phenomena more closely. There was a rhythmic clumping and the sound of heavy breathing. A man was climbing the tower, close to reaching the top with sweat beaded upon his brow. She tried to drift away, to move her occult vantage point but it was if she were affixed to this person, able to shift her viewpoint around him but unable to move away.

*Why him? He's yet to speak and I'd barely noticed him. Was it him all along?*

She tried to study his face, to see if she could recognize him as someone from her past. His features were bland, his nose flat and wide, his eyes a pale green. Average features that produced no memories. He reached the top and hefted himself over the edge, then crawled forward to inspect the sky rail through the suspension supports.

*Why? Why?!* And then she saw it. Clear and unmistakable from her all-seeing vision. Being atop the tower it was hard for the man to miss too. He rose to his knees and squinted off to a cluster of square buildings huddled amongst the snow, rocks, and ice. A tendril of smoke curled up from one of the ugly, functional buildings.

*That's where I am,* Bella thought suddenly, struck by the odd sensation of being physically one place and visually and audibly another.

The man gave a quick scan of the track and rail mounts, then began to descend the tower. His expression gave Bella hope. Worry lines creased his brow and a deep furrow was set between his pale eyes.

*He's worried there may be anarchists here,* she thought.

And then she saw Deirdre, a small slim figure too far away to recognize, but it was her all the same. Who else would be dancing in circles amongst the buildings?

*She can't be allowed to see them coming,* she realized, *who knows what she'd do to them if she gained the advantage of surprise.* It was remarkable how those boring verbal lessons of her spy training kept coming to mind. *It is what got you here,* the witty and sometimes spiteful part of her mind chimed in. *That isn't helping anyone*, the logical part of her mind added and Bella drew in a deep breath.

"Sister," she called out. "Sister, are you close?"

She heard Deirdre's faint words falter. Bella called out again. There was a moment of silence and then the rustling approach of the witch. Deirdre opened the cabin door and came inside, tromping the snow from her feet. "Did you say something?"

Bella nodded. "Yes, sister, I did."

Deirdre's brow flexed and she took a step forward. "Sister? Have you understood my kindness at last? Seen my gentle nature and the goodness of my heart and those hearts contained within it?"

Bella nodded and felt a twinge of guilt. They'd warned of the empathy which could be formed between captive and captor, but back then none of them had actually really believed it would happen to them. *Lesson learned.*

"I have, and I was wondering if I could ask a favor, kind sister."

Deirdre squinted at her. "That depends, oh yes, that depends entirely upon what you, and you, and you are going to ask." Not entirely trusting yet, then.

Bella shifted as much as possible beneath the ropes, trying to appear natural. "Well, I hesitate to ask because you've been so kind already. But I'm bored of just lying here and I was hoping you could tell me a story to pass the time."

"You're not well enough to walk just yet," Deirdre said solemnly.

"No, of course not." Bella tried her best to keep her voice cheerful and friendly. "Which is why I was hoping for a story, or a song, or a poem. I'm sure you must know something, kind sister."

Deirdre brightened immediately. "Oh, well in that case I'm sure that I can think of something, oh yes, there are words and words and words in my head and in my heart and in my parts that need to come out. Yes, let me just think of the proper order of things, those words that have power, those words that make truth from nothing but ashes and imagination." She twirled around, arms cast wide, then stopped and laughed aloud.

"There was once a lying, little sneak," she began.

Bella's heart clutched. *How could I have been so stupid. She's read my mind!*

"A clever, little fox," Deirdre continued, "living in a world of monsters and deceit. Light on its feet. Trying not to be meat." She shook her head sadly, then thrust a finger in Bella's direction. "And you, and you, and you…You have seen this little fox, sister, probably more times than you know. But you don't recognize him, no, because he charms your eyes and wets your thighs to claim his prize."

Bella's heart began returning to its normal rhythm.

Deirdre thrust both arms above her head, thumbs alongside each other and fingers splayed wide. "The sun. Burns everything. Sees everything." She lowered her hands. "And the fox hates it, because the sun alone can see him, see the lying, little sneak beneath the pretty, pretty fur." She put her hands into her hair and closed her eyes. "We all are the sun. We all are the fox. We all walk the surface of this world like a pox. Striving and conniving while the masters are dividing. The hammer falls and the anvil rings. Only time will tell what the next horror brings. Born aloft on shadowy wings."

Deirdre fell silent and then looked at Bella guiltily. "I'm not very good with humor."

Bella bit her lip. "You're an entertaining storyteller, sister." She listened for the sound of the men but only heard the wind. "Do you know anything else?"

Deirdre twirled about. "Yes, I can yes, yes, yes." She put a finger to her head. "They come from here. Far, yet so near. From my mouth to your ears."

"May I close my eyes, sister, while I listen to you speak?"

"Yes, you may. In fact, I will too. You'll do it, I'll do it, we'll all do it. It will be a story for the dark."

Bella shut her eyes, reaching out with the remote vision.

"There once was a giant with no eyes," Deirdre began. "And he walked the world clad in iron boots stained with blood, the blood of the innocents he'd innocently stepped on."

Her voice faded, mixing with the sound of boots moving through snow. The men were slowly approaching the buildings, fanned out and rifles readied. They made motions to one another with their hands, converging on the building with the smoke curling up from it. They tread carefully, unsure of who or what they would find.

Bella opened her eyes, pulling her senses back to herself.

"...would not dare to step on me, she cried and ran off to meet the giant. Now love is a curious thing, yes it is, and the giant was finally happy. He hummed a happy tune while he walked to meet his love. She ran to meet him too, calling out as she grew close. But his hum was too loud in his own ears and he crushed her to bits. He waited then, for hours and hours, thinking his love had lied to him, that she never—"

"Do you know what I would have said to him?" Bella asked.

Deirdre opened her eyes. "You've interrupted my story, sister, yes you have."

"I would have screamed to get his attention. Wouldn't you? Like this." Bella drew in a breath. "Help!" she shouted. "Help!"

"Help?" Deirdre shook her head. "That makes no sense. I'd scream, DON'T STEP ON ME!" She fell back laughing.

The door to the hut wrenched open and the man with the pale green eyes stood there with his rifle lowered. "What's going on in here, eh?"

Deirdre scrambled to her hands and knees, her teeth bared with feral aggression.

"This is private property," the man said and looked at Bella. "Why's that one tied up?"

Deirdre stood and dashed at the man, touching the side of his face before he could leap away. He screamed and tumbled out the door with face smoking and flames trailing from his open mouth. Bella couldn't see him but she heard his dying scream along with shouts from the other men.

"Witch!"

Bella closed her eyes and sent her vision outward. Fire flared from the dead man's blackened skeleton and Deirdre crouched next to it in the snow, glancing about with panic. Bella could see the men converging on her, their rifles raised and their faces terrified and angry. She wanted to stop them, to prevent the inevitable outcome, to effect the unfolding events. *This isn't what I wanted! I wanted rescue, not murder!* It was already too late. The smoldering skeleton had been the first. He certainly wouldn't be the last.

Deirdre made a dash for a nearby building and one of the men fired. The other three impulsively followed, their retorts firing in rapid succession. Deirdre spun, snow flying, and tumbled down. She lay prone with face in the snow, her breath rapid and shallow.

The men approached her slowly, reloading their rifles and pointing them at her body.

The one they called Murphy glanced around at the other cabins, windows shuttered and doors closed firm. "Do you think there's more of them?"

The foreman scanned the area and his mouth twisted into a scowl. "Mayhap, lads. Best watch ourselves."

They looked around suspiciously, the wind whistling past the buildings with a sinister shriek. Deirdre writhed in the snow, moaning softly. Smoke coiled up from the charred skeleton.

Murphy stared at the blackened bones with a look of horror. "Look what she done to Lorrie. I don't want to go like that."

"Best just burn all these cabins down, to be safe and sure," another one said.

"Aye," said the foreman. "Not a bad idea, that. We've enough oil on the sled."

*Fire?*

Bella opened her eyes and shouted once more for help.

# CHAPTER TWENTY
## *Aftermath*

The Empire dispatched airships from Verdun, and Austra, and any points in between, all of them converging upon the wreckage and survivors of the *Spirit of Innovation*. They came with soldiers and investigators, engineers and rescue workers, each tasked with a specific duty. The investigators would try to discover what happened, the engineers would inspect the track for damage and repair, the rescue workers would help facilitate the evacuation of passengers, and the soldiers would ensure that the others could do their jobs without further interruption or attack from anarchists.

A sky train pushing two passenger cars filled with soldiers was also dispatched from the mountain outpost of Istas, a special short-line tasked with securing any prisoners and pulling the *Innovation's* remaining cars back on its return.

Messages were dispatched across the nation as the Empire dealt with this unforeseen event. Who could have done such a thing? Who would have dared? Information was demanded, sought, and found to be lacking. Supposition and speculation began to devolve into accusation. The bomb had been attached in Lacroix. How involved was the Freehold of Agaria in this act? Weren't they somehow responsible by harboring anarchists and saboteurs as they hatched their evil plots against the Union? The ambassador was summoned before the duumvirate and was said to have left the meeting pale-faced and sweaty.

The massive airship *Cloudhammer* was loaded with bombs and set aloft, where it began angling its way toward the border. The nation may have been surprised by the attack but they weren't going to stand by without action.

Gears were turning, parts were in motion, the great machine of the Empire rolled onward, prepared to crush anything in its way.

Those remaining aboard the *Spirit of Innovation*, aboard the cars it had once towed at least, waited for rescue to arrive. To say they waited patiently would be to understate the various methods they used to cope with the crisis. One was critically injured trying to descend a crude rope fashioned from sheets tied together. Others got into a fistfight, accusing one another of being part of the anarchist plot. Many gathered in the smoking or dining cars, speculating endlessly about who was responsible, what they hoped to have gained, and what would happen next. More speculation was placed upon who was being held under guard in the inquisitor's car, with Muld and Weber's name coming up frequently.

Elphias steered clear of any entanglements, preferring the solitude of the observation lounge to wait for assistance to arrive. Zediah had been on his televox to the Academy nearly the entire day, answering just as many questions as he asked. Elphias got the sense that whomever he was talking to was serving as a relay of information to powers further up the hierarchy. Cobb's friend Nelson was providing what information he could, at one point even speaking on the televox directly to the Grand Inquisitor. He was still facing charges of sedition and conspiracy against the Empire, but his cooperation was buying him certain leniencies such as remaining free to move about the private car and joining sleeper. Elphias hadn't laid eyes on Arctus since he'd been taken into custody by Alisha and her relief, and that suited him fine. *I'd ruin my hands on that smug face. Shatter them from phalanges to carpals to make him as handsome as I feel inside.*

It felt strange to be waiting, to be stopped and no longer in motion beyond his own control. For days now he'd been propelled, pushed, and drawn from one event to the next. And although their journey wasn't at an end yet, Elphias hoped that the rest of the trip would be less dramatic. Or at least less problematic. The lull in the action had consequence, however, for it gave him time to dwell upon the emotions he was trying to avoid and had buried during the past few days. He tried to put the deaths out of his mind, to not let them become another anchor to his progress. That wouldn't honor Bella or Cobb. He'd grieve for them when he could properly assess it. The effort came at cost, for Elphias felt drained, hollowed out, and exhausted. It reminded him of the Purge, of the state he'd enter after long periods of patching, suturing, and amputating the wounded: too shocked to think, too tired to sleep.

He was also troubled by his last words with Zediah. The inquisitor had apologized for any delay, but told Elphias they'd be one of the last ones to leave the *Spirit of Innovation*. Zediah's duties as part of the investigation required him to remain while the other passengers were taken to Verdun.

"I hope that isn't too much trouble?" Zediah had asked.

"No, it's fine. I have nowhere to be at any particular time," Elphias had answered. And as soon as the words left his mouth he realized the pathetic nature of what they implied, and why his nature had been haunting his mind of late. He had nowhere to be, no one waiting for him, nothing at all except for where the winds blew him. He'd been living a hollow illusion for so long, that he was independent and free, when the reality was that he'd been simply drifting through life, waiting for something to happen and running from any meaningful relationships. What kind of life had he been leading? Had it really been much of a life at all? In reflection, his wandering had been a series of unremarkable days, one blending into the next. The milestones, the key memories revolved around his interactions with people. Elphias Root had basically existed as a name within the Physician's Annual and assorted papers stored within the Bureau of Records. He had no partnership, no male children to carry his name, and no longtime friends. If he had ceased to exist, no one would have noticed.

He stood up from his chair and looked out the side window. The sun was sinking, casting everything in a golden light. The distant silhouettes of airships dotted the horizon, slowly navigating to their location.

Elphias sighed. What would he do when all this was done? Perhaps he'd settle around Verdun and make a go at establishing a practice again. Perhaps he'd return to that golden bend in the river that he'd fled from. But deep down, he knew there would be no satisfaction in either option. For he did enjoy traveling and seeing new sights, and experiencing new things. It's just that he wished he had someone to share it with, friend or lover it really made no difference at this point. But how many people enjoyed living that sort of lifestyle?

Night fell. The lux lamps had been powered by the rotation of the wheels, so porters set up lanterns where light was required. Zediah had one in his office but Elphias declined the same for the observation lounge. He preferred the dark where he could easily stare through the glass at the night skies beyond. There was little cloud cover and the stars and moons shone brightly. He fell asleep at some point, awakening to the sweep of lights across the exterior of the train cars.

The airships had arrived. They hovered above, dropping lines and illuminating the area with their spotlights. There must have been a secondary power source for the train's vox system because the conductor's voice came over the speakers, telling the passengers it was time to depart in an orderly fashion. Elphias ignored the request. He wasn't sure how they'd get on to Verdun, just that Zediah would get him there when it was necessary. Once again, things were out of his hands and out of his control. He was a leaf floating on the surface of a river, drawn and pushed by the currents which surrounded him. As it had been since he'd started this whole crazy journey. He was surprised that he was becoming acclimated to the situation, but what else could he really do? Besides, eventually he'd reach the end and then it would be time to set his sights on where he wanted the rest of his life to lead.

Light grew from behind him as two porters entered the observation car, one carrying a lantern.

"Oh, forgive us, sir," the lantern bearer said, "I wasn't aware anyone was in here." He gestured toward the rear of the car. "We need to prepare for a boarding. There's soldiers coming from Istas."

"Of course," Elphias said. "Don't let me interrupt your work."

"Thank you, sir." The porter set down the lantern next to the back window and the two men began removing some bolts around the frame.

Elphias rubbed his chin. "Do you have to remove the whole window?"

"No, sir, not at all. It's actually an emergency door. There's hinges hidden behind the frame on this side. We just need to remove these fastening bolts here to open it up."

Elphias nodded. "I had no idea. Well, I'll let you get to it, I'm going to lay down in my quarters."

"Very good, sir. We'll try to keep the noise to a minimum, so as not to disturb you."

Elphias slipped through the curtains and then through the doorway into his room. It was mostly dark, lit only from the moving lights outside. He undressed and slipped on his nightshirt, then crawled onto his cot and pulled up the covers. Drowsiness washed over him and sleep began tugging him down into its mysterious currents. He closed his eyes and let his thoughts go, seeking the comforting darkness of slumber without aid of Blue Oasis.

He awoke later to the sounds of motion outside of his room. It took him a few moments to recognize the sound as the clumping of boots as soldiers passed by. He didn't realize he'd drifted back into sleep until he awoke to hear the tread of boots passing back out of the train.

"This is an outrage!" he heard Arctus protest from somewhere amongst the soldiers. "How can I be guilty when—". His voice cut off with a grunt of pain.

"Shut your lips, ladykiller, or there'll be more of the same," one of the soldiers said in a flat tone.

The soldiers moved on and soon there was only the sound of the porters refitting the window back into place. Elphias sat up and rubbed his face. He still felt hollow. Arctus may be in custody and headed for incarceration, but hanged or not the alienist's sentence would never be just. There could be no proper punishment applied to a madman like that. For what he'd done. Bella was dead.

There was motion from outside the door curtain and it pulled open. "Ah, you're awake," Zediah said. "Excellent, I was just coming to get you. It's time for us to depart."

Elphias nodded. "Let me dress and I'll be ready to go."

"Of course, I'll be waiting in my office." Zediah closed the curtain. Elphias slipped from his cot and began to don his familiar clothing. The room was mostly dark, only a faint light came from outside, presumably from the airship he'd be taking. He still had no idea what awaited him in Verdun, only that it involved death of some sort if an autopsy were involved. Given the magnitude of the destruction of the *Spirit of Innovation* and what it represented, was the matter in Verdun still relevant? Time would tell.

Elphias left his room and stepped through the curtain into Zediah's office. A lantern burned on the desk and the inquisitor stood next to it, a strange smile on his face. The inquisitor adjusted his spare pair of glasses, light reflecting from the undamaged lenses.

"We've a last minute change of plans," he said.

Elphias gave a small laugh. "As if I should be surprised by this point."

Zediah shook his head. "Nothing so drastic as our previous adventures, I assure you. We've simply picked up an unexpected passenger who will be accompanying us."

"As long as it's not Weber, I'll—"

She stepped from the darkness and into the glow of the lantern like a phantom.

"Bella?" Elphias walked to meet her, his mouth open with surprise. "Is it really you or am I dreaming?"

Her face was bruised on one side and there was a cleft in her cheek from Muld's ring. Her hair was messy and she fumbled to tuck it into some sort of order. Bella smiled. "If this were a dream I hope you'd imagine me in better condition than this."

Elphias reached out and tenderly touched the side of her face, examining the bruise. "I might not. Then I could provide you care."

Bella reached up and cupped his hand in hers. "I'm really here." She closed her eyes. "By some miracle, I'm still alive."

Elphias pulled her into a hug. They embraced each other tightly; the feel of her arms clinging to his torso and weight of her body against him was paradise.

"I thought I'd lost you…" he murmured and kissed the top of her head. Bella smelled of wood fire smoke, sweat, and most importantly—life. In such context, her scent was heavenly. He reluctantly broke the hug to step back and look at her anew.

"How?" Elphias marveled. "What happened to you?"

And so she told them both everything, from all she could remember of her encounter with Arctus and Muld in the baggage car to her rescue by the rail workers, leaving out the parts about the psychic visions. The ability seemed to have faded when Deidre died of her injuries. Bella didn't miss the strange power at all. "Then the soldier train from Istas picked me up, and now here I am."

"Remarkable," said Zediah. "So many others fell from the train too, but you're the only one to return and tell the tale."

Bella shook her head. "None of it seems real."

"I somewhat know that feeling as well," Elphias admitted. "I'm just glad you survived your ordeal."

"Me too," Bella said, meeting his gaze. "Now you two must tell me what happened after my unscheduled departure. I seem to have missed an adventure during my excursion."

"Come," Zediah said, picking up his satchel from the desk, "we can enlighten you as we board the airship. Verdun awaits."

They sailed for Verdun aboard the airship *Resolution*, an Academy vessel streamlined for fast transport by stripping it of unnecessary weight. There were a minimal number of rooms within the skeletal frame, all spartan in content and linked by narrow, railed walkways.

"I'm afraid it's not the most luxurious offering," Zediah told Elphias during a tour of the decks, "but it will get us to Verdun faster than the others."

Bella took leave of them at a sleeping cabin, seduced by the comforting mattress and darkened interior.

"Sorry, but I'm just exhausted," she told them. Besides the physical and emotional traumas of her experience, she'd also grieved when learning of Cobb's fate.

"Rest is exactly what you need right now," Elphias said, which was true. As much as he didn't want to let her out of sight now that she had returned from the presumed dead, it really was what she required.

Zediah ended the tour on the lower deck, where a circular window in the floor revealed the world below. Elphias looked down through the observation port, filled with conflicting emotions. The view was magnificent, a distant verdant landscape drifting beneath their feet, lit by starkly shadowed moonslight.

"What a grand adventure you'll have," Elphias mused, "like in them sky pirate books."

Zediah gave him a quizzical look.

"Cobb," Elphias said and smiled. "He thought you'd take me to Verdun by airship when I told him of our journey." His smile faded. "Darkly prophesied, in hindsight."

They fell silent, watching the landscape roll past for a few minutes, then Zediah rubbed his beard. "You know, this vessel isn't entirely lacking in amenities. I believe Master Cobb deserves a toast, if you'd care to join me."

Elphias nodded. "Thank you, Zediah. Yes, I'd like that very much."

Elphias followed Zediah down the narrow central passage to the inquisitor's station, a small room with a wooden standing desk and a narrow cot hinge mounted to the wall. Zediah unlocked a cabinet on the front of the desk and pulled out a bottle and two shot glasses from within. He uncorked the bottle and sniffed the contents.

"Whiskey," he beamed. "You can never be sure what you'll find in a tipple cubby."

"Is that a standard feature of inquisitor desks?" Elphias asked.

"Alcohol has its uses in our profession," Zediah smiled, "though its application for interrogative purposes has fallen out of favor on airships." He set the glasses upon the desktop and poured a shot into each, then handed one off to Elphias. "You knew him best, would you care to speak?"

Elphias gazed into the dark amber liquid half-filling his shot glass. "Brogan Cobb was an honorable man; a patriot who sacrificed his youth, and ultimately himself for the nation he loved. He deserved a normal life, but that was not his fate and he accepted it with stoicism. And though he oft discounted his own intellect, he was one of the wisest men I've ever met. Cobb was a friend, and I will miss him."

"As will I," Zediah said and raised his glass.

Elphias downed his shot. The alcohol dropped hotly into his stomach as its flavor embraced his tongue. The loss of Cobb was exactly the kind of pain he'd been trying to avoid these last ten years. Yet to have never known him would have been worse. The folly of his decision to avoid relationships and spare himself pain was made increasingly clear the longer he traveled with others. How much life had Elphias been missing out on?

Zediah sighed. "These lasterdays have been an unsettling chain of events. Especially for you. How do you fare? Are you well?"

Elphias smiled and gestured toward the bottle. "I thought interrogative purposes were out of favor."

"Ah, yes, well I'm asking as a friend, so I'm afraid there's no rules in that regard." Zediah lifted the bottle. "Perhaps another round to make it official?"

Elphias offered his glass for a refill. "As to my state of being, I'm well enough, given the circumstances."

Zediah poured them more whiskey. "Then this shall improve your mood. The Bureau of Records is producing new identification papers and a field surgeon license for you, which wasn't easy. As you probably know, they haven't issued FSLs since the Purge. They had to find the old printing plate to do it. I've also been notified your balance inquiry has been completed. The Treasury has dispatched a letter and transfer of same to the Central Bank of Verdun. It should be there by the time we arrive."

"Thank you, Zediah, that's a great relief. I was half afraid it would be boggled somehow."

"And with good reason." Zediah lifted his glass. "To kinder fates."

Elphias raised his glass and downed his drink. To kinder fates, indeed. First Bella returned from the dead, then his finances and identity recovered. Perhaps things were turning around after all.

They arrived in Verdun an hour later under overcast skies. A private cab was waiting for them outside the mooring station, ready to take them to their destination. Once they were seated the driver spurred the horses into motion and the cab started off. Their first stop was to deliver Bella to the hotel where Zediah had reserved them accommodations.

Elphias escorted Bella up to her room, making small talk along the way. They rode the elevator in silence, standing apart but staring deeply at one another. The elevator operator filled the conversational void with an endless prattle about something or other, Elphias heard none of the words. The only important thing in the world was Bella. He still couldn't believe she was truly there, the sole survivor of the fallen.

They exited the elevator and began following the room number signs. Several doors down they found Bella's room, and paused outside.

"I must say I'm looking forward to sleeping until you both return. It's been quite the ordeal," Bella admitted.

"I can't even imagine," Elphias said, "and the majority of my recent travels have been tribulations."

Bella laughed, then winced. She reached up and touched the assaulted side of her face. "I'm glad Muld is dead, and I hope Arctus suffers terribly until they hang him. Is that wrong?"

Elphias sighed. "With those two? No." He flexed his right hand, still feeling some residual pain. "Truth be told, I wish I could've punched him again as the soldiers dragged him out."

Bella's brow furrowed. "Before that snake pushed me, we left things open, you and I. Certain matters unsaid."

"Yes," Elphias said, heart pounding. Was she calling things off? Perhaps. His mouth felt dry, but he pushed on, needing to let her know how he felt. Untimely deaths had taught him that bitter lesson. "I understand if you need more time to think upon it, or if your feelings have changed. Take as much time as you require, Bella. After what you've been through you deserve that much, and more. When you've decided, I'll be there. I hope for one outcome, of course, but…well, just know my feelings won't change. Either way, I  hope we can always be friends."

Bella stared at him a long moment, face unreadable.

"What?" Elphias asked, lopsided grin crinkling his dimples. "Something on my face?"

Bella nodded, slowly. "Yes," she said, and then stepped forward and rose up to kiss him on the lips.

Elphias locked his arms tenderly around her, heart now pounding a different beat. Love, the joy of human companionship, and the wondrous intertwining of mutual passions all burned brightly within him, hotter than the flames which had claimed his vardo.

They broke the kiss and stared into each other's eyes.

"So what did you decide?" Elphias asked.

Bella laughed. "That you're a silly man. And that you should probably get back to Zediah before he thinks some other calamity has befallen us."  She reached up and gently touched the side of his face and beard. "We can talk later, yes?"

Elphias cupped her hand in his, then stepped back and kissed it as in romance tales of old. "I shall see you for dinner, m'lady," he said and then released her hand. He tipped his top hat to her, spirits soaring, then turned and reluctantly headed back toward the elevator and whatever mysterious autopsy Zediah required him to perform.

Elphias returned to the cab, and was relieved to find Zediah on a televox call instead of waiting impatiently for him.

"Good luck on your investigations. You know how I feel," Zediah said and disconnected the transmission. He took a deep breath and then noticed Elphias. "Ah, Doctor Root, excellent timing. Ready to go?"

They rode in silence for a while, and soon Elphias realized they were angling away from where the science expo was being held and making their way through back streets toward the docks.

"Now can you tell me what this is about?"

Zediah smiled and shook his head. "At this point, it would be better to just wait and see for yourself. I don't want to influence your first judgement with my own hopes and expectations."

"Fair enough," Elphias admitted and stared out the cab window. Fifteen minutes later they pulled to a stop in front of a nondescript squat building without any signs or markings on the exterior.

They climbed down from their transport and approached the structure. Zediah stopped outside the door and turned to Elphias, his face unusually serious.

"I have a confession to make, Doctor Root. I lured you here under false pretense. There is no autopsy, or rather, it's already been completed at the Academy."

"I don't understand," Elphias said. "You think I'd be use to this by now. Why bring me here then?"

"I can't tell you entirely. Not yet. But I do want to show you photographs of the specimens and their autopsy report. It wasn't all bull wash." He opened the door and held it for Elphias.

"Specimens?"

The interior was shadowed and empty, save for a table and chairs and four soldiers standing guard around a set of doors set at an angle into the floor.

Zediah gestured for Elphias to take a seat at the table. A folder lay atop it, sealed closed and bearing the Academy logo.

"As you know, I'm with Esoteric Inquiries. Do you know what we do?"

Elphias considered his question for a moment as he sat. "I hadn't given it much thought," he admitted. "But based on the word esoteric I imagine it has something to do with a specialized knowledge known or understood only by a few?"

"Very good," Zediah said and picked up the folder. "As you probably learned during your educations, the Academy is an enormous entity divided into bureaus and departments."

"I'm familiar with the Bureau of Medicine within the Department of Biology. And everyone knows the Bureau of Records. Or is known by the Bureau, I should say."

"Ah, yes. The problem with such specialized divisions, however, is that sometimes areas of study or interest fall through the gaps, as they say. Esoteric Inquiries is tasked with filling in those voids of knowledge, no matter the department or bureau. I generally work in a field of study called cryptobiology. That is, life forms that we know little about or haven't confirmed their existence."

"Such as the wood nymphs."

"Yes, exactly." Zediah opened the folder, extracted a pile of monochrome photographs, and laid them in front of Elphias.

Elphias squinted at the details, remarkably advanced over the old daguerreotypes. The clarity was amazing. As were the subjects. "What are they?" he asked.

"That is what I'm hoping you can tell me," Zediah said.

The bodies lay next to each other, three of them resting face up upon a wide table. They were in a state of decay, their flesh beginning to slip. At first Elphias took them for human males, but then began to notice the differences. Flat facial features, powerful musculature of the upper torso, and pointed ears. Closer photographs of one subject revealed sharper canine teeth and pupils slit like a cat.

"Where did they come from?" Elphias asked.

"The belly of a leviathan carcass that washed ashore." Zediah shook his head. "A stroke of luck, really. The remains of them and their raft were found lodged within the beast's gullet. Apparently it swallowed them whole, then died shortly after."

"They were on a raft?"

Zediah nodded. "Clothed in animal skins that we're still trying to analyze. They also possessed spears, bone fishing hooks, and a woven net. They appear to be a primitive race compared to us, but an intelligent and resourceful species to be sure."

"Remarkable," Elphias said and turned back to the photographs, which now displayed images from their autopsies. He marveled at the details.

There were subtle differences in their anatomical structure from what Elphias was used to seeing, but nothing abnormal. Their hearts were located to the right side of the thoracic cavity, and their internal organs and brain were slightly larger, but the ventral and dorsal cavities were remarkably similar to those found in humans.

Zediah was enthused about it all, overjoyed that they were a different species and curious about their origin.

Elphias studied the autopsy report for several minutes then sat back, stunned by the implications of these previously unknown lifeforms. He looked to Zediah and shook his head. "You've no idea where they may have come from?"

Zediah shrugged. "The fashionable theory is based on known ocean currents, trying to predict where the leviathan died and how long it took to drift here. Best guess is a land mass somewhere out in the Western Sea. That's where the search will begin anyway."

Elphias gave Zediah a look of disbelief. "Search? Have they finally developed a long range airship?"

"Not an airship, no. I'm afraid it's still classified information. Unless…" Zediah gave a sly smile.

"Are you suggesting what I think you are?"

Zediah nodded. "I told you I brought you here under pretense. It wasn't to look at these photographs. The reason I couldn't say the truth of it at the start was I had to wait until the Academy ran its necessary background checks upon you. Your lack of residency records caused them some delay."

Elphias blinked. "Background checks? Why?"

"Security clearance. How would you feel about extending your contract, or rather, entering a new one? I could use your talents, Elphias, if you're game. Your immunity to bio-hypnosis and venoms could prove invaluable. Academy physicians aren't protected against such ill persuasions, and aren't field surgeons either."

Elphias thought it through. What did he really have to do? Where did he really need to be? Nothing and nowhere as he'd realized of late. He'd gone from craving solitude to a fear of being abandoned by his companions at the end of this journey. Now he was potentially to begin another.

"Do you know what you're looking for? Can you tell me that much?"

"I expect to find another continent, or a large enough island that would explain these bodies and other evidence that has washed ashore over the years."

Elphias rubbed his jaw. *I was ready to be done with adventures. Wasn't I?* His decision was clear. "How are we to travel?"

Zediah smiled. "You're saying 'we'. Does that mean you're along for the expedition?"

Elphias nodded. "Yes, I suppose it does."

Zediah clapped his hands. "Excellent! I was hoping that would be the case."

"You still haven't answered my question of how we'll travel. Not by ship, certainly."

"It is a ship, but not of air or sea. Well, at least not the surface."

Elphias raised his eyebrows. "Something new?"

Zediah stood and motioned for Elphias to join him. They approached the soldiers, two of whom opened the angled doors for them. A set of stairs led downward. They descended the stone steps, the smell of sea water and a damp coolness to the air suggesting open water ahead. Sure enough, the stairs ended in an immense interior docking bay.

Zediah extended a hand toward the large craft floating in the enclosed water, its decks encased by metal beset with viewing ports. "I present the *Spirit of Discovery*," he said proudly.

"I've not seen the like of this," Elphias admitted. "You implied we wouldn't travel upon the surface of the sea. You don't mean …?"

Zediah nodded with pride. "The *Discovery* travels beneath the waves, running smooth and nearly silent. It's remarkable, really. They call it a submarine."

Elphias laughed at the irony of it all. He'd been forced from the comforting solitude of his vardo to a sky train, then to an airship, and now to an invention that traveled the unknown depths of the sea. He shook his head in amazement. What a fantastic era to be alive.

Elphias suddenly recalled his own words, spoken to the young boy he'd sutured ten days ago. *It's an adventure, really. You'll learn many wonderful things, see sights you can't begin to imagine, and make friends. It's an adventure to find out who you are, and who you'll become.* What new wonders awaited on the horizon? What new discoveries lay ahead? What new person would he be when it was all over? He couldn't wait to find out.

The adventure will continue in

**EMPIRE OF LIGHT 2: THE SPIRIT OF DISCOVERY**

*Wherein the heroes journey beneath the uncharted seas
to discover a strange and dangerous continent.*

• • •

Thank you for reading this novel, I hope you enjoyed the journey as much as I did. I've grown fond of these characters and look forward to seeing where the next journey takes them. I hope you'll join us on the continuing adventure as they discover an unknown land; and encounter an old enemy.

*Carcer Kane*
~Oct. 2024

www.carcerkane.com